Penguin Books
Dusky Ruth and Other Stories

Alfred Edgar Coppard was born in Folkestone in 1878.
He spent his early years in Brighton, where he attended
a Board School, and at the age of nine was sent to the
East End of London to learn the tailoring trade.
However, after three years he returned to Brighton.
Until 1919, when he became a full-time writer, he
earned his living as a clerk, educating himself by
reading poetry. In 1907 he took a clerical job at
Oxford, and soon after he began to contribute short
stories and poems to periodicals. His first collection of
short stories, *Adam & Eve & Pinch Me* (1921), were
followed by many others, including *Clorinda Walks in
Heaven* (1922), *Fishmonger's Fiddle* (1925), and *The Field of
Mustard* (1926). He also published four volumes of
poems, and his autobiography *It's Me, O Lord* was
published in 1957, the year of his death.

A. E. Coppard

Dusky Ruth and Other Stories

With an introduction
by Doris Lessing

Penguin Books

Penguin Books Ltd, Harmondsworth,
Middlesex, England
Penguin Books, 625 Madison Avenue,
New York, New York 10022, U.S.A.
Penguin Books Australia Ltd, Ringwood,
Victoria, Australia
Penguin Books Canada Ltd, 2801 John Street,
Markham, Ontario, Canada L3R 1B4
Penguin Books (N.Z.) Ltd,
182–190 Wairau Road, Auckland 10, New Zealand

This collection has been selected from the following published works:
Adam & Eve & Pinch Me (1921), *Clorinda Walks in Heaven* (1922),
The Black Dog (1923), *Fishmonger's Fiddle* (1925),
The Field of Mustard (1926), and *Silver Circus* (1928)
This collection first published by Jonathan Cape 1972
Published in Penguin Books 1974
Reprinted 1975, 1977
This collection copyright © C. D. Coppard and Julia C. Reisz, 1972
Introduction copyright © Doris Lessing, 1972

Made and printed in Great Britain by
Hunt Barnard Printing Ltd., Aylesbury, Bucks
Set in Monotype Baskerville

Contents

Contents

Introduction

By Doris Lessing

These short stories are as fine as any we have. In friends'
houses, on the shelves where the books stay which will be
kept always, you find Coppard. Talking to people, not
necessarily literary, who have read their own way into
literature, and who use books for nourishment and not
debate, Coppard's tales are found to be treasures. He wrote
a good many, some now in collections hard to come by. They
are not widely known or quoted. Yet that they can have a
general appeal was proved when recently they were adapted
for television: like Lawrence, Coppard tells a good story.

He was an exquisite craftsman, and wrote well-made
tales. But their shape was that of the growth of people or
events, so that watching one unfold, you have to cry 'What
else? Of course!' as you do in life. Coppard's work owes
everything to this quality of knowing how things must be,
how they have to work out. He understands growth. Nowhere are cataclysms or marvels, not so much as the whiff of
a foreign port or an exotic person. If there's a sailor, then he
has come back from somewhere and will be off again.

There is a steadily flowing stream in English writing
that is quiet, low in key. To this belong E. M. Forster's
tales, some of Kipling, and of H. E. Bates, many of D. H.
Lawrence; here too belong the poems of W. H. Davies and
most of Walter de la Mare. They are English, full of nature
and the countryside, straying very little into towns and
streets. Thinking of Hardy, also a country writer, helps to
see a difference. Sorrow and rebellion rage in Hardy; nothing
of the kind in Coppard, who doesn't believe in tragedy. He
was one of the people who helped me to understand that very

English man, my father, whose relationship to the country-side he was brought up in was like Coppard's. It is a sparrow's-eye view, sharp, wry, surviving, and not one that can quarrel with the savage economies of the field or the hedgerow.

I was lucky enough to meet Mr Coppard. It happened that we were once two weeks together on a delegation to the Soviet Union, which was a miniscule effort, common then, towards peace between nations. There were six of us, under conditions which made us get to know each other pretty well, one being that we were all working so hard sightseeing, and talking about what we saw, and violently disagreeing, that we slept very little. What came out strong in him was his inability to play the role 'writer'. He didn't like making speeches, he didn't like formal occasions, or conferences or big statements about literature. He did like talking half the night to an old pre-revolutionary waiter about Tolstoy, or examining the plants that grew beside the field in a collective farm. He liked flirting in a gentle humorous way with the beautiful girl doctor at the children's holiday camp. At a formal dinner he was talking to the young poet who spent much time tramping around the country by himself: Coppard knew England through walking over it.

He was a small man, light in build. At that time he was seventy-two, but looked sixty, and with a boyish face. Characteristically he would stand to one side of a scene, in observation of it, or quietly stroll around it, his face rather lifted, as it were leading with his chin, his nose alert for humbug, or for the pretensions of the rich or the powerful – about which he was not passionate but mildly derisive. The thing was, he did not have it in him to be solemn. His favourite writer was Sterne, his book *Tristram Shandy*, he was amused by philosophers and had his poets by heart.

How did this original creature evolve? He was born in 1878 at Folkestone in Kent, 'the son of George the tailor and Emily Alma the housemaid' – Alma, he was sure, from the battle of that name.

'Seventy-five years have passed since I occurred . . .' he

almost begins his autobiography, *It's Me O Lord!* – a couple of paragraphs come first, pointing out the impossibility of expecting him to tell the truth or not to puff his own work. He did not get more than halfway through his account of himself because he could not resist following every attractive by-way into anecdote.

His childhood was hard, but there is not a tincture of self-pity in his memories of it. 'In her widowhood my mother became something of a martinet; she had no time to be kind, my father's death having sunk us at once into destitution. At times she was subject to fits of wild maniacal laughter, at others to torrents of tears. In between she was always fighting against the persistent outwearing of every piece of clothing or boot we possessed, as well as the inevitable neglect we, her four youngsters, and the domesticity suffered from her twelve-hour daily absence at a laundry where she had had to start out as a plain ironer from eight o'clock to eight o'clock at twenty-seven pence a day, and where she achieved the heaven of her ambition when she was later promoted to first class at two and six per day.'

'My father was a radical, all tailors were radicals then, freethinkers to a man and scoffers at hellfire and so were all cobblers. I recall him as a nice young man of medium height and lean stature, with a chestnut beard, large reddish nose and thick disordered dark hair – indeed he was always rather untidy, for a tailor, anyway. He wore the cutaway bobtail coat proper to the time, and a billycock hat, but tailor though he was he never had more than one at any time. He never seemed to walk with any objective, but just strolled along as though in meditation, with one hand in his trousers pocket and the other folded behind his back. He loved flowers, birds, the open air and to go a-roving over the hills for mushrooms, blackberries, nuts, cowslips, whatever was reasonable and free, but being doomed, as he knew, by tuberculosis, he became careless and something of a drinker and so we were always shockingly poor.'

Coppard was nine when his father died. His schooling

then ended, because some doctor said his liver would not stand it – on which event Coppard writes: 'This interdiction was accepted almost happily and consolingly by my mother, I never went back, my schooldays were ended. That's the kind of mother to have, the kind I had, credulous, superstitious, beautiful, comic, heroic, a rare woman whom I never seem to have loved much or honoured enough.'

Coppard then became a vendor of paraffin, shouting Oil, Oil, from street to street.

He was already educating himself, loving Chaucer, Shakespeare, Milton, Wordsworth, Keats, Browning and Whitman, getting only 'a thimbleful of joy' from Byron and Shelley, hating Dryden and disliking Donne. 'In the pursuit of culture and understanding of literature I had no tutor or mentor or fellow-seeker after such righteousness. I continued to follow my instinct. What else could I have done? There were no night schools or evening classes for my purpose, I had to find my own way and my instinct seldom misled me. Certainly I was never bored, I have never in my life experienced that so common malaise. Nobody could order me to study some book because it was renowned or esteemed; I was not set to prepare any papers for scholarly or examination reasons on subjects that were of no interest to me; I obeyed no alien direction, my own was good enough always.'

He was mostly an errand boy, running for auctioneers, cheesemongers, soapsellers, carriers. He was a messenger boy for Reuter's. 'From the age of sixteen to twenty-six my life now appears to me to be a sort of kaleidoscope of running, reading, falling in love and trying to write verse.' The verse was not very good, though some got printed, but soon he came to short stories: he never wanted to write novels.

And now his life began to open up from drudgery. He went to Oxford, having like Jude a passion for the essence of the place, and he was happy there, and made friends, and married. He was a socialist, secretary to the I.L.P., spent much time walking, and then, though he loved his friends and their company, longed for solitude.

By then he had sold stories to all the literary magazines, and had a small reputation. How to manage without a salary? he wondered, deciding not to keep books, or to run around for other people ever again. He had fifty pounds. He found a minute cottage in the middle of a field near Oxford, and there he went to live and to write, throwing himself entirely on the rewards of literature, while his mother-in-law and his wife demanded: 'God above, has he gone daft?'

On the contrary, it was exactly what he should have done. 'I soon got used to my new status as a writer – having published a book I thereupon became somebody! Life at Shepherds Pit continued the same, just as delightful in the exquisite tranquillity there. I could almost believe now that the seasons never did change their character then, that summer was always there and I always in the open with the birds and the trees and the postman, the thrift of the land and the freedom.'

He was the most lovable of people, and it is evident in every word he wrote.

D.L.

Communion

He was of years calendared in unreflecting minds as tender years, and he was clothed in tough corduroy knickerbockers, once the habiliments of a huger being, reaching to the tops of some boots shod with tremendous nails and fastened by bits of fugitive string. His jacket was certainly the jacket of a child – possibly some dead one, for it was not his own – and in lieu of a collar behold a twist of uncoloured, unclean flannel. Pink face, pink hands, yellow hair, a quite un-redeemable dampness about his small nose – altogether he was a country boy.

'What are you doing there, Tom Prowse?' asked Grainger, the sexton, entering to him suddenly one Saturday after-noon. The boy was sitting on a bench in the empty nave, hands on knees, looking towards the altar. He rose to his feet and went timidly through the doorway under the stern glance of that tall tall man, whose height enabled him to look around out of a grave when it was completely dug. 'You pop on out of 'ere,' said Grainger, threateningly, but to himself, when the boy had gone.

Walking into the vestry Grainger emptied his pockets of a number of small discarded bottles and pots of various shapes and uses – ink bottles, bottles for gum and meat extract, fish-paste pots, and tins which had contained candy. He left them there. The boy, after he had watched him go away, came back and resumed his seat behind one of the round piers.

A lady dressed in black entered and, walking to the front stall under the pulpit, knelt down. The boy stared at the motionless figure for a long time until his eyes ached and the

intense silence made him cough a little. He was surprised
at the booming hollow echo and coughed again. The lady
continued bowed in her place; he could hear her lips whispering sibilantly: the wind came into the porch with sudden gust
and lifted the arms at the door. Turning he knocked his
clumsy boots against the bench. After that the intense silence
came back again, humming in his ears and almost stopping
his breath, until he heard footsteps on the gravel path. The
vicar's maid entered and went towards the vestry. She
wished to walk softly when she observed the kneeling lady
but her left shoe squeaked stubbornly as she moved, and both
heels and soles echoed in sharp tones along the tiles of the
chancel. The boy heard the rattle of a bucket handle and saw
the maid place the bucket beside the altar and fetch flowers
and bottles and pots from the vestry. Some she stood upon
the table of the altar; others, tied by pieces of string, she
hung in unique positions upon the front and sides, filling
them with water from the pail as she did so; and because the
string was white, and the altar was white, and the ugly
bottles were hidden in nooks of moss, it looked as if the very
cloth of the altar sprouted with casual bloom.

Not until the maid had departed did the lady who had
been bowed so long lift up her head adoringly towards the
brass cross; the boy overheard her deep sigh; then she, too,
went away, and in a few moments more the boy followed and
walked clumsily, thoughtfully, to his home.

His father was the village cobbler. He was a widower,
and he was a freethinker too; no mere passive rejector of
creeds, but an active opponent with a creed of his own,
which if less violent was not less bigoted than those he so
witheringly decried. The child Tom had never been allowed
to attend church; until today, thus furtively, he had never
even entered one, and in the day school religious instruc-
tion had been forbidden by his atheistic father. But while
faith goes on working its miracles the whirligigs of unfaith
bring on revenges. The boy now began to pay many secret
visits to the church. He would walk under the western tower

and slip his enclosing palms up and down the woolly rope handles, listen to the slow beat of the clock, and rub with his wristband the mouldings of the brass lectern with the ugly bird on a ball and the three singular chubby animals at the foot, half ox, half dog, displaying monstrous teeth. He scrutinized the florid Georgian memorial fixed up the wall, recording the virtues, which he could not read, of a departed Rodney Giles; made of marble, there were two naked fat little boys with wings; they pointed each with one hand towards the name, and with the other held a handkerchief each to one tearful eye. This was very agreeable to young Prowse, but most he loved to sit beside one of the pillars – the stone posties, he called them – and look at the window above the altar where for ever half a dozen angels postured rhythmically upon the ladder of Jacob.

One midsummer evening, after evensong, he entered for his usual meditation. He had no liking for any service or ritual; he had no apprehension of the spiritual symbols embodied in the building; he only liked to sit there in the quiet, gazing at things in a dumb sort of way, taking, as it were, a bath of holiness. He sat a long time; indeed, so still was he, he might have been dozing as the legions of dead parishioners had dozed during interminable dead sermons. When he went to the door – the light having grown dim – he found it was locked. He was not at all alarmed at his situation: he went and sat down again. In ten minutes or so he again approached the door . . . it was still locked. Then he walked up the aisle to the chancel steps and crossed the choir for the first time. Choristers' robes were in the vestry, and soon, arrayed in cassock and surplice, he was walking with a singular little dignity to his old seat by one of the pillars. He sat there with folded hands, the church growing gloomier now; he climbed into the pulpit and turned over the leaves of the holy book; he sat in the choir stalls, pretended to play the organ, and at last went before the altar and, kneeling at the rails, clasped his orthodox hands and murmured, as he had heard others murmuring there, a rigma-role of his scholastic hours:

> Thirty days hath September,
> April, June and November.
> All the rest have thirty-one,
> Excepting February alone,
> And leap year coming once in four,
> February then has one day more.

Re-entering the vestry, he observed on a shelf in a niche a small loaf wrapped in a piece of linen. He felt hungry and commenced to devour the bread, and from a goblet there he drank a little sip of sweet tasting wine. He liked the wine very much, and drank more and more of it.

There was nothing else to be done now in the darkness, so he went on to the soft carpet within the altar rails, and, piling up a few of the praying mats from the choir – little red cushions they were, stamped with black fleur-de-lys, which he admired much in the daylight – he fell asleep.

And he slept long and deeply until out of some wonderful place he began to hear the word 'Ruffian, ruffian,' shouted with anger and harshness. He was pulled roughly to his feet, and apprehension was shaken into his abominable little head.

The morning sunlight was coming through the altar window, and the vicar's appearance was many-coloured as a wheelwright's door; he had a green face, and his surplice was scaled with pink and purple gouts like a rash from some dreadful rainbow. And dreadful indeed was the vicar as he thrust the boy down the altar steps into the vestry, hissing as he did, 'Take off those things!' and darting back to throw the cushions into proper places to support the knees of the expected devotees.

'Now, how did you get in here?' he demanded, angrily.

The boy hung up the cassock: 'Someone locked me in last night, sir.'

'Who was it?'

'I dunno, sir, they locked me in all night.'

His interrogator glared at him for a moment in silence,

and the boy could not forbear a yawn. Threat the vicar seized him by the ear and, pulling it with such animation as to contort his own features as well as the child's, dragged him to the vestry door, gurgling with uncontrolled vexation, 'Get out of this. Get out . . . you . . . you beast!'

As the boy went blinking down the nave the tenor bell began to ring; the stone posties looked serene and imperturbable in new clean sunlight, and that old blackbird was chirping sweetly in the lilac at the porch.

The Princess of Kingdom Gone

Long ago a princess ruled over a very tiny kingdom, too small, indeed, for ambition. Had it been larger she might have been a queen, and had it been seven times larger, so people said, she would certainly have been an empress. As it was, the barbarians referred to her country as 'that field!', or put other indignities upon it which, as she was high-minded, the princess did not heed, or, if she did heed, had too much pride to acknowledge.

In other realms her mansion, her beautiful mansion, would have been called a castle, or even a palace, so high was the wall, crowned with pink tiles, that enclosed and protected it from evil. The common gaze was warded from the door by a grove of thorns and trees, through which an avenue curved a long way round from the house to the big gate. The gate was of knotted oak, but it had been painted and grained most cleverly to represent some other fabulous wood. There was this inscription upon it: NO HAWKERS, NO CIRCULARS, NO GRATUITIES. Everybody knew the princess had not got any of these things, but it was because they also knew the mansion had no throne in it that people sneered, really – but how unreasonable; you might just as well grumble at a chime that hadn't got a clock! As the princess herself remarked – 'What *is* a throne without highmindedness!' – hinting, of course, at certain people whom I dare not name. Behind the mansion lay a wondrous garden, like the princess herself above everything in beauty. A very private bower was in the midst of it, guarded with corridors of shaven yew and a half-circle hedge of arbutus and holly. A slim river flowed, not by dispensation, but by accident, through the bower, and the bed and bank of it, screened by cypresses, had been lined, not by accident but by design – so strange are the workings of destiny – with tiles and elegant steps for a bathing pool. Here the princess, when the blazon of the sun was enticing, used to take off her robes of silk and her garments of linen and walk about the turf of the bower around the squinancy tree before slipping into the dark velvet water.

One day when she stepped out from the pool she discovered a lot of crimson flower petals clinging to her white skin. 'How beautiful they are,' she cried, picking up her mirror, 'and where do they come from?' As soon as convenient she inquired upon this matter of her Lord Chancellor, a man named Smith who had got on very well in life but was a bit of a smudge.

'Crimson petals in the bath!'

'Yes, they have floated down with the stream.'

'How disgusting! Very! I'll make instant inquiries!'

He searched and he searched – he was very thorough was Smith – but though his researches took no end of time, and he issued a bulky dossier commanding all and sundry to attach the defiant person of the miscreant or miscreants who had defiled the princess's bath stream or pool with refuse detritus or scum, offering, too, rewards for information leading to his her or their detection, conviction, and ultimate damnation, they availed him not. The princess continued to bathe and to emerge joyfully from the stream covered with petals and looking as wonderful as a crimson leopard. She caught some of the petals with a silver net; she dried them upon the sunlight and hid them in the lining of her bed, for they were full of acrid but pleasing odours. So she herself early one morning walked abroad, early indeed, and passed along the river until she came to the field adjoining the mansion. Very sweet and strange the world seemed in the quiet after dawn. She stopped beside a half-used rick to look about her; there was a rush of surprised wings behind the stack and a thousand starlings fled up into the air. She heard their wings beating the air until they had crossed the river and dropped gradually into an elm tree like a black shower. Then she perceived a tall tree shining with crimson blooms and long dark boughs bending low upon the river. Near it a tiny red cottage stood in the field like a painted box, surrounded by green triangular bushes. It was a respectable looking cottage, named River View. On her approach the door suddenly opened, and a youth with a towel, just that and nothing more, emerged. He took flying rejoicing leaps towards the flaming tree, sprung upon its lowest limb and flung himself into the stream. He glided there like a rod of ivory, but a crimson shower fell from the quivering tree and veiled the pleasing boy until he climbed out upon the opposite bank and stood covered, like a leopard, with splendid crimson scars. The princess dared peer no longer; she retraced her steps, musing homewards to breakfast and was rude to Smith because he was such a fool not to have discovered the young man who lived next door under the mysterious tree.

At the earliest opportunity she left a card at River View. Narcissus was the subject's name, and in due time he came to dinner, and they had green grapes and black figs, nuts like sweet wax and wine like melted amethysts. The princess loved him so much that he visited her very often and stayed very late. He was only a poet and she a princess, so she could not possibly marry him although this was what she very quickly longed to do; but as she was only a princess, and he a poet clinking his golden spurs, he did not want to be married to her. He had thick curling locks of hair red as copper, the mild eyes of a child, and a voice that could out-sing a thousand delightful birds. When she heard his soft laughter in the dim delaying eve he grew strange and alluring to the princess. She knew it was because he was so beautiful that everybody loved him and wanted to win and keep him, but he had no inclination for anything but his art – which was to express himself. That was very sad for the princess; to be able to retain nothing of him but his poems, his fading images, while he himself eluded her as the wind eludes all detaining arms, forest and feather, briar and down of a bird. He did not seem to be a man at all but just a fairy image that slipped from her arms, gone, like brief music in the moonlight, before she was aware.

When he fell sick she watched by his bed.

'Tell me,' she murmured, her wooing palms caressing his flaming hair, 'tell me you love me.'

All he would answer was, 'I dream of loving you, and I love dreaming of you, but how can I tell if I love you?'

Very tremulous but arrogant she demanded of him, 'Shall I not know if you love me at all?'

'Ask the fox in your brake, the hart upon your mountain. I can never know if you love *me*.'

'I have given you my deepest vows, Narcissus; love like this is wider than the world.'

'The same wind blows in desert as in grove.'

'You do not love at all.'

'Words are vain, princess, but when I die, put these white hands like flowers about my heart; if I dream the unsleeping dream I will tell you there.'

'My beloved,' she said, 'if you die I will put upon your grave a shrine of silver, and in it an ark of gold jewelled with green garnets and pink sapphires. My spirit should dwell in it alone and wait for you; until you came back again I could not live.'

The poet died.

The princess was wild with grief, but she commanded her Lord Chancellor and he arranged magnificent obsequies. The shrine of silver and the ark of jewelled gold were ordered, a grave dug in a new planted garden more wonderful than the princess's bower, and a TO LET bill appeared in the window of River View. At last Narcissus, with great pomp, was buried, the shrine and the ark of gold were clapped down upon him, and the princess in blackest robes was led away on the arm of Smith – Smith was wonderful.

The sun that evening did not set – it mildly died out of

the sky. Darkness came into the meadows, the fogs came out of them and hovered over the river and the familiar night sounds began. The princess sat in the mansion with a lonely heart from which all hopes were receding; no, not receding, she could see only the emptiness from which all her hopes had gone.

At midnight the spirit of Narcissus in its cerecloth rose up out of the grave, frail as a reed; rose out of its grave and stood in the cloudy moonlight beside the shrine and the glittering ark. He tapped upon the jewels with his fingers but there was no sound came from it, no fire, no voice. 'O holy love,' sighed the ghost, 'it is true what I feared, it is true, alas, it is true!' And lifting again his vague arm he crossed out the inscription on his tomb and wrote there instead with a grey and crumbling finger his last poem:

> Pride and grief in your heart,
> Love and grief in mine.

Then he crept away until he came to the bower in the princess's garden. It was all silent and cold; the moon was touching with brief beam the paps of the plaster Diana. The ghost laid himself down to rest forever beneath the squinancy tree, to rest and to wait; he wanted to forestall time's inscrutable awards. He sank slowly into the earth as a knot of foam slips through the beach of the seashore. Deep down he rested and waited.

Day after day, month after month, the constant princess went to her new grove of lamentation. The grave garden was magnificent with holy flowers, the shrine polished and glistening, the inscription crisp and clear – the ghost's erasure being vain for mortal eyes. In the ark she knew her spirit brooded and yearned, she fancied she could see its tiny flame behind the garnets and sapphires, and in a way this gave her happiness. Meanwhile her own once happy bower was left to neglect. The bolt rusted in its gate, the shrubs rioted, tree trunks were crusted with oozy fungus, their boughs cracked to decay, the rose fell rotten, and toads and vermin lurked in the desolation of the glades. 'Twas pitiful; 'twas as if the heart of the princess had left its pleasant bower and had indeed gone to live in her costly shrine.

In the course of time she was forced to go away on business of state and travelled for many months; on her return the face of the Lord Chancellor was gloomy with misery. The golden ark had been stolen. Alarm and chagrin filled the princess. She went to the grave. It too had now grown weedy and looked forlorn. It was as if her own heart had been stolen away from her. 'Oh,' she moaned, 'what does it matter!' and, turning away, went home to her bower. There, among that sad sight, she saw a strange new tree almost in bloom. She gave orders for the pool to be cleansed and the bower restored to its former beauty. This was done, and on a bright day when the blazon of the sun was kind she went into the bower again, flung her black robes from her, and slipped like a rod of ivory into the velvet water. There were no blooms to gather now, though she searched with her silver net, but as she walked from the pool her long hair caught in the boughs of the strange tall squinancy tree, and in the disentangling it showered upon her beautiful crimson blooms that as they fell lingered upon her hips, her sweet shoulders, and kissed her shining knees.

Weep not my Wanton

Air and light on Sack Down at summer sunset were soft
as ointment and sweet as milk; at least, that is the notion
the down might give to a mind that bloomed within its
calm horizons, some happy victim of romance it might be,
watching the silken barley moving in its lower fields with
the slow movement of summer sea, reaching no harbour,
having no end. The toilers had mostly given over; their
ploughs and harrows were left to the abandoned fields;
they had taken their wages and gone, or were going, home;
but at the crown of the hill a black barn stood by the roadside,
and in its yard, amid sounds of anguish, a score of young
boar pigs were being gelded by two brown lads and a gipsy
fellow. Not half a mile of distance here could enclose you
the compass of their cries. If a man desired peace he would
step fast down the hill towards Arwall with finger in ear until
he came to quiet at a bank overlooking slopes of barley, and
could perceive the fogs of June being born in the standing
grass beyond.

Four figures, a labourer and his family, travelled slowly
up the road proceeding across the hill, a sound mingling
dully with their steps – the voice of the man. You could
not tell if it were noise of voice or of footsteps that first
came into your ear, but it could be defined on their advance
as the voice of a man upbraiding his little son.

'You're a naughty, naughty – you're a vurry, *vurry*
naughty boy! Oi can't think what's comen tyeh!'

The father towered above the tiny figure shuffling under
his elbow, and kept his eyes stupidly fixed upon him. He
saw a thin boy, a spare boy, a very shrunken boy of seven

or eight years, crying quietly. He let no grief out of his lip, but his white face was streaming with dirty tears. He wore a man's cap, an unclean sailor jacket, large knickerbockers that made a mockery of his lean joints, a pair of women's button boots, and he looked straight ahead.

'The idear! To go and lose a sixpence like that then! Where dye think yer'll land yerself, ay? Wher'd I be if I kept on losing sixpences, ay? A creature like you, ay!' and lifting his heavy hand the man struck the boy a blow behind with shock enough to disturb a heifer. They went on, the child with sobs that you could feel rather than hear. As they passed the black barn the gipsy bawled encouragingly: 'Selp me, father, that's a good 'un, wallop his trousers!'

But the man ignored him, as he ignored the yell of the pig and the voice of the lark rioting above them all; he continued his litany:

'You're a naughty, naughty *boy*, an' I dunno what's comen tyeh!'

The woman, a poor slip of a woman she was, walked behind them with a smaller child: she seemed to have no desire to shield the boy or to placate the man. She did not seem to notice them, and led the toddling babe, to whom she gabbled, some paces in the rear of the man of anger. He was a great figure with a bronzed face; his trousers were tied at the knee, his wicker bag was slung over his shoulder. With his free and massive hand he held the hand of the boy. He was slightly drunk, and walked with his legs somewhat wide, at the beginning of each stride lifting his heel higher than was required, and at the end of it placing his foot firmly but obliquely inwards. There were two bright medals on the breast of his waistcoat, presumably for valour; he was perhaps a man who would stand upon his rights and his dignities, such as they were – but then he was drunk. His language, oddly unprofane, gave a subtle and mean point to his decline from the heroic standard. He only ceased his complaining to gaze swayingly at the boy; then he struck him. The boy, crying quietly, made no effort to avoid or resist him.

'You understand me, you bad boy! As long as you're with me you got to come under collar. And wher'll you be next I *dunno*, a bad creature like you, ay! An' then to turn roun' an' answer me! *I dunno!* I dunno *what's* comen tyeh. Ye know ye lost that sixpence through glammering about. Wher d'ye lose it, ay? Wher dy'e lose it, ay?'

At these questions he seized the boy by the neck and shook him as a child does a bottle of water. The baby behind them was taken with little gusts of laughter at the sight, and the woman cooed back playfully at her.

'George, George!' yelled the woman.

The man turned round.

'Look after Annie!' she yelled again.

'What's up?' he called.

Her only answer was a giggle of laughter as she disappeared behind a hedge. The child toddled up to its father and took his hand, while the quiet boy took her other hand with relief. She laughed up into their faces, and the man resumed his homily.

'He's a bad, bad boy. He's a vurry *naughty* bad boy!'

By and by the woman came shuffling after them; the boy looked furtively around and dropped his sister's hand.

'Carm on, me beauty!' cried the man, lifting the girl to his shoulder. 'He's a bad boy; you 'ave a ride on your daddy.' They went on alone, and the woman joined the boy. He looked up at her with a sad face.

'O, my Christ, Johnny!' she said, putting her arms round the boy, 'what's 'e bin doin' to yeh? Yer face is all blood!'

'It's only me nose, mother. Here,' he whispered, 'here's the tanner.'

They went together down the hill towards the inn, which had already a light in its windows. The screams from the barn had ceased, and a cart passed them full of young pigs, bloody and subdued. The hill began to resume its old dominion of soft sounds. It was nearly nine o'clock, and one anxious farmer still made hay although, on this side of the down, day had declined, and with a greyness that came not from the sky, but crept up from the world. From the quiet hill, as the last skein of cocks was carted to the stack, you could hear dimly men's voices and the rattle of their gear.

Adam & Eve & Pinch Me

... and in the whole of his days, vividly at the end of the afternoon – he repeated it again and again to himself – the kind country spaces had *never* absorbed *quite* so rich a glamour of light, so miraculous a bloom of clarity. He could feel streaming in his own mind, in his bones, the same crystalline brightness that lay upon the land. Thoughts and images went flowing through him as easily and amiably as fish swim in their pools; and as idly, too, for one of his specutions took up the theme of his family name. There was such an agreeable oddness about it, just as there was about all the luminous sky today, that it touched him as just a little remarkable. What *did* such a name connote, signify, or symbolize? It was a rann of a name, but it had euphony! Then again, like the fish, his ambulating fancy flashed into other shallows, and he giggled as he paused, peering at the buds in the brake. Turning back towards his house again he could see, beyond its roofs, the spire of the church tinctured richly as the vane: all round him was a new grandeur upon the grass of the fields, and the spare trees had shadows below that seemed to support them in the manner of a plinth, more real than themselves, and the dykes and any chance heave of the level fields were underlined, as if for special emphasis, with long shades of mysterious blackness.

With a little drift of emotion that had at other times assailed him in the wonder and ecstasy of pure light, Jaffa Codling pushed through the slit in the back hedge and stood within his own garden. The gardener was at work. He could hear the voices of the children about the lawn at the other side of the house. He was very happy, and the place was beautiful, a fine white many-windowed house rising from a lawn bowered with plots of mould, turreted with shrubs, and overset with a vast walnut tree. This house had deep clean eaves, a roof of faint coloured slates that, after rain, glowed dully, like onyx or jade, under the red chimneys, and half-way up at one end was a balcony set with black balusters. He went to a French window that stood open and stepped into the dining room. There was no one within, and, on that lonely instant, a strange feeling of emptiness dropped upon him. The clock ticked almost as if it had been caught in some indecent act; the air was dim and troubled after that glory outside. Well, now, he would go up at once to his study and write down for his new book the ideas and images he had accumulated – beautiful rich thoughts they were – during that wonderful afternoon. He went to mount the stairs and he was passed by one of the maids; humming a silly song she brushed past him rudely, but he was an easy-going man – maids were unteachably tiresome – and reaching the landing he sauntered towards his room. The door stood slightly open and he could hear voices within. He put his hand upon the door . . . it would not open any farther. What the devil . . . he pushed – like the bear in the tale – and he pushed, and he pushed – was there something against it on the other side? He put his shoulder to it . . . some wedge must be there, and *that* was extraordinary. Then his whole apprehension was swept up and whirled as by an avalanche – Mildred, his wife, was in there; he could hear her speaking to a man in fair soft tones and the rich phrases that could be used only by a woman yielding a deep affection to him. Codling kept still. Her words burned on his mind and thrilled him as if spoken to himself. There was a movement in the room, then utter silence. He again thrust savagely at the partly open door, but he could not stir it. The silence within continued. He beat upon the door with his fists, crying, 'Mildred, Mildred!' There was no response, but he could hear the rocking arm-chair commence to swing to and fro. Pushing his hand round the edge of the door he tried to thrust his head between the opening. There was not space for this, but he could just peer into the corner of a mirror hung near, and this is what he saw: the chair at one end of its swing, a man sitting in it, and upon one arm of it Mildred, the beloved woman, with her lips upon the man's face, caressing him with her hands. Codling made another effort to get into the room — as vain as it was violent. 'Do you hear me, Mildred?' he shouted. Apparently neither of them heard him; they rocked to and fro while he gazed stupefied. What, in the name of God . . . What this . . . was she bewitched . . . were there such things after all as magic, devilry!

He drew back and held himself quite steadily. The chair stopped swaying, and the room grew awfully still. The sharp ticking of the clock in the hall rose upon the house like the tongue of some perfunctory mocker. Couldn't they hear the clock? . . . Couldn't they hear his heart? He had to put his hand upon his heart, for, surely, in that great silence inside there, they would hear its beat, growing so loud now that it seemed almost to stun him! Then in a queer way he found himself reflecting, observing, analysing his own actions and intentions. He found some of them to be just a little spurious, counterfeit. He felt it would be easy, so perfectly easy to flash in one blast of anger and annihilate the two. He would do nothing of the kind. There was no occasion for it. People didn't really do that sort of thing, or, at least, not with a genuine passion. There was no need for anger. His curiosity was satisfied, quite satisfied, he was certain, he had not the remotest interest in the man. A welter of unexpected thoughts swept upon his mind as he stood there. As a writer of books he was often stimulated by the emotions and impulses of other people, and now his own surprise was beginning to intrigue him, leaving him, O, quite unstirred emotionally, but interesting him profoundly.

He heard the maid come stepping up the stairway again, humming her silly song. He did not want a scene, or to be caught eavesdropping, and so turned quickly to another door. It was locked. He sprang to one beyond it; the handle would not turn. 'Bah! what's *up* with 'em?' But the girl was now upon him, carrying a tray of coffee things. 'O, Mary!' he exclaimed casually, 'I . . .' To his astonishment the girl stepped past him as if she did not hear or see him, tapped upon the door of his study, entered, and closed the door behind her. Jaffa Codling then got really angry. 'Hell! were the blasted servants in it!' He dashed to the door again and tore at the handle. It would not even turn, and, though he wrenched with fury at it, the room was utterly sealed against him. He went away for a chair with which to smash the effrontery of that door. No, he wasn't angry, either with his wife or this fellow – Gilbert, she had called him – who had a strangely familiar aspect as far as he had been able to take it in; but when one's servants . . . faugh!

The door opened and Mary came forth smiling demurely. He was a few yards farther along the corridor at that moment. 'Mary!' he shouted, 'leave the door open!' Mary carefully closed it and turned her back on him. He sprang after her with bad words bursting from him as she went towards the stairs and flitted lightly down, humming all the way as if in derision. He leaped downwards after her three steps at a time, but she trotted with amazing swiftness into the kitchen and slammed the door in his face. Codling stood, but kept his hands carefully away from the door, kept them behind him. 'No, no,' he whispered cunningly, 'there's something fiendish about door handles today, I'll go and get a bar, or a butt of timber,' and, jumping out into the garden for some such thing, the miracle happened to him. For it was nothing else than a miracle, the unbelievable, the impossible, simple and laughable if you will, but having as much validity as any miracle can ever invoke. It was simple and laughable because by all the known physical laws he should have collided with his gardener, who happened to pass the window with his wheelbarrow as Codling jumped out on to the path. And it was unbelievable that they should not, and impossible that they *did* not collide; and it was miraculous, because

Codling stood for a brief moment in the garden path and the wheelbarrow of Bond, its contents, and Bond himself passed apparently through the figure of Codling as if he were so much air, as if he were not a living breathing man but just a common ghost. There was no impact, just a momentary breathlessness. Codling stood and looked at the retreating figure going on utterly unaware of him. It is interesting to record that Codling's first feelings were mirthful. He giggled. He was jocular. He ran along in front of the gardener, and let him pass through him once more; then after him again; he scrambled into the man's barrow, and was wheeled about by this incomprehensible thick-headed gardener who was dead to all his master's efforts to engage his attention. Presently he dropped the wheelbarrow and went away, leaving Codling to cogitate upon the occurrence. There was no room for doubt, some essential part of him had become detached from the obviously not less vital part. He felt he was essential because he was responding to the experience, he was reacting in the normal way to normal stimuli, although he happened for the time being to be invisible to his fellows and unable to communicate with them. How had it come about – this queer thing? How could he discover what part of him had cut loose, as it were? There was no question of this being death; death wasn't funny, it wasn't a joke; he had still all his human instincts. You didn't get angry with a faithless wife or joke with a fool of a gardener if you were dead, certainly not! He had realised enough of himself to know he was the usual man of instincts, desires, and pro-hibitions, complex and contradictory; his family history for a million or two years would have denoted that, not explicitly – obviously impossible – but suggestively. He had found himself doing things he had no desire to do, doing things he had a desire *not* to do, thinking thoughts that had no contig-uous meanings, no meanings that could be related to his general experience. At odd times he had been chilled – aye, and even agreeably surprised – at the immense potential evil in himself. But still, this was no mere Jekyll and Hyde

affair, that a man and his own ghost should separately inhabit the same world was a horse of quite another colour.
The other part of him was alive and active somewhere . . .
as alive . . . as alive . . . yes, as *he* was, but dashed if he knew
where! What a lark when they got back to each other and
compared notes! In his tales he had brooded over so many
imagined personalities, followed in the track of so many
psychological enigmas that he *had* felt at times a stranger to
himself. What if, after all, that brooding had given him the
faculty of projecting this figment of himself into the world
of men. Or was he some unrealized latent element of being
without its natural integument, doomed now to drift over
the ridge of the world for ever. Was it his personality, his
spirit? Then how was the dashed thing working? Here was
he with the most wonderful happening in human experience,
and he couldn't differentiate or disinter things. He was like
a new Adam flung into some old Eden.

There was Bond tinkering about with some plants a
dozen yards in front of him. Suddenly his three children
came round from the other side of the house, the youngest
boy leading them, carrying in his hand a small sword which
was made, not of steel, but of some more brightly shining
material; indeed it seemed at one moment to be of gold,
and then again of flame, transmuting everything in its
neighbourhood into the likeness of flame, the hair of the
little girl Eve, a part of Adam's tunic; and the fingers of the
boy Gabriel as he held the sword were like pale tongues of
fire. Gabriel, the youngest boy, went up to the gardener
and gave the sword into his hands, saying: 'Bond, is this
sword any good?' Codling saw the gardener take the weapon
and examine it with a careful sort of smile; his great gnarled
hands became immediately transparent, the blood could
be seen moving diligently about the veins. Codling was so
interested in the sight that he did not gather in the gardener's
reply. The little boy was dissatisfied and repeated his question, 'No, but Bond, *is* this sword any good?' Codling rose,
and stood by invisible. The three beautiful children were

3

grouped about the great angular figure of the gardener in his soiled clothes, looking up now into his face, and now at the sword, with anxiety in all their puckered eyes. 'Well, Marse Gabriel,' Codling could hear him reply, 'as far as a sword goes, it may be a good un, or it may be a bad un, but, good as it is, it can never be anything but a bad thing.' He then gave it back to them; the boy Adam held the haft of it, and the girl Eve rubbed the blade with curious fingers. The younger boy stood looking up at the gardener with unsatisfied gaze. 'But, Bond, *can't* you say if this sword's any *good*?' Bond turned to his spade and trowels. 'Mebbe the shape of it's wrong, Marse Gabriel, though it seems a pretty handy size.' Saying this he moved off across the lawn. Gabriel turned to his brother and sister and took the sword from them; they all followed after the gardener and once more Gabriel made inquiry: 'Bond, is this sword any *good*?' The gardener again took it and made a few passes in the air like a valiant soldier at exercise. Turning then, he lifted a bright curl from the head of Eve and cut it off with a sweep of the weapon. He held it up to look at it critically and then let it fall to the ground. Codling sneaked behind him and, picking it up, stood stupidly looking at it. 'Mebbe, Marse Gabriel,' the gardener was saying, 'it ud be better made of steel, but it has a smartish edge on it.' He went to pick up the barrow but Gabriel seized it with a spasm of anger, and cried out: 'No, no, Bond, will you say, just yes or no, Bond, is this sword any *good*?' The gardener stood still, and looked down at the little boy, who repeated his question – 'just yes or no, Bond!' 'No, Marse Gabriel!' 'Thank you, Bond,' replied the child with dignity, 'that's all we wanted to know,' and, calling to his mates to follow him, he ran away to the other side of the house.

Codling stared again at the beautiful lock of hair in his hand, and felt himself grow so angry that he picked up a strange looking flowerpot at his feet and hurled it at the retreating gardener. It struck Bond in the middle of the back and, passing clean through him, broke on the wheel of his barrow, but Bond seemed to be quite unaware of this catastrophe. Codling rushed after, and, taking the gardener by the throat, he yelled, 'Damn you, will you tell me what all this means?' But Bond proceeded calmly about his work un-noticing, carrying his master about as if he were a clinging vapour, or a scarf hung upon his neck. In a few moments, Codling dropped exhausted to the ground. 'What . . . O Hell . . . what, what am I to do?' he groaned, 'What has happened to me? What shall I *do*? What *can* I do?' He looked at the broken flowerpot. 'Did I invent that?' He pulled out his watch. 'That's a real watch, I hear it ticking, and it's six o'clock.' Was he dead or disembodied or mad? What was this infernal lapse of identity? And who the devil, yes, who was it upstairs with Mildred? He jumped to his feet and hurried to the window; it was shut; to the door, it was fastened; he was powerless to open either. Well! well! this was experimental psychology with a vengeance, and he began to chuckle again. He'd have to write to McDougall about it. Then he turned and saw Bond wheeling across the lawn towards him again. '*Why* is that fellow always shoving that infernal green barrow around?' he asked, and, the fit of fury seizing him again, he rushed towards Bond, but, before he reached him, the three children danced into the garden again, crying, with great excitement, 'Bond, O, Bond!' The gardener stopped and set down the terrifying barrow; the children crowded about him, and Gabriel held out another shining thing, asking: 'Bond, is this box any good?' The gardener took the box and at once his eyes lit up with interest and delight. 'O, Marse Gabriel, where'd ye get it? Where'd ye get it?' 'Bond,' said the boy impatiently, 'is the box any *good*?' 'Any good?' echoed the man, 'Why, Marse Gabriel, Marse Adam, Miss Eve, look yere!' Holding it down in front of them, he lifted the lid from the box and a bright coloured bird flashed out and flew round and round above their heads. 'O,' screamed Gabriel with delight, 'it's a kingfisher!' 'That's what it is,' said Bond, 'a kingfisher!' 'Where?' asked Adam. 'Where?'

asked Eve. 'There it flies – round the fountain – see it? see it!' 'No,' said Adam. 'No,' said Eve.

'O, do, do, see it,' cried Gabriel, 'here it comes, it's coming!' and, holding his hands on high, and standing on his toes, the child cried out as happy as the bird which Codling saw flying above them.

'I can't see it,' said Adam.

'Where is it, Gaby?' asked Eve.

'O, you stupids,' cried the boy. '*There* it goes. There it goes . . . there . . . it's gone!'

He stood looking brightly at Bond, who replaced the lid.

'What shall we do now?' he exclaimed eagerly. For reply, the gardener gave the box into his hand, and walked off with the barrow. Gabriel took the box over to the fountain. Codling, unseen, went after him, almost as excited as the boy; Eve and her brother followed. They sat upon the stone tank that held the falling water. It was difficult for the child to unfasten the lid; Codling attempted to help him, but he was powerless. Gabriel looked up into his father's face and smiled. Then he stood up and said to the others:

'Now, *do* watch it this time.'

They all knelt carefully beside the water. He lifted the lid and, behold, a fish like a gold carp, but made wholly of fire, leaped from the box into the fountain. The man saw it dart down into the water, he saw the water bubble up behind it, he heard the hiss that the junction of fire and water produces, and saw a little track of steam follow the bubbles about the tank until the figure of the fish was consumed and disappeared. Gabriel, in ecstasies, turned to his sister with blazing happy eyes, exclaiming:

'There! Evey!'

'What was it?' asked Eve, nonchalantly, 'I didn't see anything.'

'More didn't I,' said Adam.

'Didn't you see that lovely fish?'

'No,' said Adam.

'No,' said Eve.

'O, stupids,' cried Gabriel, 'it went right past the bottom of the water.'

'Let's get a fishin' hook,' said Adam.

'No, no, no,' said Gabriel, replacing the lid of the box. 'O, no.'

Jaffa Codling had remained on his knees staring at the water so long that, when he looked around him again, the children had gone away. He got up and went to the door, and that was closed; the windows, fastened. He went moodily to a garden bench and sat on it with folded arms. Dusk had begun to fall into the shrubs and trees, the grass to grow dull, the air chill, the sky to muster its gloom. Bond had overturned his barrow, stalled his tools in the lodge, and gone to his home in the village. A curious cat came round the house and surveyed the man who sat chained to his seven-horned dilemma. It grew dark and fearfully silent. Was the world empty now? Some small thing, a snail perhaps, crept among the dead leaves in the hedge, with a sharp, irritating noise. A strange flood of mixed thoughts poured through his mind until at last one idea disentangled itself, and he began thinking with tremendous fixity of little Gabriel. He wondered if he could brood or meditate, or 'will' with sufficient power to bring him into the garden again. The child had just vaguely recognized him for a moment at the waterside. He'd try that dodge, telepathy was a mild kind of a trick after so much of the miraculous. If he'd lost his blessed body, at least the part that ate and smoked and talked to Mildred . . . He stopped as his mind stumbled on a strange recognition . . . What a joke, of course . . . idiot . . . not to have seen *that*. He stood up in the garden with joy . . . of course, *he* was upstairs with Mildred, it was himself, the other bit of him, that Mildred had been talking to. What a howling fool he'd been.

He found himself concentrating his mind on the purpose of getting the child Gabriel into the garden once more, but it was with a curious mood that he endeavoured to establish this relationship. He could not fix his will into any calm intensity of power, or fixity of purpose, or pleasurable mental ecstasy. The utmost force seemed to come with a malicious threatening splenetic 'entreaty'. That damned snail in the hedge broke the thread of his meditation; a dog began to bark sturdily from a distant farm; the faculties of his mind became joggled up like a child's picture puzzle, and he brooded unintelligibly upon such things as skating and steam engines, and Elizabethan drama so lapped about with themes like jealousy and chastity. Really now, Shakespeare's Isabella was the most consummate snob in . . . He looked up quickly to his wife's room and saw Gabriel step from the window to the balcony as if he were fearful of being seen. The boy lifted up his hands and placed the bright box on the rail of the balcony. He looked up at the faint stars for a moment or two, and then carefully released the lid of the box. What came out of it and rose into the air appeared to Codling to be just a piece of floating light, but as it soared above the roof he saw it grow to be a little ancient ship, with its hull and fully set sails and its three masts all of faint primrose flame colour. It cleaved through the air, rolling slightly as a ship through the wave, in widening circles above the house, making a curving ascent until it lost the shape of a vessel and became only a moving light hurrying to some sidereal shrine. Codling glanced at the boy on the balcony, but in that brief instant something had happened, the ship had burst like a rocket and released three coloured drops of fire which came falling slowly, leaving beautiful grey furrows of smoke in their track. Gabriel leaned over the rail with outstretched palms, and, catching the green star and the blue one as they drifted down to him, he ran with a rill of laughter back into the house. Codling sprang forward just in time to catch the red star; it lay vividly blasting his own palm for a monstrous second, and then, slipping through, was gone. He stared at the ground, at the balcony, the sky, and then heard an exclamation . . . his wife stood at his side.

'Gilbert! How you frightened me!' she cried, 'I thought

you were in your room; come along in to dinner.' She took his arm and they walked up the steps into the dining room together. 'Just a moment,' said her husband, turning to the door of the room. His hand was upon the handle, which turned easily in his grasp, and he ran upstairs to his room. He opened the door. The light was on, the fire was burning brightly, a smell of cigarette smoke about, pen and paper upon his desk, the Japanese book-knife, the gilt matchbox, everything all right, no one there. He picked up a book from his desk . . . *Monna Vanna*. His bookplate was in it – *Ex Libris – Gilbert Cannister*. He put it down beside the green dish; two yellow oranges were in the green dish, and two most deliberately green Canadian apples rested by their side. He went to the door and swung it backwards and forwards quite easily. He sat on his desk trying to piece the thing together, glaring at the print and the book-knife and the smart matchbox, until his wife came up behind him exclaiming: 'Come along, Gilbert!'

'Where are the kids, old man?' he asked her, and, before she replied, he had gone along to the nursery. He saw the two cots, his boy in one, his girl in the other. He turned whimsically to Mildred, saying, 'There *are* only two, *are* there?' Such a question did not call for reply, but he confronted her as if expecting some assuring answer. She was staring at him with her bright beautiful eyes.

'Are there?' he repeated.

'How strange you should ask me that now!' she said . . . 'If you're a very good man . . . perhaps . . .'

'Mildred!'

She nodded brightly.

He sat down in the rocking chair, but got up again saying to her gently – 'We'll call him Gabriel.'

'But, suppose –'

'No, no,' he said, stopping her lovely lips, 'I know all about him.' And he told her a pleasant little tale.

Dusky Ruth

At the close of an April day, chilly and wet, the traveller came to a country town. In the Cotswolds, though the towns are small and sweet and the inns snug, the general habit of the land is bleak and bare. He had newly come upon upland roads so void of human affairs, so lonely, that they might have been made for some forgotten uses by departed men, and left to the unwitting passage of such strangers as himself. Even the unending walls, built of old rough laminated rock, that detailed the far-spreading fields, had grown very old again in their courses; there were dabs of darkness, buttons of moss, and fossils on every stone. He had passed a few neighbourhoods, sometimes at the crook of a stream, or at the cross of debouching roads, where old habitations, their gangrenated thatch riddled with bird holes, had not been so much erected as just spattered about the place. Beyond these signs an odd lark or blackbird, the ruckle of partridges, or the nifty gallop of a hare, had been the only mitigation of the living loneliness that was almost as profound by day as by night. But the traveller had a care for such times and places. There are men who love to gaze with the mind at things that can never be seen, feel at least the throb of a beauty that will never be known, and hear over immense bleak reaches the echo of that which is no celestial music, but only their own hearts' vain cries; and though his garments clung to him like clay it was with deliberate questing step that the traveller trod the single street of the town, and at last entered the inn, shuffling his shoes in the doorway for a moment and striking the raindrops from his hat. Then he turned into a small smoking-room. Leather-lined benches, much worn, were fixed to the wall under the window and in other odd corners and nooks behind mahogany tables. One wall was furnished with all the congenial gear of a bar, but without any intervening counter. Opposite a bright fire was burning, and a neatly dressed young woman sat before it in a Windsor chair, staring at the flames. There was no other inmate of the room, and as he entered the girl rose up and greeted him. He found that he could be accommodated for the night, and in a few moments his hat and scarf were removed and placed inside the fender, his wet overcoat was taken to the kitchen, the landlord, an old fellow, was lending him a roomy pair of slippers, and a maid was setting supper in an adjoining room.

He sat while this was doing and talked to the barmaid. She had a beautiful, but rather mournful face, as it was lit by the firelight, and when her glance was turned away from it her eyes had a piercing brightness. Friendly and well-spoken as she was, the melancholy in her aspect was noticeable – perhaps it was the dim room, or the wet day, or the long hours ministering a multitude of cocktails to thirsty gallantry.

When he went to his supper he found cheering food and drink, with pleasant garniture of silver and mahogany. There were no other visitors, he was to be alone; blinds were drawn, lamps lit, and the fire at his back was comforting. So he sat long about his meal until a white-faced maid came to clear the table, discoursing to him of country things as she busied about the room. It was a long narrow room, with a sideboard and the door at one end and the fireplace at the other. A bookshelf, almost devoid of books, contained a number of plates; the long wall that faced the windows was almost destitute of pictures, but there were hung upon it, for some inscrutable but doubtless sufficient reason, many dish-covers, solidly shaped, of the kind held in such mysterious regard and known as 'willow pattern'; one was even hung upon the face of a map. Two musty prints were mixed with them, presentments of horses having a stilted, extravagant physique and bestridden by images of inhuman and incommunicable dignity, clothed in whiskers, coloured jackets, and tight white breeches.

He took down the books from the shelf, but his interest was speedily exhausted, and the almanacs, the county directory, and various guide-books were exchanged for the *Cotswold Chronicle*. With this, having drawn the deep chair to the hearth, he whiled away the time. The newspaper amused him with its advertisements of stock shows, farm auctions, travelling quacks and conjurers, and there was a lengthy account of the execution of a local felon, one Timothy Bridger, who had murdered an infant in some shameful circumstances. This dazzling crescendo proved rather trying to the traveller; he threw down the paper.

The town was all quiet as the hills, and he could hear no sounds in the house. He got up and went across the hall to the smoke room. The door was shut, but there was light within, and he entered. The girl sat there much as he had seen her on his arrival, still alone, with feet on fender. He shut the door behind him, sat down, and crossing his legs puffed at his pipe, admired the snug little room and the pretty figure of the girl, which he could do without embarrassment as her meditative head, slightly bowed, was turned away from him. He could see something of her, too, in the mirror at the bar, which repeated also the agreeable contours of bottles of coloured wines and rich liqueurs – so entrancing in form and aspect that they seemed destined to charming histories, even in disuse – and those of familiar outline containing mere spirits or small beer, for which are reserved the harsher destinies of base oils, horse medicines, disinfectants, and cold tea. There were coloured glasses for bitter wines, white glasses for sweet, a tiny leaden sink beneath them, and the four black handles of the beer engine.

The girl wore a light blouse of silk, a short skirt of black velvet, and a pair of very thin silk stockings that showed the flesh of instep and shin so plainly that he could see they were reddened by the warmth of the fire. She had on a pair of dainty cloth shoes with high heels, but what was wonderful about her was the heap of rich black hair piled at the back of her head and shadowing the dusky neck. He sat puffing his pipe and letting the loud tick of the clock fill the quiet room. She did not stir and he could move no muscle. It was as if he had been willed to come there and wait silently. That, he felt now, had been his desire all the evening; and here, in her presence, he was more strangely stirred than by any event he could remember.

In youth he had viewed women as futile pitiable things that grew long hair, wore stays and garters, and prayed incomprehensible prayers. Viewing them in the stalls of the theatre from his vantage-point in the gallery, he always disliked the articulation of their naked shoulders. But still, there was a god in the sky, a god with flowing hair and exquisite eyes, whose one stride with an ardour grandly rendered took him across the whole round hemisphere to which his buoyant limbs were bound like spokes to the eternal rim and axle, his bright hair burning in the pity of the sunsets and tossing in the anger of the dawns.

Master traveller had indeed come into this room to be with this woman; she as surely desired him, and for all its accidental occasion it was as if he, walking the ways of the world, had suddenly come upon . . . what so imaginable with all permitted reverence as, well, just a shrine; and he, admirably humble, bowed the instant head.

Were there no other people within? The clock indicated a few minutes to nine. He sat on, still as stone, and the woman might have been of wax for all the movement or sound she made. There was allurement in the air between them; he had forborne his smoking, the pipe grew cold between his teeth. He waited for a look from her, a movement to break the trance of silence. No footfall in streets or house, no voice in the inn but the clock beating away as if pronouncing a doom. Suddenly it rasped out nine large notes, a bell in the town repeated them dolefully, and a cuckoo no farther than the kitchen mocked them with three times three. After that came the weak steps of the old landlord along the hall, the slam of doors, the clatter of lock and bolt, and then the silence returning unendurably upon them.

He arose and stood behind her; he touched the black hair. She made no movement or sign. He pulled out two or three combs, and dropping them into her lap let the whole mass tumble about his hands. It had a curious harsh touch in the unravelling, but was so full and shining; black as a rook's wings it was. He slid his palms through it. His fingers searched it and fought with its fine strangeness; into his mind there travelled a serious thought, stilling his wayward fancy – this was no wayward fancy, but a rite accomplished itself! (*Run, run, silly man, y'are lost!*) But having got so far he burnt his boats, leaned over, and drew her face back to him. And at that, seizing his wrists, she gave him back ardour for ardour, pressing his hands to her bosom, while the kiss was sealed and sealed again. Then she sprang up and picking his hat and scarf from the fender said:

'I have been drying them for you, but the hat has shrunk a bit, I'm sure – I tried it on.'

He took them from her and put them behind him; he leaned lightly back upon the table, holding it with both his hands behind him; he could not speak.

'Aren't you going to thank me for drying them?' she asked, picking her combs from the rug and repinning her hair.

'I wonder why we did that?' he asked, shamedly.

'It is what I'm thinking too,' she said.

'You were so beautiful about . . . about it, you know.'

She made no rejoinder, but continued to bind her hair, looking brightly at him under her brows. When she had finished she went close to him.

'Will that do?'

'I'll take it down again.'

'No, no, the old man or the old woman will be coming in.'

'What of that?' he said, taking her into his arms, 'tell me your name.'

She shook her head, but she returned his kisses and stroked

his hair and shoulders with beautifully melting gestures.

'What is your name, I want to call you by your name?' he said; 'I can't keep calling you Lovely Woman, Lovely Woman.'

Again she shook her head and was dumb.

'I'll call you Ruth then, Dusky Ruth, Ruth of the black, beautiful hair.'

'That is a nice-sounding name – I knew a deaf and dumb girl named Ruth; she went to Nottingham and married an organ-grinder – but I should like it for my name.'

'Then I give it to you.'

'Mine is so ugly.'

'What is it?'

Again the shaken head and the burning caress.

'Then you shall be Ruth; will you keep that name?'

'Yes. If you give me the name I will keep it for you.'

Time had indeed taken them by the forelock, and they looked upon a ruddled world.

'I stake my one talent,' he said jestingly, 'and behold it returns me fortyfold; I feel like the boy who catches three mice with one piece of cheese.'

At ten o'clock the girl said:

'I must go and see how *they* are getting on,' and she went to the door.

'Are we keeping them up?'

She nodded.

'Are you tired?'

'No, I am not tired.'

She looked at him doubtfully.

'We ought not to stay in here; go into the coffee-room and I'll come there in a few minutes.'

'Right,' he whispered gaily, 'we'll sit up all night.'

She stood at the door for him to pass out, and he crossed the hall to the other room. It was in darkness except for the flash of the fire. Standing at the hearth he lit a match for the lamp, but paused at the globe; then he extinguished the match.

'No, it's better to sit in the firelight.'

He heard voices at the other end of the house that seemed to have a chiding note in them.

'Lord,' he thought, 'she is getting into a row?'

Then her steps came echoing over the stone floors of the hall; she opened the door and stood there with a lighted candle in her hand; he stood at the other end of the room, smiling.

'Good night,' she said.

'O no, no! come along,' he protested, but not moving from the hearth.

'Got to go to bed,' she answered.

'Are they angry with you?'

'No.'

'Well, then, come over here and sit down.'

'Got to go to bed,' she said again, but she had meanwhile put her candlestick upon the little sideboard and was trimming the wick with a burnt match.

'O, come along, just half an hour,' he protested. She did not answer but went on prodding the wick of the candle.

'Ten minutes, then,' he said, still not going towards her.

'Five minutes,' he begged.

She shook her head, and picking up the candlestick turned to the door. He did not move, he just called her name: 'Ruth!'

She came back then, put down the candlestick and tip-toed across the room until he met her. The bliss of the embrace was so poignant that he was almost glad when she stood up again and said with affected steadiness, though he heard the tremor in her voice:

'I must get you your candle.'

She brought one from the hall, set it on the table in front of him, and struck the match.

'What is my number?' he asked.

'Number six room,' she answered, prodding the wick vaguely with her match, while a slip of white wax dropped over the shoulder of the new candle. 'Number six ... next to mine.'

The match burnt out; she said abruptly 'Good night,' took up her own candle and left him there.

In a few moments he ascended the stairs and went into his room. He fastened the door, removed his coat, collar, and slippers, but the rack of passion had seized him and he moved about with no inclination to sleep. He sat down, but there was no medium of distraction. He tried to read the newspaper which he had carried up with him, and without realizing a single phrase he forced himself to read again the whole account of the execution of the miscreant Bridger. When he had finished this he carefully folded the paper and stood up, listening. He went to the parting wall and tapped thereon with his finger tips. He waited half a minute, one minute, two minutes; there was no answering sign. He tapped again, more loudly, with his knuckles, but there was no response, and he tapped many times. He opened his door as noiselessly as possible; along the dark passage there were slips of light under the other doors, the one next his own, and the one beyond that. He stood in the corridor listening to the rumble of old voices in the farther room, the old man and his wife going to their rest. Holding his breath fearfully, he stepped to *her* door and tapped gently upon it. There was no answer, but he could somehow divine her awareness of him; he tapped again; she moved to the door and whispered 'No, no, go away.' He turned the handle, the door was locked.

'Let me in,' he pleaded. He knew she was standing there an inch or two beyond him.

'Hush,' she called softly. 'Go away, the old woman has ears like a fox.'

He stood silent for a moment.

'Unlock it,' he urged; but he got no further reply, and feeling foolish and baffled he moved back to his own room, cast his clothes from him, doused the candle and crept into the bed with soul as wild as a storm-swept forest, his heart beating a vagrant summons. The room filled with strange heat, there was no composure for mind or limb, nothing but flaming visions and furious embraces.

'Morality ... what is it but agreement with your own soul?'

So he lay for two hours – the clocks chimed twelve – listening with foolish persistency for *her* step along the corridor, fancying every light sound – and the night was full of them – was her hand upon the door.

Suddenly – and then it seemed as if his very heart would abash the house with its thunder – he could hear distinctly someone knocking on the wall. He got quickly from his bed and stood at the door, listening. Again the knocking was heard, and having half-clothed himself he crept into the passage, which was now in utter darkness, trailing his hand along the wall until he felt her door; it was standing open. He entered her room and closed the door behind him. There was not the faintest gleam of light, he could see nothing. He whispered 'Ruth!' and she was standing there. She touched him, but not speaking. He put out his hands, and they met round her neck; her hair was flowing in its great wave about her; he put his lips to her face and found that her eyes were streaming with tears, salt and strange and disturbing. In the close darkness he put his arms about her with no thought but to comfort her; one hand had plunged through the long harsh tresses and the other across her hips before he realised that she was ungowned; then he was aware of the softness of her breasts and the cold naked sleekness of her shoulders. But she was crying there, crying silently with great tears, her strange sorrow stifling his desire.

'Ruth, Ruth, my beautiful dear!' he murmured soothingly. He felt for the bed with one hand, and turning back the quilt and sheets he lifted her in as easily as a mother does her child, replaced the bedding, and, in his clothes, he lay stretched beside her comforting her. They lay so, innocent as children, for an hour, when she seemed to have gone to sleep. He rose then and went silently to his room, full of weariness.

In the morning he breakfasted without seeing her, but as he had business in the world that gave him just an hour longer at the inn before he left it for good and all, he went into the smoke-room and found her. She greeted him with curious gaze, but merrily enough, for there were other men there now, farmers, a butcher, a registrar, an old, old man. The hour passed, but not these men, and at length he donned his coat, took up his stick, and said goodbye. Her shining glances followed him to the door, and from the window as far as they could view him.

The Cherry Tree

There was uproar somewhere among the backyards of Australia Street. It was so alarming that people at their midday meal sat still and stared at one another. A fortnight before murder had been done in the street, in broad daylight, with a chopper; people were nervous. An upper window was thrown open and a startled and startling head exposed.

'It's that young devil, Johnny Flynn, again! Killing rats!' shouted Mrs Knatchbole, shaking her fist towards the Flynns' backyard. Mrs Knatchbole was ugly; she had a goitred neck and a sharp skinny nose with an orb shining at its end, constant as grief.

'You wait, my boy, till your mother comes home, you just wait!' invited this apparition, but Johnny was gazing sickly at the body of a big rat slaughtered by the dogs of his friend George. The uproar was caused by the quarrelling of the dogs, possibly for honours, but more probably, as is the custom of victors, for loot.

'Bob down!' warned George, but Johnny bobbed up to catch the full anger of those baleful Knatchbole eyes. The urchin put his fingers promptly to his nose.

'Look at that for eight years old!' screamed the lady. 'Eight years old 'e is! As true as God's my maker I'll . . .'

The impending vow was stayed and blasted for ever, Mrs Knatchbole being taken with a fit of sneezing, whereupon the boys uttered some derisive 'Haw haws!'

So Mrs Knatchbole met Mrs Flynn that night as she came from work, Mrs Flynn being a widow who toiled daily and dreadfully at a laundry and perforce left her children, except for their school hours, to their own devices. The encounter was an emphatic one and the tired widow promised to admonish her boy.

'But it's alright, Mrs Knatchbole, he's going from me in a week, to his uncle in London he is going, a person of wealth, and he'll be no annoyance to ye then. I'm ashamed that he misbehaves but he's no bad boy really.'

At home his mother's remonstrances reduced Johnny to repentance and silence; he felt base indeed; he wanted to do something great and worthy at once to offset it all; he wished he had got some money, he'd have gone and bought her a bottle of stout – he knew she liked stout.

'Why do ye vex people so, Johnny?' asked Mrs Flynn wearily. 'I work my fingers to the bone for ye, week in and week out. Why can't ye behave like Pomony?'

His sister was a year younger than him; her name was Mona, which Johnny's elegant mind had disliked. One day he re-baptized her; Pomona she became and Pomona she remained. The Flynns sat down to supper. 'Never mind about all that, mum,' said the boy, kissing her as he passed her chair, 'talk to us about the cherry tree!' The cherry tree, luxuriantly blooming, was the crown of the mother's memories of her youth and her father's farm; around the myth of its wonderful blossoms and fruit she could weave garlands of romance, and to her own mind, as well as to the minds of her children, it became a heavenly symbol of her old lost home, grand with acres and delightful with orchard and full pantry. What wonder that in her humorous narration the joys were multiplied and magnified until even Johnny was obliged to intervene. 'Look here, how many horses *did* your father have, mum . . . really, though?' Mrs Flynn became vague, cast a furtive glance at this son of hers and then gulped with laughter until she recovered her ground with: 'Ah, but there *was* a cherry tree!' It was a grand supper – actually a polony and some potatoes. Johnny knew this was because he was going away. Ever since it was known that he was to go to London they had been having something special like this, or sheep's trotters, or a pig's tail. Mother seemed to grow kinder and kinder to him. He wished he had some money, he would like to buy her a bottle of stout – he knew she liked stout.

Well, Johnny went away to live with his uncle, but alas he was only two months in London before he was returned to his mother and Pomony. Uncle was an engine-driver who disclosed to his astounded nephew a passion for gardening. This was incomprehensible to Johnny Flynn. A great roaring boiling locomotive was the grandest thing in the world. Johnny had rides on it, so he knew. And it was easy for him to imagine that every gardener cherished in the darkness of his disappointed soul an unavailing passion for a steam engine, but how an engine-driver could immerse himself in the mushiness of gardening was a baffling problem. However, before he returned home he discovered one important thing from his uncle's hobby, and he sent the information to his sister:

Dear Pomona,

Uncle Harry has got a alotment and grow veggutables. He says what makes the mold is worms. You know we puled all the worms out off our garden and chukked them over Miss Natchbols wall. Well you better get some more quick a lot ask George to help you and I bring som seeds home when I comes next week by the xcursion on Moms birthday

Yours sincerely brother
John Flynn

On mother's birthday Pomona met him at the station. She kissed him shyly and explained that mother was going to have a half-holiday to celebrate the double occasion and would be home with them at dinner time.

'Pomona, did you get them worms?'

Pomona was inclined to evade the topic of worms for the garden, but fortunately her brother's enthusiasm for another gardening project tempered the wind of his indignation. When they reached home he unwrapped two parcels he had brought with him; he explained his scheme to his sister; he led her into the garden. The Flynns' backyard, mostly paved with bricks, was small, and so the enclosing walls, truculently capped by chips of glass, although too low for privacy were yet too high for the growth of any cherishable plant. Johnny had certainly once reared a magnificent exhibit of two cowslips, but these had been mysteriously destroyed by the Knatchbole cat. The dank little enclosure was charged with sterility; nothing flourished there except a lot of beetles and a dauntless evergreen bush, as tall as Johnny, displaying a profusion of thick shiny leaves that you could split on your tongue and make squeakers with. Pomona showed him how to do this and they then busied themselves in the garden until the dinner siren warned them that mother would be coming home. They hurried into the kitchen and Pomona quickly spread the cloth and the plates of food upon the table, while Johnny placed conspicuously in the centre, after laboriously extracting the stopper with a fork and a hair-pin, a bottle of stout brought from London. He had been much impressed by numberless advertisements upon the hoardings respecting this attractive beverage. The children then ran off to meet their mother and they all came home together with great hilarity. Mrs Flynn's attention having been immediately drawn to the sinister decoration of her dining table, Pomona was requested to pour out a glass of the nectar. Johnny handed this gravely to his parent, saying.

'Many happy returns of the day, Mrs Flynn!'

'O, dear, dear!' gasped his mother merrily, 'you drink first!'

'Excuse me, no, Mrs Flynn,' rejoined her son, 'many happy returns of the day!'

When the toast had been honoured Pomona and Johnny looked tremendously at each other.

'Shall we?' exclaimed Pomona. 'O yes,' decided Johnny; 'come on, mum, in the garden, something marvellous!'

She followed her children into the dull little den, and by happy chance the sun shone grandly for the occasion. Behold the dauntless evergreen bush had been stripped of its leaves and upon its blossomless twigs the children had hung numerous couples of ripe cherries, white and red and black.

'What do you think of it, mum?' they cried, snatching some of the fruit and pressing it into her hands, 'what do you think of it?'

'Beautiful!' replied Mrs Flynn in a tremulous voice. The children stared silently at their mother until she could bear it no longer. She turned and went sobbing into the kitchen.

The Black Dog

I

Having pocketed his fare the freckled rustic took himself and his antediluvian cab back to the village limbo from which they had briefly emerged. Loughlin checked his luggage into the care of the porter, an angular man with one eye who was apparently the only other living being in this remote minute station, and sat down in the platform shade. July noon had a stark eye-tiring brightness, and a silence so very deep – when that porter ceased his intolerable clatter – that Loughlin could hear footsteps crunching on the road half a mile away. The train was late. There were no other passengers. Nothing to look at except his trunks, two shiny rails in the grim track, red hollyhocks against white palings on the opposite bank.

The holiday in this quiet neighbourhood had delighted him, but its crowning experience had been too brief. On the last day but one the loveliest woman he had ever known had emerged almost as briefly as that cabman. Some men are constantly meeting that woman. Not so the Honourable Gerald Loughlin, but no man turns his back tranquilly on destiny even if it is but two days old and already some half-dozen miles away. The visit had come to its end, Loughlin had come to his station, the cab had gone back to its lair, but on reflection he could find no other reasons for going away and denying himself the delight of this proffered experience. Time was his own, as much as he could buy of it, and he had an income that enabled him to buy a good deal.

Moody and hesitant he began to fill his pipe when the one-eyed porter again approached him.

'Take a pipe of that?' said Loughlin, offering him the pouch.

'Thanky, sir, but I can't smoke a pipe; a cigarette I take now and again, thanky, sir, not often, just to keep me from cussing and damning. My wife buys me a packet sometimes, she says I don't swear so much then, but I don't know, I has to knock 'em off soon's they make me feel bad, and then, damn it all, I be worsen ever . . .'

'Look here,' said the other, interrupting him, 'I'm not going by this train after all. Something I have forgotten. Now look after my bags and I'll come along later, this afternoon.' He turned and left the station as hurriedly as if his business was really of the high importance the porter immediately conceived it to be.

The Honourable Gerald, though handsome and honest, was not a fool. A fool is one who becomes distracted between the claims of instinct and common sense; the larger foolishness is the peculiar doom of imaginative people, artists and their kind, while the smaller foolishness is the mark of all those who have nothing but their foolishness to endorse them. Loughlin responded to this impulse unhesitatingly but without distraction, calmly and directly as became a well-bred bachelor in the early thirties. He might have written to the young beauty with the queer name, Orianda Crabbe, but that course teemed with absurdities and difficulties for he was modest, his romantic imagination weak, and he had only met her at old Lady Tillington's a couple of days before. Of this mere girl, just twenty-three or twenty-four, he knew nothing save that they had been immediately and vividly charming to each other. That was no excuse for presenting himself again to the old invalid of Tillington Park, it would be impossible for him to do so, but there had been one vague moment of their recalled intercourse, a glimmering intimation, which just seemed to offer a remote possibility of achievement, and so he walked on in the direction of the park.

Tillington was some miles off and the heat was oppressive. At the end of an hour's stroll he stepped into The Three Pigeons at Denbury and drank a deep drink. It was quiet and deliciously cool in the taproom there, yes, as silent as that little station had been. Empty the world seemed today, quite empty; he had not passed a human creature. Happily bemused he took another draught. Eighteen small panes of glass in that long window and perhaps as many flies buzzing in the room. He could hear and see a breeze saluting the bright walled ivy outside and the bushes by a stream. This drowsiness was heaven, it made so clear his recollection of Orianda. It was impossible to particularize but she was in her way, her rather uncultured way, just perfection. He had engaged her upon several themes, music, fishing (Loughlin loved fishing), golf, tennis, and books; none of these had particularly stirred her but she had brains, quite an original turn of mind. There had been neither time nor opportunity to discover anything about her, but there she was, staying there, that was the one thing certain, apparently indefinitely, for she described the park in a witty detailed way even to a certain favourite glade which she always visited in the afternoons. When she had told him that, he could swear she was not finessing; no, no, it was a most engaging simplicity, a frankness that was positively marmoreal.

He would certainly write to her; yes, and he began to think of fine phrases to put in a letter, but could there be anything finer, now, just at this moment, than to be sitting with her in this empty inn. It was not a fair place, though it was clean, but how she would brighten it, yes! there were two long settles and two short ones, two tiny tables and eight spittoons (he *had* to count them), and somehow he felt her image flitting adorably into this setting, defeating with its native glory all the scrupulous beer-smelling impoverishment. And then, after a while, he would take her, and they would lie in the grass under a deep-bosomed tree and speak of love. How beautiful she would be. But she was not there, and so he left the inn and crossed the road to a church, pleasant and tiny and tidy, white-walled and clean-ceilinged. A sparrow chirped in the porch, flies hummed in the nave, a puppy was barking in the vicarage garden. How trivial, how absurdly solemn, everything seemed. The thud of the great pendulum in the tower had the sound of a dead man beating on a bar of spiritless iron. He was tired of the vapid tidiness of these altars with their insignificant tapestries, candlesticks of gilded wood, the bunches of pale flowers oppressed by the rich glow from the windows. He longed for an altar that should be an inspiring symbol of belief, a place of green and solemn walls with a dark velvet shrine sweeping aloft to the peaked roof unhindered by tarnishing lustre and tedious linen. Holiness was always something richly dim. There was no more holiness here than in the tough hassocks and rush-bottomed chairs; not here, surely, the apple of Eden flourished. And yet, turning to the lectern, he noted the large prayer book open at the office of marriage. He idly read over the words of the ceremony, filling in at the gaps the names of Gerald Wilmot Loughlin and Orianda Crabbe.

What a fool! He closed the book with a slam and left the church. Absurd! You *couldn't* fall in love with a person as sharply as all that, could you? But why not? Unless fancy was charged with the lightning of gods it was nothing at all.

Tramping away still in the direction of Tillington Park he came in the afternoon to that glade under a screen of trees spoken of by the girl. It was green and shady, full of scattering birds. He flung himself down in the grass under a deep-bosomed tree. She had spoken delightfully of this delightful spot.

When she came, for come she did, the confrontation left him very unsteady as he sprang to his feet. (Confound that potation at The Three Pigeons! Enormously hungry, too!) But he was amazed, entranced, she was so happy to see him again. They sat down together, but he was still bewildered and his confusion left him all at sixes and sevens. Fortunately her own rivulet of casual chatter carried them on until he suddenly asked, 'Are you related to the Crabbes of Cotterton – I fancy I know them?'

'No, I think not, no, I am from the south country, near the sea, nobody at all, my father keeps an inn.'

'An inn! How extraordinary! How very . . . very . . .'

'Extraordinary?' Nodding her head in the direction of the hidden mansion she added, 'I am her companion.'

'Lady Tillington's?'

She assented coolly, was silent, while Loughlin ransacked his brains for some delicate reference that would clear him over this . . . this . . . cataract. But he felt stupid – that confounded potation at The Three Pigeons! Why, that was where he had thought of her so admirably, too. He asked if she cared for the position, was it pleasant, and so on. Heavens, what an astonishing creature for a domestic; quite positively lovely, a compendium of delightful qualities, this girl, so frank, so simple!

'Yes, I like it, but home is better. I should love to go back to my home, to father, but I can't, I'm still afraid – I ran away from home three years ago, to go with my mother. I'm like my mother, she ran away from home too.'

Orianda picked up the open parasol which she had dropped, closed it in a thoughtful manner, and laid its crimson folds beside her. There was no other note of colour in her white attire; she was without a hat. Her fair hair had a quenching tinge upon it that made it less bright than gold, but more rare. Her cheeks had the colour of homely flowers, the lily and the pink. Her teeth were as even as the peas in a newly opened pod, as clear as milk.

'Tell me about all that. May I hear it?'

'I have not seen him or heard from him since, but I love him very much now.'

'Your father?'

'Yes, but he is stern, a simple man, and he is so just. We live at a tiny old inn at the end of a village near the hills. The Black Dog. It is thatched and has tiny rooms. It's painted all over with pink, pink whitewash.'

'Ah, I know.'

'There's a porch, under a sycamore tree, where people

sit, and an old rusty chain hanging on a hook just outside the door.'

'What's that for?'

'I don't know what it is for, horses, perhaps, but it is always there, I always see that rusty chain. And on the opposite side of the road there are three lime trees and behind them is the yard where my father works. He makes hurdles and ladders. He is the best hurdle maker in three counties, he has won many prizes at the shows. It is splendid to see him working at the willow wood, soft and white. The yard is full of poles and palings, spars and faggots, and long shavings of the thin bark like seaweed. It smells so nice. In the spring the chaffinches and wrens are singing about him all day long; the wren is lovely, but in the summer of course it's the whitethroats come chippering, and yellow-hammers.'

'Ah, blackbirds, thrushes, nightingales!'

'Yes, but it's the little birds seem to love my father's yard.'

'Well then, but why did you, why did you run away?'

'My mother was much younger, and different from father; she was handsome and proud too, and in all sorts of ways superior to him. They got to hate each other; they were so quiet about it, but I could see. Their only common interest was me, they both loved me very much. Three years ago she ran away from him. Quite suddenly, you know; there was nothing at all leading up to such a thing. But I could not understand my father, not then, he took it all so calmly. He did not mention even her name to me for a long time, and I feared to intrude; you see, I did not understand, I was only twenty. When I did ask about her he told me not to bother him, forbade me to write to her. I didn't know where she was, but he knew, and at last I found out too.'

'And you defied him, I suppose?'

'No, I deceived him. He gave me money for some purpose – to pay a debt – and I stole it. I left him a letter and ran away to my mother. I loved her.'

'O well, that was only to be expected,' said Loughlin. 'It was all right, quite right.'

'She was living with another man. I didn't know. I was a fool.'

'Good lord! That was a shock for you,' Loughlin said. 'What did you do?'

'No, I was not shocked, she was so happy. I lived with them for a year . . .'

'Extraordinary!'

'And then she died.'

'Your mother died!'

'Yes, so you see I could not stop with my . . . I could not stay where I was, and I couldn't go back to my father.'

'I see, no, but you want to go back to your father now.'

'I'm afraid. I love him, but I'm afraid. I don't blame my mother, I feel she was right, quite right – it was such happiness. And yet I feel, too, that father was deeply wronged. I can't understand that, it sounds foolish. I should so love to go home again. This other kind of life doesn't seem to eclipse me – things have been extraordinarily kind – I don't feel out of my setting, but still it doesn't satisfy, it is polite and soft, like silk, perhaps it isn't barbarous enough, and I want to live, somehow – well, I have not found what I wanted to find.'

'What did you want to find?'

'I shan't know until I have found it. I do want to go home now, but I am full of strange feelings about it. I feel as if I was bearing the mark of something that can't be hidden or disguised of what my mother did, as if I were all a burning recollection for him that he couldn't fail to see. He is good, a just man. He . . . he is the best hurdle maker in three counties.'

While listening to this daughter of a man who made ladders the Honourable Gerald had been swiftly thinking of an intriguing phrase that leaped into his mind. Social plesiomorphism, that was it! Caste was humbug, no doubt, but even if it was conscious humbug it was there, really there, like the patterned frost upon a window pane, beautiful though a little incoherent, and conditioned only by the size and number of your windows. (Eighteen windows in that pub!) But what did it amount to, after all? It was stuck upon your clear polished outline for every eye to see, but within was something surprising as the sight of a badger in church – until you got used to the indubitable relation of such badgers to such churches. Fine turpitudes!

'My dear girl,' he burst out, 'your mother and you were right, absolutely. I am sure life is enhanced not by amassing conventions, but by destroying them. And your feeling for your father is right, too, rightest of all. Tell me . . . let me . . . may I take you back to him?'

The girl's eyes dwelt upon his with some intensity.

'Your courage is kind,' she said, 'but he doesn't know you, nor you him.' And to that she added, 'You don't even know me.'

'I have known you for ten thousand years. Come home to him with me, we will go back together. Yes, you can explain. Tell him,' the Honourable Gerald had got the bit between his teeth now, 'tell him I'm your sweetheart, will you – will you?'

'Ten thousand . . . ! Yes, I know; but it's strange to think you have only seen me just once before!'

'Does that matter? Everything grows from that one small moment into a world of . . . well of . . . boundless admiration.'

'I don't want,' said Orianda, reopening her crimson parasol, 'to grow into a world of any kind.'

'No, of course you don't. But I mean the emotion is irresistible, "the desire of the moth for the star," that sort of thing, you know, and I immolate myself, the happy victim of your attractions.'

'All that has been said before.' Orianda adjusted her parasol as a screen for her raillery.

'I swear,' said he, 'I have not said it before, never to a living soul.'

Fountains of amusement beamed in her brilliant eyes. She was exquisite; he was no longer in doubt about the colour of her eyes – though he could not describe them. And the precise shade of her hair was – well, it was extraordinarily beautiful.

'I mean – it's been said to me!'

'O damnation! Of course it's been said to you. Ah, and isn't that my complete justification? But you agree, do you not? Tell me if it's possible. Say you agree, and let me take you back to your father.'

'I think I would like you to,' the jolly girl said, slowly.

II

On an August morning a few weeks later they travelled down together to see her father. In the interim Orianda had resigned her appointment, and several times Gerald had met her secretly in the purlieus of Tillington Park. The girl's cool casual nature fascinated him not less than her appearance. Admiration certainly outdistanced his happiness, although that also increased; but the bliss had its shadow, for the outcome of their friendship seemed mysteriously to depend on the outcome of the proposed return to her father's home, devotion to that project forming the first principle, as it were, of their intercourse. Orianda had not dangled before him the prospect of any serener relationship; she took his caresses as naturally and undemonstratively as a pet bird takes a piece of sugar. But he had begun to be aware of a certain force behind all her charming naïveté; the beauty that exhaled the freshness, the apparent fragility, of a drop of dew had none the less a savour of tyranny which he vowed should never, least of all by him, be pressed to vulgar exercise.

When the train reached its destination Orianda confided calmly that she had preferred not to write to her father. Really she did not know for certain whether he was alive or even living on at the old home she so loved. And there was a journey of three miles or more which Orianda proposed to walk. So they walked.

The road lay across an expanse of marshy country and

approached the wooded uplands of her home only by numerous eccentric divagations made necessary by culverts that drained the marsh. The day was bright; the sky, so vast an arch over this flat land, was a very oven for heat; there were cracks in the earth, the grass was like stubble. At the mid journey they crossed a river by its wooden bridge, upon which a boy sat fishing with stick and string. Near the water was a long white hut with a flag; a few tethered boats floated upon the stream. Gerald gave a shilling to a travelling woman who carried a burden on her back and shuffled slowly upon the harsh road sighing, looking neither to right nor left; she did not look into the sky, her gaze was fastened upon her dolorous feet, one two, one two, one two; her shift, if she had such a garment, must have clung to her old body like a shrimping net.

In an hour they had reached the uplands and soon, at the top of a sylvan slope where there was shade and cooling air, Gerald saw a sign hung upon a sycamore tree, THE BLACK DOG BY NATHANIEL CRABBE. The inn was small, pleasant with pink wash and brown paint, and faced across the road a large yard encircled by hedges, trees, and a gate. The travellers stood peeping into the enclosure which was stocked with new ladders, hurdles, and poles of various sizes. Amid them stood a tall burly man at a block, trimming with an axe the butt of a willow rod. He was about fifty, clad in rough country clothes, a white shirt, and a soft straw hat. He had mild simple features coloured, like his arms and neck, almost to the hue of a bay horse.

'Hullo!' called the girl. The man with the axe looked round at her unrecognizingly. Orianda hurried through the gateway. 'Father!' she cried.

'I did not know. I was not rightly sure of ye,' said the man, dropping the axe, 'such a lady you've grown.'

As he kissed his daughter his heavy discoloured hands rested on her shoulders, her gloved ones lay against his breast. Orianda took out her purse.

'Here is the money I stole, father.'

4

She dropped some coins one by one into his palm. He counted them over, and saying simply 'Thank you, my dear,' put them into his pocket.'

'I'm dashed!' – thought Loughlin, who had followed the girl – 'it's exactly how *she* would take it; no explanation, no apology. They do not know what reproach means. Have they no code at all?'

She went on chatting with her father, and seemed to have forgotten her companion.

'You mean you want to come back!' exclaimed her father eagerly, 'come back here? That would be grand, that would. But look, tell me what I am to do. I've – you see – this is how it is –'

He spat upon the ground, picked up his axe, rested one foot upon the axe-block and one arm upon his knee. Orianda sat down upon a pile of the logs.

'This is how it is . . . be you married?'

'Come and sit here, Gerald,' called the girl. As he came forward Orianda rose and said: 'This is my very dear friend, father, Gerald Loughlin. He has been so kind. It is he who has given me the courage to come back. I wanted to for so long. O, a long time, father, a long time. And yet Gerald had to drag me here in the end.'

'What was you afraid of, my girl?' asked the big man.

'Myself.'

The two visitors sat upon the logs. 'Shall I tell you about mother?' asked the girl.

Crabbe hesitated; looked at the ground.

'Ah, yes, you might,' he said.

'She died, did you know?'

The man looked up at the trees with their myriads of unmoving leaves; each leaf seemed to be listening.

'She died?' he said softly. 'No, I did not know she died.'

'Two years ago,' continued the girl, warily, as if probing his mood.

'Two years!' He repeated it without emotion. 'No. I did not know she died. 'Tis a bad job.' He was quite still, his mind seemed to be turning over his own secret memories, but what he bent forward and suddenly said was, 'Don't say anything about it in there.' He nodded towards the inn.

'No?' Orianda opened her crimson parasol.

'You see,' he went on, again resting one foot on the axe-block and addressing himself more particularly to Gerald, 'I've . . . this is how it is. When I was left alone I could not get along here, not by myself. That's for certain. There's the house and the bar and the yard – I'd to get help, a young woman from Brighton. I met her at Brighton.' He rubbed the blade of the axe reflectively across his palm – 'And she manages house for me now, you see.'

He let the axe fall again and stood upright. 'Her name's Lizzie.'

'O, quite so, you could do no other,' Gerald exclaimed cheerfully, turning to the girl. But Orianda said softly, 'What a family we are! He means he is living with her. And so you don't want your undutiful daughter after all, father?' Her gaiety was a little tremulous.

'No, no!' he retorted quickly, 'you must come back, you must come back, if so be you can. There's nothing I'd like better, nothing on this mortal earth. My God, if something don't soon happen I don't know what *will* happen.' Once more he stooped for the axe. 'That's right, Orianda, yes, yes, but you've no call to mention to her' – he glared uneasily at the inn doorway – 'that . . . that about your mother.'

Orianda stared up at him though he would not meet her gaze.

'You mean she doesn't know?' she asked, 'you mean she would want you to marry her if she did know?'

'Yes, that's about how it is with us.'

Loughlin was amazed at the girl's divination. It seemed miraculous, what a subtle mind she had, extraordinary! And how casually she took the old rascal's – well, what could you call it? – effrontery, shame, misdemeanour, helplessness. But was not her mother like it too? He had grasped nothing at all of the situation yet, save that Nathaniel

Crabbe appeared to be netted in the toils of this house-keeper, this Lizzie from Brighton. Dear Orianda was 'dished' now, poor girl. She could not conceivably return to such a menage.

Orianda was saying: 'Then I may stay, father, mayn't I, for good with you?'

Her father's eyes left no doubt of his pleasure.

'Can we give Gerald a bedroom for a few days? Or do we ask Lizzie?'

'Ah, better ask her,' said the shameless man. 'You want to make a stay here, sir?'

'If it won't incommode you,' replied Loughlin.

'O, make no doubt about that, to be sure no, I make no doubt about that.'

'Have you still got my old bedroom?' asked Orianda, for the amount of dubiety in his air was in prodigious antagonism to his expressed confidence.

'Why yes, it may happen,' he replied slowly.

'Then Gerald can have the spare room. It's all wainscot and painted dark blue. It's a shrimp of a room, but there's a preserved albatross in a glass case as big as a van.'

'I make no doubt about that,' chimed in her father, straightening himself and scratching his chin uneasily, 'you must talk to Lizzie.'

'Splendid!' said Gerald to Orianda, 'I've never seen an albatross.'

'We'll ask Lizzie,' said she, 'at once.'

Loughlin was experiencing not a little inward distress at this turn in the affair, but it was he who had brought Orianda to her home, and he would have to go through with the horrid business.

'Is she difficult, father?'

'No, she's not difficult, not difficult, so to say, you must make allowance.'

The girl was implacable. Her directness almost froze the blood of the Honourable Loughlin.

'Are you fond of her? How long has she been here?'

'O, a goodish while, yes, let me see – no, she's not difficult, if that's what you mean – three years, perhaps.'

'Well, but that's long enough!'

(Long enough for what – wondered Loughlin?)

'Yes, it is longish.'

'If you really want to get rid of her you could tell her . . .'

'Tell her what?'

'You know what to tell her!'

But her father looked bewildered and professed his ignorance.

'Take me in to her,' said Orianda, and they all walked across to The Black Dog. There was no one within; father and daughter went into the garden while Gerald stayed behind in a small parlour. Through the window that looked upon a grass plot he could see a woman sitting in a deck chair under a tree. Her face was turned away so that he saw only a curve of pink cheek and a thin mound of fair hair tossed and untidy. Lizzie's large red fingers were slipping a sprig of watercress into a mouth that was hidden round the corner of the curve. With her other hand she was caressing a large brown hen that sat on her lap. Her black skirt wrapped her limbs tightly, a round hip and a thigh being rigidly outlined, while the blouse of figured cotton also seemed strained upon her buxom breast, for it was torn and split in places. She had strong white arms and holes in her stockings. When she turned to confront the others it was easy to see that she was a foolish, untidy, but still a rather pleasant woman of about thirty.

'How do you do, Lizzie?' cried Orianda, offering a cordial hand. The hen fluttered away as, smiling a little wanly, the woman rose.

'Who is it, 'Thaniel?' she asked.

Loughlin heard no more, for some men came noisily into the bar and Crabbe hurried back to serve them.

III

In the afternoon Orianda drove Gerald in the gig back to the station to fetch the baggage.

'Well, what success, Orianda?' he asked as they jogged along.

'It would be perfect but for Lizzie – that *was* rather a blow. But I should have foreseen her – Lizzies are inevitable. And she *is* difficult – she weeps. But, O I am glad to be home again. Gerald, I feel I shall not leave it, ever.'

'Yes, Orianda,' he protested, 'leave it for me. I'll give your nostalgia a little time to fade. I think it was a man named Pater said, "All life is a wandering to find home." You don't want to omit the wandering?'

'Not if I have found my home again?'

'A home with Lizzie!'

'No, not with Lizzie.' She flicked the horse with the whip. 'I shall be too much for Lizzie; Lizzie will resume her wandering. She's as stupid as a wax widow in a show. Nathaniel is tired of Lizzie, and Lizzie of Nathaniel. The two wretches! But I wish she did not weep.'

Gerald had not observed any signs of tearfulness in Lizzie at the midday dinner; on the contrary, she seemed rather a jolly creature, not that she had spoken much beyond 'Yes, 'Thaniel, no, 'Thaniel,' or Gerald, or Orianda, as the case had been. Her use of his Christian name, which had swept him at once into the bosom of the family, shocked him rather pleasantly. But he did not know what had taken place between the two women; perhaps Lizzie had already perceived and tacitly accepted her displacement.

He was wakened next morning by unusual sounds, chatter of magpies in the front trees, and the ching of hammers on a bulk of iron at the smithy. Below his window a brown terrier stood on its barrel barking at a goose. Such common simple things had power to please him, and for a few days everything at The Black Dog seemed planned on this scale of novel enjoyment. The old inn itself, the log yard, harvesting, the chatter of the evening topers, even the village Sunday delighted him with its parade of Phyllis and Corydon, though it is true Phyllis wore a pink frock, stockings of faint blue, and walked like a man, while Corydon had a bowler hat and walked like a bear. He helped 'Thaniel with axe, hammer, and plane, but best of all was to serve mugs of beer nightly in the bar and to drop the coins into the drawer of money. The rest of the time he spent with Orianda whom he wooed happily enough, though without establishing any marked progress. They roamed in fields and in copses, lounged in lanes, looking at things and idling deliciously, at last returning home to be fed by Lizzie, whose case somehow hung in the air, faintly deflecting the perfect stream of felicity.

In their favourite glade a rivulet was joined by a number of springs bubbling from a pool of sand and rock. Below it the enlarged stream was dammed into a small lake once used for turning a mill, but now, since the mill was dismantled, covered with arrow heads and lily leaves, surrounded by inclining trees, bushes of rich green growth, terraces of willow herb, whose fairy-like pink steeples Orianda called 'codlins and cream,' and catmint with knobs of agreeable odour. A giant hornbeam tree had fallen and lay half buried in the lake. This, and the black poplars whose vacillating leaves underscored the solemn clamour of the outfall, gave to it the very serenity of desolation.

Here they caught sight of the two woodpeckers bathing in the springs, a cock and his hen, who had flown away yaffling, leaving a pretty mottled feather tinged with green floating there. It was endless pleasure to watch each spring bubble upwards from a pouch of sand that spread smoke-like in the water, turning each cone into a midget Vesuvius. A wasp crawled laboriously along a flat rock lying in the pool. It moved weakly, as if, marooned like a mariner upon some unknown isle, it could find no way of escape; only, this isle was no bigger than a dish in an ocean as small as a cart-wheel. The wasp seemed to have forgotten that it had wings, it creepingly examined every inch of the rock until it came to a patch of dried dung. Proceeding still as wearily it paused upon a dead leaf until a breeze blew leaf and insect into the water. The wasp was overwhelmed by the rush from the bubbles, but at last it emerged, clutching the woodpecker's floating feather and dragged itself into safety as a swimmer heaves himself into a boat. In a moment it preened its wings, flew back to the rock, and played at Crusoe again. Orianda picked the feather from the pool.

'What a fool that wasp is,' declared Gerald, 'I wonder what it is doing?

Orianda, placing the feather in his hat, told him it was probably wandering to find home.

One day, brightest of all days, they went to picnic in the marshes, a strange place to choose, all rank with the musty smell of cattle, and populous with grasshoppers that burred below you and millions, quadrillions of flies that buzzed above. But Orianda loved it. The vast area of coarse pasture harboured not a single farmhouse, only a shed here and there marking a particular field, for a thousand shallow brooks flowed like veins from all directions to the arterial river moving through its silent leagues. Small frills of willow curving on the river brink, and elsewhere a temple of lofty elms, offered the only refuge from sun or storm. Store cattle roamed unchecked from field to field, and in the shade of gaunt rascally bushes sheep were nestling. Green reeds and willow herb followed the watercourses with endless efflorescence, beautiful indeed.

In the late afternoon they had come to a spot where they could see their village three or four miles away, but between them lay the inexorable barrier of the river without a bridge. There was a bridge miles away to the right, they had crossed it earlier in the day; and there was another bridge on the left, but that also was miles distant.

'Now what are we to do?' asked Orianda. She wore a white muslin frock, a country frock, and a large straw hat with poppies, a country hat. They approached a column of trees. In the soft smooth wind the foliage of the willows was tossed into delicate greys. Orianda said they looked like cock-shy heads on spindly necks. She would like to shy at them, but she was tired. 'I know what we *could* do.' Orianda glanced around the landscape, trees, and bushes; the river was narrow, though deep, not more than forty feet across, and had high banks.

'You can swim, Gerald?'

Yes, Gerald could swim rather well.

'Then let's swim it, Gerald, and carry our own clothes over.'

'Can you swim, Orianda?'

Yes, Orianda could swim rather well.

'All right then,' he said. 'I'll go down here a little way.'

'O, don't go far, I don't want you to go far away, Gerald,' and she added softly, 'my dear.'

'No, I won't go far,' he said, and sat down behind a bush a hundred yards away. Here he undressed, flung his shoes one after the other across the river, and swimming on his back carried his clothes over in two journeys. As he sat drying in the sunlight he heard a shout from Orianda. He peeped out and saw her sporting in the stream quite close below him. She swam with a graceful overarm stroke that tossed a spray of drops behind her and launched her body as easily as a fish's. Her hair was bound in a handkerchief. She waved a hand to him. 'You've done it! Bravo! What courage! Wait for me. Lovely.' She turned away like an eel, and at every two or three strokes she spat into the air a gay little fountain of water. How extraordinary she was. Gerald wished he had not hurried. By and by he slipped into the water again and swam upstream. He could not see her.

'Have you finished?' he cried.

'I have finished, yes.' Her voice was close above his head. She was lying in the grass, her face propped between her palms, smiling down at him. He could see bare arms and shoulders.

'Got your clothes across?'

'Of course.'

'All dry?'

She nodded.

'How many journeys? I made two.'

'Two,' said Orianda briefly.

'You're all right then.' He wafted a kiss, swam back, and dressed slowly. Then as she did not appear he wandered along to her humming a discreet and very audible hum as he went. When he came upon her she still lay upon the grass most scantily clothed.

'I beg your pardon,' he said hastily, and full of surprise and modesty walked away. The unembarrassed girl called after him, 'Drying my hair.'

'All right' – he did not turn round – 'no hurry.'

But what sensations assailed him. They aroused in his decent gentlemanly mind not exactly a tumult, but a flux of emotions, impressions, and qualms; doubtful emotions, incredible impressions, and torturing qualms. That alluring picture of Orianda, her errant father, the abandoned Lizzie! Had the water perhaps heated his mind though it had cooled his body? He felt he would have to urge her, drag her if need be, from this Black Dog. The setting was fair enough and she was fair, but lovely as she was not even she could escape the brush of its vulgarity, its plebeian pressure.

And if all this has, or seems to have, nothing, or little enough to do with the drying of Orianda's hair, it is because the Honourable Gerald was accustomed to walk from grossness with an averted mind.

'Orianda,' said he, when she rejoined him, 'when are you going to give it up? You cannot stay here . . . with Lizzie . . . can you?'

'Why not?' she asked, sharply tossing back her hair. 'I stayed with my mother, you know.'

'That was different from this. I don't know how, but it must have been.'

73

She took his arm. 'Yes, it was. Lizzie I hate, and poor stupid father loves her as much as he loves his axe or his handsaw. I hate her meekness, too. She has taken the heart out of everything. I must get her away.'

'I see your need, Orianda, but what can you do?'

'I shall lie to her, lie like a libertine. And I shall tell her that my mother is coming home at once. No Lizzie could face that.'

He was silent. Poor Lizzie did not know that there was now no Mrs Crabbe.

'You don't like my trick, do you?' Orianda shook his arm caressingly.

'It hasn't any particular grandeur about it, you know.'

'Pooh! You shouldn't waste grandeur on clearing up a mess. This is a very dirty Eden.'

'No, all's fair, I suppose.'

'But it isn't war, you dear, if that's what you mean. I'm only doing for them what they are naturally loth to do for themselves.' She pronounced the word 'loth' as if it rimed with moth.

'Lizzie,' he said, 'I'm sure about Lizzie. I'll swear there is still some fondness in her funny little heart.'

'It isn't love, though; she's just sentimental in her puffy kind of way. My dear Honourable, you don't know what love is.' He hated her to use his title, for there was then always a breath of scorn in her tone. Just at odd times she seemed to be – not vulgar, that was unthinkable – she seemed to display a contempt for good breeding. He asked with a stiff smile, 'What *is* love?'

'For me,' said Orianda, fumbling for a definition, 'for me it is a compound of anticipation and gratitude. When either of these two ingredients is absent love is dead.'

Gerald shook his head, laughing. 'It sounds like a malignant bolus that I shouldn't like to take. I feel that love is just self-sacrifice. Apart from the taste of the thing or the price of the thing, why and for what this anticipation, this gratitude?'

'For the moment of passion, of course. Honour thy moments of passion and keep them holy. But O, Gerald Loughlin,' she added mockingly, 'this you cannot understand, for you are not a lover; you are not, no, you are not even a good swimmer.' Her mockery was adorable, but baffling.

'I do not understand you,' he said. Now why in the whole world of images should she refer to his swimming? He *was* a good swimmer. He was silent for a long time and then again he began to speak of marriage, urging her to give up her project and leave Lizzie in her simple peace.

Then, not for the first time, she burst into a strange perverse intensity that may have been love but might have been rage, that was toned like scorn and yet must have been a jest.

'Lovely Gerald, you must never marry, Gerald, you are too good for marriage. All the best women are already married, yes, they are – to all the worst men.' There was an infinite slow caress in her tone but she went on rapidly. 'So I shall never marry you, how should I marry a kind man, a good man? I am a barbarian, and want a barbarian lover, to crush and scarify me, but you are so tender and I am so crude. When your soft eyes look on me they look on a volcano.'

'I have never known anything half as lovely,' he broke in.

Her sudden emotion, though controlled, was unconcealed and she turned away from him.

"My love is a gentleman, but with him I should feel like a wild bee in a canary cage.'

'What are you saying!' cried Gerald, putting his arms around her. 'Orianda!'

'O yes, we do love in a mezzotinted kind of way. You could do anything with me short of making me marry you, anything, Gerald.' She repeated it tenderly. 'Anything. But short of marrying me I could make you do nothing.' She turned from him again for a moment or two. Then she took his arm and as they walked on she shook it and said chaffingly, 'And what a timid swimmer my Gerald is.'

But he was dead silent. That flux of sensations in his mind had taken another twist, fiery and exquisite. Like rich clouds they shaped themselves in the sky of his mind, fancy's bright towers with shining pinnacles.

Lizzie welcomed them home. Had they enjoyed themselves – yes, the day had been fine – and so they had enjoyed themselves – well, well, that was right. But throughout the evening Orianda hid herself from him, so he wandered almost distracted about the village until in a garth he saw some men struggling with a cow. Ropes were twisted around its horns and legs. It was flung to the earth. No countryman ever speaks to an animal without blaspheming it, although if he be engaged in some solitary work and inspired to music, he invariably sings a hymn in a voice that seems to have some vague association with wood pulp. So they all blasphemed and shouted. One man, with sore eyes, dressed in a coat of blue fustian and brown cord trousers, hung to the end of a rope at an angle of forty-five degrees. His posture suggested that he was trying to pull the head off the cow. Two other men had taken turns of other rope around some stout posts, and one stood by with a handsaw.

'What are you going to do?' asked Gerald.

'Its harns be bent, yeu see,' said the man with the saw, 'they be going into its head. 'Twill blind or madden the beast.'

So they blasphemed the cow, and sawed off its crumpled horns.

When Gerald went back to the inn Orianda was still absent. He sat down but he could not rest. He could never rest now until he had won her promise. That lovely image in the river spat fountains of scornful fire at him. 'Do not leave me, Gerald,' she had said. He would never leave her, he would never leave her. But the men talking in the inn scattered his fiery thoughts. They discoursed with a vacuity whose very endlessness was transcendent. Good God! Was there ever a living person more magnificently inane than old Tottel, the registrar. He would have inspired a stork to protest. Of course, a man of his age should not have worn a cap, a small one especially; Tottel himself was small, and it made him look rumpled. He was bandy: his intellect was bandy too.

'Yes,' Mr Tottel was saying, 'it's very interesting to see interesting things, no matter if it's man, woman, or a object. The most interesting man as I ever met in my life I met on my honeymoon. Years ago. He made a lifelong study of railways, that man, knew 'em from Alpha to . . . to . . . what is it?'

'Abednego,' said someone.

'Yes, the trunk lines, the fares, the routes, the junctions of anywheres in England or Scotland or Ireland or Wales. London, too, the Underground. I tested him, every station in correct order from South Kensington to King's Cross. A strange thing! Nothing to do with railways in 'imself, it was just his 'obby. Was a Baptist minister, really, but still a most interesting man.'

Loughlin could stand it no longer, he hurried away into the garden. He could not find her. Into the kitchen – she was not there. He sat down excited and impatient, but he must wait for her, he wanted to know, to know at once. How divinely she could swim! What was it he wanted to know? He tried to read a book there, a ragged dusty volume about the polar regions. He learned that when a baby whale is born it weighs at least a ton. How horrible!

He rushed out into the field full of extravagant melancholy and stupid distraction. That! All that was to be her life here! This was your rustic beauty, idiots and railways, boors who could choke an ox and chop off its horns – maddening doubts, maddening doubts – foul-smelling rooms, darkness, indecency. She held him at arm's length still, but she was dove-like, and he was grappled to her soul with hoops of steel, yes, indeed.

But soon this extravagance was allayed. Dim loneliness came imperceivably into the fields and he turned back. The birds piped oddly; some wind was caressing the higher foliage, turning it all one way, the way home. Telegraph poles ahead looked like half-used pencils; the small cross on the steeple glittered with a sharp and shapely permanence.

When he came to the inn Orianda was gone to bed.

IV

The next morning an air of uneasy bustle crept into the house after breakfast, much going in and out and up and down in restrained perturbation.

Orianda asked him if he could drive the horse and trap to the station. Yes, he thought he could drive it.

'Lizzie is departing,' she said, 'there are her boxes and things. It is very good of you, Gerald, if you will be so kind. It is a quiet horse.'

Lizzie, then, had been subdued. She was faintly affable during the meal, but thereafter she had been silent; Gerald could not look at her until the last dreadful moment had come and her things were in the trap.

'Good-bye, 'Thaniel,' she said to the innkeeper, and kissed him.

'Good-bye, Orianda,' and she kissed Orianda, and then climbed into the trap beside Gerald, who said 'Click click,' and away went the nag.

Lizzie did not speak during the drive – perhaps she was in tears. Gerald would have liked to comfort her, but the nag was unusually spirited and clacked so freshly along that he did not dare turn to the sorrowing woman. They trotted down from the uplands and into the windy road over the marshes. The church spire in the town ahead seemed to change its position with every turn of that twisting route. It would have a background now of high sour-hued down, now of dark woodland, anon of nothing but sky and cloud; in a few miles farther there would be the sea. Hereabout there were no trees, few houses, the world was vast and bright, the sky vast and blue. What was prettiest of all was a windmill turning its fans steadily in the draught from the sea. When they crossed the river its slaty slow-going flow was broken into blue waves.

At the station Lizzie dismounted without a word and Gerald hitched the nag to a tree. A porter took the luggage and labelled it while Gerald and Lizzie walked about the platform. A calf with a sack over its loins, tied by the neck to a pillar, was bellowing deeply; Lizzie let it suck at her finger for a while, but at last she resumed her walk and talked with her companion.

'She's a fine young thing, clever, his daughter; I'd do anything for her, but for him I've nothing to say. What can I say? What could I do? I gave up a great deal for that man, Mr Loughlin – I'd better not call you Gerald any more now – a great deal. I knew he'd had trouble with his wicked wife, and now to take her back after so many years, eh! It's beyond me, I know how he hates her. I gave up everything for him, I gave him what he can't give back to me, and he hates her; you know?'

'No, I did not know. I don't know anything of this affair.'

'No, of course, you would not know anything of this affair,' said Lizzie with a sigh. 'I don't want to see him again. I'm a fool, but I got my pride, and that's something to the good, it's almost satisfactory, ain't it?'

As the train was signalled she left him and went into the booking office. He marched up and down, her sad case affecting him with sorrow. The poor wretch, she had given up so much and could yet smile at her trouble. He himself had never surrendered to anything in life – that was what life demanded of you – surrender. For reward it gave you love, this swarthy, skin-deep love that exacted remorseless penalties. What German philosopher was it who said 'Woman pays the debt of life not by what she does, but by what she suffers'? The train rushed in. Gerald busied himself with the luggage, saw that it was loaded, but did not see its owner. He walked rapidly along the carriages, but he could not find her. Well, she was sick of them all, probably hiding from him. Poor woman. The train moved off, and he turned away.

But the station yard outside was startlingly empty, horse and trap were gone. The tree was still there, but with a man leaning against it, a dirty man with a dirty pipe and a dirty smell. Had he seen a horse and trap?

'A brown mare?'

'Yes.'

'Trap with yaller wheels?'

'That's it.'

'O ah, a young ooman druv away in that . . .'

'A young woman!'

'Ah, two minutes ago.' And he described Lizzie. 'Out yon,' said the dirty man, pointing with his dirty pipe to the marshes.

Gerald ran until he saw a way off on the level winding road the trap bowling along at a great pace; Lizzie was lashing the cob.

'The damned cat!' He puffed large puffs of exasperation and felt almost sick with rage, but there was nothing now to be done except walk back to The Black Dog, which he began to do. Rage gave place to anxiety, fear of some unthinkable disaster, some tragic horror at the inn.

'What a clumsy fool! All my fault, my own stupidity!' He groaned when he crossed the bridge at the half distance. He halted there: 'It's dreadful, dreadful!' A tremor in his blood, the shame of his foolishness, the fear of catastrophe, all urged him to turn back to the station and hasten away from these miserable complications.

But he did not do so, for across the marshes at the foot of the uplands he saw the horse and trap coming back furiously towards him. Orianda was driving it.

'What has happened?' she cried, jumping from the trap. 'O, what fear I was in, what's happened?' She put her arms around him tenderly.

'And I was in great fear,' he said with a laugh of relief. 'What has happened?'

'The horse came home, just trotted up to the door and stood still. Covered with sweat and foam, you see. The trap was empty. We couldn't understand it, anything, unless you had been flung out and were bleeding on the road somewhere. I turned the thing back and came on at once.' She was without a hat; she had been anxious and touched him fondly. 'Tell me what's the scare?'

He told her all.

'But Lizzie was not in the trap,' Orianda declared excitedly. 'She has not come back. What does it mean, what does she want to do? Let us find her. Jump up, Gerald.'

Away they drove again, but nobody had seen anything of Lizzie. She had gone, vanished, dissolved, and in that strong warm air her soul might indeed have been blown to Paradise. But they did not know how or why. Nobody knew. A vague search was carried on in the afternoon, guarded though fruitless inquiries were made, and at last it seemed clear, tolerably clear, that Lizzie had conquered her mad impulse or intention or whatever it was, and walked quietly away across the fields to a station in another direction.

v

For a day or two longer time resumed its sweet slow delightfulness, though its clarity was diminished and some of its enjoyment dimmed. A village woman came to assist in the mornings, but Orianda was now seldom able to leave the inn; she had come home to a burden, a happy, pleasing burden, that could not often be laid aside, and therefore a somewhat lonely Loughlin walked the high and the low of the country by day and only in the evenings sat in the parlour with Orianda. Hope too was slipping from his heart as even the joy was slipping from his days, for the spirit of vanished Lizzie, defrauded and indicting, hung in the air of the inn, an implacable obsession, a triumphant foreboding that was proved a prophecy when some boys fishing in the mill dam hooked dead Lizzie from the pool under the horn-beam tree.

Then it was that Loughlin's soul discovered to him a mass of feelings – fine sympathy, futile sentiment, a passion for righteousness, morbid regrets – from which a tragic bias was born. After the dread ordeal of the inquest, which gave a passive verdict of Found Drowned, it was not possible for him to stem this disloyal tendency of his mind. It laid that drowned figure accusatively at the feet of his beloved girl, and no argument or sophistry could disperse the venal savour that clung to the house of The Black Dog. 'To analyse or assess a person's failings or deficiencies,' he declared to himself, 'is useless, not because such blemishes are immovable, but because they affect the mass of beholders in divers ways. Different minds perceive utterly variant figures in the same being. To Brown Robinson is a hero, to Jones a snob, to Smith a fool. Who then is right? You are lucky if you can put your miserable self in relation at an angle where your own deficiencies are submerged or minimized, and wise if you can maintain your vision of that interesting angle.' But embedded in Loughlin's modest intellect there was a stratum of probity that was rock to these sprays of the casuist; and although Orianda grew more alluring than ever, he packed his bag, and on a morning she herself drove him in the gig to the station.

Upon that miserable departure it was fitting that rain should fall. The station platform was piled with bushel baskets and empty oil barrels. It rained with a quiet remorse-lessness. Neither spoke a word, no one spoke, no sound was uttered but the faint flicking of the raindrops. Her kiss to him was long and sweet, her goodbye almost voiceless.

'You will write?' she whispered.

'Yes, I will write.'

But he does not do so. In London he has not forgotten, but he cannot endure the thought of that countryside – to be far from the madding crowd is to be mad indeed. It is only after some trance of recollection, when his fond experience is all delicately and renewingly there, that he wavers; but time and time again he relinquishes or postpones his return. And sometimes he thinks he really will write a letter to his friend who lives in the country.

But he does not do so.

The Tiger

I

The tiger was coming at last; the almost fabulous beast, the subject of so much conjecture for so many months, was at the docks twenty miles away. Yak Pedersen had gone to fetch it, and Barnabe Woolf's Menagerie was about to complete its unrivalled collection by the addition of a full-grown Indian tiger of indescribable ferocity, newly trapped in the forest and now for the first time exhibited, and so on, and so on. All of which, as it happened, was true. On the previous day Pedersen the Dane and some helpers had taken a brand new four-horse exhibition waggon, painted and carved with extremely legendary tigers lapped in blood – even the bars were gilded – to convey this unmatchable beast to its new masters. The show had had to wait a long time for a tiger, but it had got a beauty at last, a terror indeed by all accounts, though it is not to be imagined that every-thing recorded of it by Barnabe Woolf was truth and nothing but truth. Showmen do not work in that way.

Yak Pedersen was the tamer and menagerie manager, a tall, blond, angular man about thirty-five, of dissolute and savage blood himself, with the very ample kind of moustache that bald men often develop; yes, bald, in-temperate, lewd, and an interminable smoker of Cuban cigarettes, which seemed constantly to threaten a conflagra-tion in that moustache. Marie the Cossack hated him, but Yak loved her with a fierce deep passion. Nobody knew why she was called Marie the Cossack. She came from Canning Town – everybody knew that, and her proper name was Fascota, Mrs Fascota, wife of Jimmy Fascota, who was the architect and carpenter and builder of the show. Jimmy was not much to look at, so little in fact that you couldn't help wondering what it was Marie had seen in him when she could have had the King of Poland, as you might say, almost for the asking. But still Jimmy was the boss ganger of the show, and even that young gentleman in frock coat and silk hat who paraded the platform entrance to the arena and rhodomontadoed you into it, often against your will, by the seductive recital of the seven ghastly wonders of the world, all certainly to be seen, to be seen inside, waiting to be seen, must be seen, roll up – even he was subject to the commands of Jimmy Fascota when the time came to dismantle and pack up the show, although the transfer of his activities involved him temporarily in a change, a horrid change, of attire and language. Marie was not a lady, but she was not for Pedersen anyway. She swore like a factory foreman, or a young soldier, and when she got tipsy she was full of freedoms. By the power of God she was beautiful, and by the same gracious power she was virtuous. Her husband knew it; he knew all about master Pedersen's passion, too, and it did not even interest him. Marie did feats in the lion cages, whipping poor decrepit beasts, desiccated by captivity, through a hoop or over a stick of wood and other kindergarten disportings; but there you are, people must live, and Marie lived that way. Pedersen was always wooing her. Sometimes he was gracious and kind, but at other times when his failure wearied him he would be cruel and sardonic, with a suggestive tongue whose vice would have scourged her were it not that Marie was impervious, or too deeply inured to mind it. She always grinned at him and fobbed him off with pleasantries, whether he was amorous or acrid.

'God Almighty!' he would groan, 'she is not good for me, this Marie. What can I do for her? She is burning me alive and the Skaggerack could not quench me, not all of it. The devil! What can I do with this? Some day I shall smash her across the eyes, yes, across the eyes.'

So you see the man really loved her.

When Pedersen returned from the docks the car with its

captive was dragged to a vacant place in the arena, and the wooden front panel was let down from the bars. The marvellous tiger was revealed. It sprung into a crouching attitude as the light surprised the appalling beauty of its smooth fox-coloured coat, its ebony stripes, and snowy pads and belly. The Dane, who was slightly drunk, uttered a yell and struck the bars of the cage with his whip. The tiger did not blench, but all the malice and ferocity in the world seemed to congregate in its eyes and impress with a pride and ruthless grandeur the colossal brutality of its face. It did not move its body, but its tail gradually stiffened out behind it as stealthily as fire moves in the forest undergrowth, and the hair along the ridge of its back rose in fearful spikes. There was the slightest possible distension of the lips, and it fixed its marvellous baleful gaze upon Pedersen. The show people were hushed into silence, and even Pedersen was startled. He showered a few howls and curses at the tiger, who never ceased to fix him with eyes that had something of contempt in them and something of a horrible presage. Pedersen was thrusting a sharp spike through the bars when a figure stepped from the crowd. It was an old Negro, a hunchback with a white beard, dressed in a red fez, long tunic of buff cotton, and blue trousers. He laid both his hands on the spike and shook his head deprecatingly, smiling all the while. He said nothing, but there was nothing he could say – he was dumb.

'Let him alone, Yak; let the tiger alone, Yak!' cried Barnabe Woolf. 'What is this feller?'

Pedersen with some reluctance turned from the cage and said: 'He is come with the animal.'

'So?' said Barnabe. 'Vell, he can go. Ve do not vant any black feller.'

'He cannot speak – no tongue – it is gone,' Yak replied.

'No tongue! Vot, have they cut him out?'

'I should think it,' said the tamer. 'There was two of them, a white keeper, but that man fell off the ship one night and they do not see him any more. This chap he feed it and look after it. No information of him, dumb you see, and a foreigner; don't understand. He have no letters, no money, no name, nowheres to go. Dumb, you see, he has nothing, nothing but a flote. The captain said to take him away with us. Give a job to him, he is a proposition.'

'Vot is he got you say?'

'Flote.' Pedersen imitated with his fingers and lips the actions of a flute-player.

'O ya, a vloot! Vell, ve don't vant no vloots now; ve feeds our own tigers, don't ve, Yak?' And Mr Woolf, oily but hearty – and well he might be so for he was beautifully rotund, hair like satin, extravagantly clothed, and rich with jewellery – surveyed first with a contemplative grin, and then compassionately, the figure of the old Negro, who stood unsmiling with his hands crossed humbly before him. Mr Woolf was usually perspiring, and usually being addressed by perspiring workmen, upon whom he bellowed orders and such anathemas as reduced each recipient to the importance of a potato, and gave him the aspect of a consumptive sheep. But today Mr Woolf was affable and calm. He took his cigar from his mouth and poured a flood of rich grey air from his lips. 'O ya, look after him a day, or a couple of days.' At that one of the boys began to lead the hunchback away as if he were a horse. 'Come on, Pompoon,' he cried, and thenceforward the unknown Negro was called by that name.

Throughout the day the tiger was the sensation of the show, and the record of its ferocity attached to the cage received thrilling confirmation whenever Pedersen appeared before the bars. The sublime concentration of hatred was so intense that children screamed, women shuddered, and even men held their breath in awe. At the end of the day the beasts were fed. Great hacks of bloody flesh were forked into the bottoms of the cages, the hungry victims pouncing and snarling in ecstasy. But no sooner were they served than the front panel of each cage was swung up, and the inmate in the seclusion of his den slaked his appetite and slept. When the public had departed the lights were put out and the doors of the arena closed. Outside in the darkness only its great rounded oblong shape could be discerned, built high of painted wood, roofed with striped canvas, and adorned with flags. Beyond this match-box coliseum was a row of caravans, tents, naphtha flares, and buckets of fire on which suppers were cooking. Groups of the show-people sat or lounged about, talking, cackling with laughter, and even singing. No one observed the figure of Pompoon as he passed silently on the grass. The outcast, doubly chained to his solitariness by the misfortune of dumbness and strange nationality, was hungry. He had not tasted food that day. He could not understand it any more than he could understand the speech of these people. In the end caravan, nearest the arena, he heard a woman quietly singing. He drew a shining metal flute from his breast, but stood silently until the singer ceased. Then he repeated the tune very accurately and sweetly on his flute. Marie the Cossack came to the door in her green silk tights and high black boots with gilded fringes; her black velvet doublet had plenty of gilded buttons upon it. She was a big, finely moulded woman, her dark and splendid features were burned healthily by the sun. In each of her ears two gold discs tinkled and gleamed as she moved. Pompoon opened his mouth very widely and supplicatingly; he put his hand upon his stomach and rolled his eyes so dreadfully that Mrs Fascota sent her little daughter Sophy down to him with a basin of soup and potatoes. Sophy was partly undressed, in bare feet and red petticoat. She stood gnawing the bone of a chicken, and grinning at the black man as he swallowed and dribbled as best he could without a spoon. She cried out: 'Here, he's going to eat the bloody basin and all, mum!' Her mother cheerfully ordered her to 'give him those fraggiments, then!' The child did so, pausing now and again to laugh at the satisfied roll of the old man's eyes. Later on Jimmy Fascota found him a couple of sacks, and Pompoon slept upon them beneath their caravan. The last thing the old man saw was Pedersen carrying a naphtha flare, unlocking a small door leading into the arena, and closing it with a slam after he had entered. Soon the light went out.

II

After a week the show shifted and Pompoon accompanied it. Mrs Kavanagh, who looked after the birds, was, a little fortunately for him, kicked in the stomach by a mule and had to be left at an infirmary. Pompoon, who seemed to understand birds, took charge of the parakeets, love-birds, and other highly-coloured fowl, including the quetzal with green mossy head, pink breast, and flowing tails, and the primrose-breasted toucans with bills like a butcher's cleaver.

The show was always moving on and moving on. Putting it up and taking it down was a more entertaining affair than the exhibition itself. With Jimmy Fascota in charge, and the young man of the frock coat in an ecstasy of labour, half-clothed husky men swarmed up the rigged frameworks, dismantling poles, planks, floors, ropes, roofs, staging, tearing at bolts and bars, walking at dizzying altitudes on narrow boards, swearing at their mates, staggering under vast burdens, sweating till they looked like seals, packing and disposing incredibly of it all, furling the flags, rolling up the filthy awnings, then Right O! for a market town twenty miles away.

In the autumn the show would be due at a great gala town in the north, the supreme opportunity of the year, and by that time Mr Woolf expected to have a startling headline about a new tiger act and the intrepid tamer. But somehow Pedersen could make no progress at all with this. Week after week went by, and the longer he left that initial entry into the cage of the tiger, notwithstanding the comforting support of firearms and hot irons, the more remote appeared the possibility of its capitulation. The tiger's hatred did not manifest itself in roars and gnashing of teeth, but by its rigid implacable pose and a slight flexion of its protruded claws. It seemed as if endowed with an imagination of bloodlust, Pedersen being the deepest conceivable excitation of this. Week after week went by and the show people became aware that Pedersen, their Pedersen, the unrivalled, the dauntless tamer, had met his match. They were proud of the beast. Some said it was Yak's bald crown that the tiger disliked, but Marie swore it was his moustache, a really remarkable piece of hirsute furniture, that he would not have parted with for a pound of gold – so he said. But whatever it was – crown, moustache, or the whole conglomerate Pedersen – the tiger remarkably loathed it and displayed his loathing, while the unfortunate tamer had no more success with it than he had ever had with Marie the Cossack, though there was at least a good humour in her treatment of him which was horribly absent from the attitude of the beast. For a long time Pedersen blamed the hunchback for it all. He tried to elicit from him by gesticulations in front of the cage the secret of the creature's enmity, but the barriers to their intercourse were too great to be overcome, and to all Pedersen's illustrative frenzies Pompoon would only shake his sad head and roll his great eyes until the Dane would cuff him away with a curse of disgust and turn to find the eyes of the tiger, the dusky, smooth-skinned tiger with bitter bars of ebony, fixed upon him with tenfold malignity. How he longed in his raging impotence to transfix the thing with a sharp spear through the cage's gilded bars, or to bore a hole into its vitals with a red-hot iron! All the traditional treatment in such cases, combined first with starvation and then with rich feeding, proved unavailing. Pedersen always had the front flap of the cage left down at night so that he might, as he thought, establish some kind of working arrangement between them by the force of propinquity. He tried to sleep on a bench just outside the cage, but the horror of the beast so penetrated him that he had to turn his back upon it. Even then the intense enmity pierced the back of his brain and forced him to seek a bench elsewhere out of range of the tiger's vision.

Meanwhile, the derision of Marie was not concealed – it was even blatant – and to the old contest of love between herself and the Dane was now added a new contest of personal courage, for it had come to be assumed, in some undeclarable fashion, that if Yak Pedersen could not tame that tiger, then Marie the Cossack would. As this situation crystallized daily the passion of Pedersen changed to jealousy and hatred. He began to regard the smiling Marie in much the same way as the tiger regarded him.

'The hell-devil! May some lightning scorch her like a toasted fish!'

But in a short while this mood was displaced by one of anxiety; he became even abject. Then, strangely enough, Marie's feelings underwent some modification. She was proud of the chance to subdue and defeat him, but it might be at a great price – too great a price for her. Addressing herself in turn to the dim understanding of Pompoon she had come to perceive that he believed the tiger to be not merely quite untamable, but full of mysterious dangers. She could not triumph over the Dane unless she ran the risk he feared to run. The risk was colossal then, and with her realization of this some pity for Yak began to exercise itself in her; after all, were they not in the same boat? But the more she sympathized the more she jeered. The thing had to be done somehow.

Meanwhile Barnabe Woolf wants that headline for the big autumn show, and a failure will mean a nasty interview with that gentleman. It may end by Barnabe kicking Yak Pedersen out of his wild beast show. Not that Mr Woolf is so gross as to suggest that. He senses the difficulty, although his manager in his pride will not confess to any. Mr Woolf declares that his tiger is a new tiger; Yak must watch out for him, be careful. He talks as if it were just a question of giving the cage a coat of whitewash. He never hints at contingencies; but still, there is his new untamed tiger, and there is Mr Yak Pedersen, his wild beast tamer – at present.

III

One day the menagerie did not open. It had finished an engagement, and Jimmy Fascota had gone off to another town to arrange the new pitch. The show folk made holiday about the camp, or flocked into the town for marketing or carousals. Mrs Fascota was alone in her caravan, clothed in her jauntiest attire. She was preparing to go into the town when Pedersen suddenly came silently in and sat down.

'Marie,' he said, after a few moments, 'I give up that tiger. To me he has given a spell. It is like a mesmerize.' He dropped his hands upon his knees in complete humiliation. Marie did not speak, so he asked, 'What you think?'

She shrugged her shoulders, and put her brown arms akimbo. She was a grand figure so, in a cloak of black satin and a huge hat trimmed with crimson feathers.

'If *you* can't trust him,' she said, 'who can?'

'It is myself I am not to trust. Shameful! But that tiger will do me, yes, so I will not conquer him. It's bad, very, very bad, is it not so? Shameful, but I will not do it!' he declared excitedly.

'What's Barnabe say?'

'I do not care, Mr Woolf can think what he can think! Damn Woolf! But for what I do think of my own self . . . Ah!' He paused for a moment, dejected beyond speech. 'Yes, miserable it is, in my own heart very shameful, Marie. And what you think of me, yes, that too!'

There was a note in his voice that almost confounded her – why, the man was going to cry! In a moment she was all melting compassion and bravado.

'You leave the devil to me, Yak. What's come over you, man? God love us, I'll tiger him!'

But the Dane had gone as far as he could go. He could admit his defeat, but he could not welcome her all too ready amplification of it.

'Na, na, you are good for him, Marie, but you beware.

He is not a tiger; he is beyond everything, foul – he has got a foul heart and a thousand demons in it. I would not bear to see you touch him; no, no, I would not bear it!'

'Wait till I come back this afternoon – you wait!' cried Marie, lifting her clenched fist. 'So help me, I'll tiger him, you'll see!'

Pedersen suddenly awoke to her amazing attraction. He seized her in his arms. 'Na, na, Marie! God above! I will not have it.'

'Aw, shut up!' she commanded, impatiently, and pushing him from her she sprang down the steps and proceeded to the town alone.

She did not return in the afternoon; she did not return in the evening; she was not there when the camp closed up for the night. Sophy, alone, was quite unconcerned. Pompoon sat outside the caravan while the flame of the last lamp was perishing weakly above his head. He now wore a coat of shag-coloured velvet. He was old and looked very wise, often shaking his head, not wearily, but as if in doubt. The flute lay glittering upon his knees and he was wiping his lips with a green silk handkerchief when barefoot Sophy in her red petticoat crept behind him, unhooked the lamp, and left him in darkness. Then he departed to an old tent the Fascotas had found for him.

When the mother returned the camp was asleep in its darkness and she was very drunk. Yak Pedersen had got her. He carried her into the arena, and bolted and barred the door.

IV

Marie Fascota awoke next morning in broad daylight; through chinks and rents in the canvas roof of the arena the brightness was beautiful to behold. She could hear a few early risers bawling outside, while all around her the caged beasts and birds were squeaking, whistling, growling, and snarling. She was lying beside the Dane on a great bundle of straw. He was already awake when she became aware of him, watching her with amused eyes.

'Yak Pedersen! Was I drunk?' Marie asked dazedly in low husky tones, sitting up. 'What's this, Yak Pedersen? Was I drunk? Have I been here all night?'

He lay with his hands behind his head, smiling in the dissolute ugliness of his abrupt yellow skull so incongruously bald, his moustache so profuse, his nostrils and ears teeming with hairs.

'Can't you speak?' cried the wretched woman. 'What game do you call this? Where's my Sophy, and my Jimmy – is he back?'

Again he did not answer; he stretched out a hand to caress her. Unguarded as he was, Marie smashed down both her fists full upon his face. He lunged back blindly at her and they both struggled to their feet, his fingers clawing in her thick strands of hair as she struck at him in frenzy. Down rolled the mass and he seized it; it was her weakness, and she screamed. Marie was a rare woman – a match for most men – but the capture of her hair gave her utterly into his powerful hands. Uttering a torrent of filthy oaths, Pedersen pulled the yelling woman backwards to him and grasping her neck with both hands gave a murderous wrench and flung her to the ground. As she fell Marie's hand clutched a small cage of fortune-telling birds. She hurled this at the man, but it missed him; the cage burst against a pillar and the birds scattered in the air.

'Marie! Marie!' shouted Yak, 'Listen! listen!'

Remorsefully he flung himself before the raging woman who swept at him with an axe, her hair streaming, her eyes blazing with the fire of a thousand angers.

'Drunk, was I!' she screamed at him. 'That's how ye got me, Yak Pedersen? Drunk, was I!'

He warded the blow with his arm, but the shock and pain of it was so great that his own rage burst out again, and leaping at the woman he struck her a horrible blow across the eyes. She sunk to her knees and huddled there without a sound, holding her hands to her bleeding face, her loose hair covering it like a net. At the pitiful sight the Dane's grief conquered him again, and bending over her imploringly he said: 'Marie, my love, Marie! Listen! It is not true! Swear me to God, good woman, it is not true, it is not possible! Swear me to God!' he raged distractedly. 'Swear me to God!' Suddenly he stopped and gasped. They were in front of the tiger's cage, and Pedersen was as if transfixed by that fearful gaze. The beast stood with hatred concentrated in every bristling hair upon its hide, and in its eyes a malignity that was almost incandescent. Still as a stone, Marie observed this, and began to creep away from the Dane, stealthily, stealthily. On a sudden, with incredible agility, she sprang up the steps of the tiger's cage, tore the pin from the catch, flung open the door, and, yelling in madness, leapt in. As she did so, the cage emptied. In one moment she saw Pedersen grovelling on his knees, stupid, and the next . . .

All the hidden beasts, stirred by instinctive knowledge of the tragedy, roared and raged. Marie's eyes and mind were open to its horror. She plugged her fingers into her ears; screamed; but her voice was a mere wafer of sound in that pandemonium. She heard vast crashes of someone smashing in the small door of the arena, and then swooned upon the floor of the cage.

The bolts were torn from their sockets at last, the slip door swung back, and in the opening appeared Pompoon, alone, old Pompoon, with a flaming lamp and an iron spear. As he stepped forward into the gloom he saw the tiger, dragging something in its mouth, leap back into its cage.

Mordecai and Cocking

Two men sat one afternoon beside a spinney of beeches near the top of a wild bare down. Old shepherd Mordecai was admonishing a younger countryman, Eustace Cocking, now out of work, who held beside him in leash a brindled whippet dog, sharp featured and lean, its neck clipped in a broad leather collar. The day was radiant, the very air had bloom; bright day is never so bright as upon these lonely downs, and the grim face of storm never so tragic elsewhere. From the beeches other downs ranged in every direction, nothing but downs in beautiful abandoned masses. In a valley below the men a thousand sheep were grazing; they looked no more than a handful of white beach randomly scattered.

'The thing's forbidden, Eustace; it always has and always will be, I say, and thereby 'tis wrong.'

'Well, if ever I doos anything wrong I allus feel glad of it next morning.'

' 'Tis against law, Eustace, and to be against law is the downfall of mankind. What I mean to say – I'm a national man.'

'The law! Foo! That's made by them as don't care for my needs, and don't understand my rights. Is it fair to let them control your mind as haven't got a grip of their own? I worked for yon farmer a matter of fourteen years, hard, I tell you, I let my back sweat . . .'

The dog at his side was restless; he cuffed it impatiently. 'And twice a week my wife she had to go to farmhouse; twice a week; doing up their washing and their muck – Lie down!' he interjected sternly to the querulous dog – 'two days in every seven. Then the missus says to my wife, "I shall want you to come four days a week in future, Mrs Cocking; the house is too much of a burden for me." My wife says, "I can't come no oftener, ma'am; I'd not have time to look after my own place, my husband, and the six children, Ma'am." Then missus flew into a passion. "Oh, so you won't come, eh!"

' "I'd come if I could, ma'am," my wife says, "and gladly, but it ain't possible, you see." '

' "Oh, very well!" says the missus. And that was the end of that, but come Saturday, when the boss pays me: "Cocking," he says, "I shan't want you no more arter next week." No explanation, mind you, and I never asked for none. I know'd what 'twas for, but I don't give a damn. What meanness, Mordecai! Of course I don't give a damn whether I goes or whether I stops; you know my meaning – I'd much rather stop; my home's where I be known; but I don't give a damn. 'Tain't the job I minds so much as to let him have that power to spite me so at a moment after fourteen years because of his wife's temper. 'Tis not decent. 'Tis under-grading a man.'

There was no comment from the shepherd. Eustace continued: 'If that's your law, Mordecai, I don't want it. I ignores it.'

'And that you can't do,' retorted the old man. 'God A'mighty can look after the law.'

'If He be willing to take the disgrace of it, Mordecai Stavely, let Him.'

The men were silent for a long time, until the younger cheerfully asked, 'How be poor old Harry Mixen?'

'Just alive.'

Eustace leaned back, munching a strig of grass reflectively and looking at the sky. 'Don't seem no sign of rain, however?'

'No.'

The old man who said 'No' hung his melancholy head, and pondered; he surveyed his boots, which were of harsh hard leather with deep soles. He then said, 'We ought to thank God we had such mild weather at the back end of the year. If you remember, it came a beautiful autumn and a softish winter. Things are growing now; I've seen oats as high as my knee; the clover's lodged in places. It will be all good if we escape the east winds – hot days and frosty nights.'

The downs, huge and bare, stretched in every direction, green and grey, gentle and steep, their vast confusion enlightened by a small hanger of beech or pine, a pond, or more often a derelict barn; for among the downs there are barns and garners ever empty, gone into disuse and abandoned. They are built of flint and red brick, with a roof of tiles. The rafters often bear an eighteenth-century date. Elsewhere in this emptiness even a bush will have a name, and an old stone becomes a track mark. Upon the soft tufts and among the triumphant furze live a few despised birds, chats and finches and that blithe screamer the lark, but above all, like veins upon the down's broad breast, you may perceive the run-way of the hare.

'Why can't a man live like a hare?' broke out the younger man. 'I'd not mind being shot at a time and again. It lives a free life, anyway, not like a working man with a devil on two legs always cracking him on.'

'Because,' said Mordecai, 'a hare is a vegetarian creature, what's called a ruminant, chewing the cud and dividing not the hoof. And,' he added significantly, 'there be dogs.'

'It takes a mazin' good dog to catch ever a hare on its own ground. Most hares could chase any dog ever born, believe you me, if they liked to try at that.'

'There be traps and wires!'

'Well, we've no call to rejoice, with the traps set for a man, and the wires a-choking him.'

At that moment two mating hares were roaming together on the upland just below the men. The doe, a small fawn creature, crouched coyly before the other, a large nut-brown hare with dark ears. Soon she darted away, sweeping before him in a great circle, or twisting and turning as easily as a snake. She seemed to fly the faster, but when his muscular pride was aroused he swooped up to her shoulder, and, as if in loving derision, leaped over her from side to side as she ran. She stopped as sharply as a shot upon its target and faced him, quizzing him gently with her nose. As they sat thus the dark-eared one perceived not far off a squatting figure; it was another hare, a tawny buck, eyeing their dalliance. The doe commenced to munch the herbage; the nut-brown one hobbled off to confront this wretched, rash, intruding fool. When they met both rose upon their haunches, clawing and scraping and patting at each other with as little vigour as mild children put into their quarrels – a rigmarole of slapping hands. But, notwithstanding the delicacy of the treatment, the interloper, a meek enough fellow, succumbed, and the conqueror loped back to his nibbling mistress.

Yet, whenever they rested from their wooing flights, the tawny interloper was still to be seen near by. Hapless mourning seemed to involve his hunched figure; he had the aspect of a deferential, grovelling man; but the lover saw only his provocative, envious eye – he swept down upon him. Standing up again, he slammed and basted him with puny velvet blows until he had salved his indignation, satisfied his connubial pride, or perhaps merely some strange fading instinct – for it seemed but a mock combat, a ritual to which they conformed.

Away the happy hare would prance to his mate, but as often as he came round near that shameless spy he would pounce upon him and beat him to the full, like a Turk or like a Russian. But though he could beat him and disgrace him, he could neither daunt nor injure him. The vanquished miscreant would remain watching their wooing with the eye of envy – or perhaps of scorn – and hoping for a miracle to happen.

And a miracle did happen. Cocking, unseen, near the beeches released his dog. The doe shot away over the curve of the hill and was gone. She did not merely gallop, she seemed to pass into ideal flight, the shadow of wind itself.

Her fawn body, with half-cocked ears and unperceivable convulsion of the leaping haunches, soared across the land with the steady swiftness of a gull. The interloping hare, in a blast of speed, followed hard upon her traces. But Cocking's hound had found at last the hare of its dreams, a nut-brown, dark-eared, devil-guided, eluding creature, that fled over the turf of the hill as lightly as a cloud. The long leaping dog swept in its track with a stare of passion, following in great curves the flying thing that grew into one great throb of fear all in the grand sunlight on the grand bit of a hill. The lark stayed its little flood of joy and screamed with notes of pity at the protracted flight; and bloodless indeed were they who could view it unmoved, nor feel how sweet a thing is death if you be hound, how fell a thing it is if you be hare. Too long, O delaying death, for this little heart of wax; and too long, O delaying victory, for that pursuer with the mouth of flame. Suddenly the hound faltered, staggered a pace or two, then sank to the grass, its lips dripping blood. When Cocking reached him the dog was dead. He picked the body up.

'It's against me, like everything else,' he muttered.

But a voice was calling 'Oi! Oi!' He turned to confront a figure rapidly and menacingly approaching.

'I shall want you, Eustace Cocking,' cried the gamekeeper, 'to come and give an account o' yourself.'

The Wife of Ted Wickham

Perhaps it is a mercy we can't see ourselves as others see us. Molly Wickham was a remarkably pretty woman in days gone by; maybe she is wiser since she has aged, but when she was young she was foolish. She never seemed to realize it, but I wasn't deceived.

So said the cattle-dealer, a healthy looking man, massive, morose, and bordering on fifty. He did not say it to anybody in particular, for it was said – it was to himself he said it – privately, musingly, as if to soothe the still embittered recollection of a beauty that was foolish, a fondness that was vain.

Ted Wickham himself was silly, too, when he married her. Must have been extraordinarily touched to marry a little soft, religious, teetotal party like her, and him a great sporting cock of a man, just come into a public-house business that his aunt had left him, The Half Moon, up on the Bath Road. He always ate like an elephant, but she'd only the appetite of a scorpion. And what was worse, he was a true blood conservative while all her family were a set of radicals that you couldn't talk sense to: if you only so much as mentioned the name of Gladstone they would turn their eyes up to the ceiling as if he was a saint in glory. Blood is thicker than water, I know, but it's unnatural stuff to drink so much of. Grant their name was. They christened her Pamela, and as if that wasn't cruel enough they messed her initials up by giving her the middle name of Isabel.

But she was a handsome creature, on the small side, but sound as a roach and sweet as an apple tree in bloom. Pretty enough to convert Ted, and I thought she would convert him, but she was a cussed woman – never did what you would expect of her – and so she didn't even try. She gave up religion herself, gave it up altogether and went to church no more. That was against her inclination, but of course it was only right, for Ted never could have put up with that. Wedlock's one thing and religion's two: that's odd and even: a little is all very well if it don't go a long ways. Parson Twamley kept calling on her for a year or two afterwards, trying to persuade her to return to the fold – he couldn't have called oftener if she had owed him a hundred pound – but she would not hear of it, she would not go. He was not much of a parson, not one to wake anybody up, but he had a good delivery, and when he'd the luck to get hold of a sermon of any sense his delivery was very good, very good indeed. She would say, 'No, sir, my feelings aren't changed one bit, but I won't come to church any more, I've my private reasons.' And the parson would glare across at old Ted as if he were a Belzeboob, for Ted always sat and listened to the parson chattering to her. Never said a word himself, always kept his pipe stuck in his jaw. Ted never persuaded her in the least, just left it to her, and she would come round to his manner of thinking in the end, for though he never actually said it, she always knew what his way of thinking was. A strange thing, it takes a real woman to do that, silly or no! At election times she would plaster the place all over with Tory bills, do it with her own hands!

Still, there's no stability in meekness of that sort, a weathervane can only go with wind and weather, and there was no sense in her giving in to Ted as she did, not in the long run, for he couldn't help but despise her. A man wants something or other to whet the edge of his life on; and he did despise her, I know.

But she was a fine creature in her way, only her way wasn't his. A beautiful woman, too, well limbered up, with lovely hair, but always a very proper sort, a milksop – Ted told me once that he had never seen her naked. Well, can you wonder at the man? And always badgering him to do things that could not be done at the time. To have The Half Moon painted, or enlarged, or insured: she'd keep on badgering him, and he could not make her see that any god's amount of money spent on paint wouldn't improve the taste of liquor.

'I can see as far into a quart pot as the King of England,' he says, 'and I know that if this bar was four times as big as 'tis a quart wouldn't hold a drop more then than it does now.'

'No, of course,' she says.

'Nor a drop less neither,' says Ted. He showed her that all the money expended on improvements and insurance and such things were so much off something else. Ted was a generous chap – liked to see plenty of everything, even though he had to give some of it away. But you can't make some women see some things.

'Not a roof to our heads, nor a floor to our feet, nor a pound to turn round on if a fire broke out,' Molly would say.

'But why should a fire break out?' he'd ask her. 'There never has been a fire here, there never ought to be a fire here, and what's more, there never will be a fire here, so why should there be a fire?'

And of course she let him have his own way, and they never had a fire there while he was alive, though I don't know that any great harm would have been done anyways, for after a few years trade began to slacken off, and the place got dull, and what with the taxes it was not much more than a bread and cheese business. Still, there's no matter of that: a man don't ask for a bed of roses: a world without some disturbance or anxiety would be like a duck-pond where the ducks sleep all day and are carried off at night by the foxes.

Molly was like that in many things, not really contrary, but no tact. After Ted died she kept on at The Half Moon for a year or two by herself, and regular as clockwork every month Pollock, the insurance manager, would drop in and try for to persuade her to insure the house or the stock or the furniture, any mortal thing. Well, believe you, when she had only got herself to please in the matter that woman wouldn't have anything to say to that insurance – she never did insure, and never would.

'I wouldn't run such a risk; upon my soul it's flying in the face of possibilities, Mrs Wickham' – he was a palavering chap, that Pollock; a tall fellow with sandy hair, and he always stunk of liniment for he had asthma on the chest – 'A very grave risk, it is indeed,' he would say, 'the Meazers' family was burnt clean out of hearth and home last St Valentine's day, and if they hadn't taken up a policy what would have become of those Meazers?'

'I dunno,' Molly says – that was the name Ted give her – 'I dunno, and I'm sorry for unfortunate people, but I've my private reasons.'

She was always talking about her private reasons, and they must have been devilish private, for not a soul on God's earth ever set eyes on them.

'Well, Mrs Wickham,' says Pollock, 'they'd have been a tidy ways up Queer Street, and ruin's a long-lasting affair,' Pollock says. He was a rare palavering chap, and he used to talk about Gladstone, too, for he knew her family history; but that didn't move her, and she did not insure.

'Yes, I quite agree,' she says, 'but I've my private reasons.'

Sheer female cussedness! But where her own husband couldn't persuade her Pollock had no chance at all. And then, of course, two years after Ted died she did go and have a fire there. The Half Moon was burnt clean out, rafters and railings, and she had to give it up and shift into the little bullseye business where she is now, selling bullseyes to infants and ginger beer to boy scholars on bicycles. And what does it all amount to? Why, it don't keep her in hairpins. She had the most beautiful hair once. But that's telling the story back foremost.

Ted was a smart chap, a particular friend of mine (so

was Molly), and he could have made something of himself
and of his business, perhaps, if it hadn't been for her. He
was a sportsman to the backbone; cricket, shooting, fishing,
always game for a bit of life, any mortal thing – what was
there he couldn't do? And a perfect demon with women,
I've never seen the like. If there was a woman for miles
around as he couldn't come at, then you could bet a crown
no one else could. He had the gift. Well, when one woman
ain't enough for a man, twenty ain't too many. He and me
were in a tight corner together more than once, but he never
went back on a friend, his word was his Bible oath. And there
was he all the while tied up to this soft wife of his, who never
once let on she knew of it at all, though she knowed much.
And never would she cast the blink of her eyes – splendid
eyes they were, too – on any willing stranger, nor even a
friend, say, like myself; it was all Ted this and Ted that,
though I was just her own age and Ted was twelve years
ahead of us both. She didn't know her own value, wouldn't
take her opportunities, hadn't the sense, as I say, though she
had got everything else. Ah, she was a woman to be looking
at once, and none so bad now; she wears well.

But she was too pious and proper, it aggravated him,
but Ted never once laid a finger on her and never uttered
one word of reproach though he despised her; never grudged
her a thing in reason when things were going well with him.
It's God Almighty's own true gospel – they never had a
quarrel in all the twelve years they was wed, and I don't
believe they ever had an angry word, but how he kept his
hands off her I don't know. I couldn't have done it, but I
was never married – I was too independent for that work.
He'd contradict her sometimes, for she *would* talk, and Ted
was one of your silent sorts, but *she* – she would talk for ever
more. She was so artful that she used to invent all manners
of tomfoolery on purpose to make him contradict her;
believe you, she did, even on his death bed.

I used to go and sit with him when he was going, poor
Ted, for I knew he was done for; and on the day he died,

she said to him – and I was there and I heard it, 'Is there anything you would like me to do, dear?' And he said, 'No.' He was almost at his last gasp, he had strained his heart, but she was for ever on at him, even then, an unresting woman. It was in May, I remember it, a grand bright afternoon outside, but the room itself was dreadful, it didn't seem to be afternoon at all; it was unbearable for a strong man to be dying in such fine weather, and the carts going by, and though we were a watching him, it seemed more as if something was watching us.

And she says to him again: 'Isn't there anything you would like me to do?'

Ted says to her: 'Ah! I'd like to hear you give one downright good-damn curse. Swear, my dear!'

'At what?' she says.

'Me, if you like.'

'What for?' she says. I can see her now, staring at him.

'For my sins.'

'What sins?' she says.

Now did you ever hear anything like that? What sins! After a while she began at him once more.

'Ted, if anything happens to you I'll never marry again.'

'Do what you like,' says he.

'I'll not do that,' she says, and she put her arms round him, 'for you'd not rest quiet in your grave, would you, Ted?'

'Leave me alone,' he says, for he was a very crusty sick man, very crusty, poor Ted, but could you wonder? 'You leave me alone and I'll rest sure enough.'

'You can be certain,' she cries, 'that I'd never, never do that, I'd never look at another man after you, Ted, never; I promise it solemnly.'

'Don't bother me, don't bother at all.' And poor Ted give a grunt and turned over on his side to get away from her.

At that moment some gruel boiled over on the hob – gruel and brandy was all he could take. She turned to look after it, and just then old Ted gave a breath and was gone, dead. She turned like a flash, with the steaming pot in her hand, bewildered for a moment. She saw he had gone. Then she put the pot back gently on the fender, walked over to the window and pulled down the blind. Never dropped a tear, not one tear.

Well, that was the end of Ted. We buried him, one or two of us. There was an insurance on his life for fifty pounds, but Ted had long before mortgaged the policy and so there was next to nothing for her. But what else could the man do? (Molly always swore the bank defrauded her!) She put a death notice in the paper, how he was dead, and the date, and what he died of: 'after a long illness, nobly and patiently borne.' Of course, that was sarcasm, she never meant one word of it, for he was a terror to nurse, the worst that ever was; a strong man on his back is like a wasp in a bottle. But every year, when the day comes round – and it's ten years now since he died – she puts a memorial notice in the same paper about her loving faithful husband and the long illness nobly and patiently borne!

And then, as I said, the insurance man and the parson began to call again on that foolish woman, but she would not alter her ways for any of them. Not one bit. The things she had once enjoyed before her marriage, the things she had wanted her own husband to do but were all against his grain, these she could nohow bring herself to do when he was dead and gone and she was alone and free to do them. What a farce human nature can be! There was an Italian hawker came along with rings in his ears and a coloured cart full of these little statues of Cupid, and churches with spires a yard long and red glass in them, and heads of some of the great people like the Queen and General Gordon.

'Have you got a head of Lord Beaconsfield?' Molly asks him.

He goes and searches in his cart and brings her out a beautiful head on a stand, all white and new, and charges her half a crown for it. Few days later the parson calls on the job of persuading her to return to his flock now that she was free to go once more. But no. She says: 'I can never change now, sir, it may be all wrong of me, but what my man thought was good enough for me, and I somehow cling to that. It's all wrong, I suppose, and you can't understand it, sir, but it's all my life.'

Well, Twamley chumbled over an argument or two, but he couldn't move her; there's no mortal man could ever move that woman except Ted – and he didn't give a damn.

'Well,' says parson, 'I have hopes, Mrs Wickham, that you will come to see the matter in a new light, a little later on perhaps. In fact, I'm sure you will, for look, there's that bust,' he says, and he points to it on the mantelpiece. 'I thought you and he were all against Gladstone, but now you've got his bust upon your shelf; it's a new one, I see.'

'No, no, that isn't Gladstone,' cried Molly, all of a tremble, 'that isn't Gladstone, it's Lord Beaconsfield!'

'Indeed, but pardon me, Mrs Wickham, that is certainly a bust of Mr Gladstone.'

So it was. This Italian chap had deceived the silly creature and palmed her off with any bust that come handy, and it happened to be Gladstone. She went white to the teeth, and gave a sort of scream, and dashed the little bust in a hundred pieces on the hearth in front of the minister there. O, he had a very vexing time with her.

That was years ago. And then came the fire, and then the bullseye shop. For ten years now I've prayed that woman to marry me, and she just tells me: No. She says she pledged her solemn word to Ted as he lay a-dying that she would not wed again. It was his last wish – she says. But it's a lie, a lie, for I heard them both. Such a lie! She's a mad woman, but fond of him still in her way, I suppose. She liked to see Ted make a fool of himself, liked him better so. Perhaps that's what she don't see in me. And what I see in her – I can't imagine. But it's a something, something in her that sways me now just as it swayed me then, and I doubt but it will sway me for ever.

Tribute

Two honest young men lived in Braddle, worked together at the spinning mills at Braddle, and courted the same girl in the town of Braddle, a girl named Patience who was poor and pretty. One of them, Nathan Regent, who wore cloth uppers to his best boots, was steady, silent and dignified, but Tony Vassall, the other, was such a happy-go-lucky fellow that he soon carried the goodwill of Patience in his heart, in his handsome face, in his pocket at the end of his nickel watch chain, or wherever the sign of requited love is carried by the happy lover. The virtue of steadiness, you see, can be measured only by the years, and this Tony had put such a hurry into the tender bosom of Patience: silence may very well be golden, but it is a currency not easy to negotiate in the kingdom of courtship; dignity is so much less than simple faith that it is unable to move even one mountain, it charms the hearts only of bank managers and bishops.

So Patience married Tony Vassall and Nathan turned his attention to other things, among them to a girl who had a neat little fortune – and Nathan married that.

Braddle is a large gaunt hill covered with dull little houses, and it has flowing from its side a stream which feeds a gigantic and beneficent mill. Without that mill – as everybody in Braddle knew, for it was there that everybody in Braddle worked – the heart of Braddle would cease to beat. Tony went on working at the mill. So did Nathan in a way, but he had a cute ambitious wife, and what with her money and influence he was soon made a manager of one of the departments. Tony went on working at the mill.

In a few more years Nathan's steadiness so increased his opportunities that he became joint manager of the whole works. Then his colleague died; he was appointed sole manager, and his wealth became so great that eventually Nathan and Nathan's wife bought the entire concern. Tony went on working at the mill. He now had two sons and a daughter, Nancy, as well as his wife Patience, so that even his possessions may be said to have increased although his position was no different from what it had been for twenty years.

The Regents, now living just outside Braddle, had one child, a daughter named Olive, of the same age as Nancy. She was very beautiful and had been educated at a school to which she rode on a bicycle until she was eighteen.

About that time, you must know, the country embarked upon a disastrous campaign, a war so calamitous that every sacrifice was demanded of Braddle. The Braddle mills were worn from their very bearings by their colossal efforts, increasing by day or by night, to provide what were called the sinews of war. Almost everybody in Braddle grew white and thin and sullen with the strain of constant labour. Not quite everybody, for the Regents received such a vast increase of wealth that their eyes sparkled; they scarcely knew what to do with it; their faces were neither white nor sullen.

'In times like these,' declared Nathan's wife, 'we must help our country still more, still more we must help; let us lend our money to the country.'

'Yes,' said Nathan.

So they lent their money to their country. The country paid them tribute, and therefore, as the Regent wealth continued to flow in, they helped their country more and more; they even lent the tribute back to the country and received yet more tribute for that.

'In times like these,' said the country, 'we must have more men, more men we must have.' And so Nathan went and sat upon a Tribunal; for, as everybody in Braddle knew, if the mills of Braddle ceased to grind, the heart of Braddle would cease to beat.

'What can we do to help our country?' asked Tony Vassall of his master, 'we have no money to lend.'

'No?' was the reply. 'But you can give your strong son Dan.'

Tony gave his son Dan to the country.

'Good-bye, dear son,' said his father, and his brother and his sister Nancy said 'Good-bye.' His mother kissed him.

Dan was killed in battle; his sister Nancy took his place at the mill.

In a little while the neighbours said to Tony Vassall: 'What a fine strong son is your young Albert Edward!'

And Tony gave his son Albert Edward to the country.

'Good-bye, dear son,' said his father; his sister kissed him, his mother wept on his breast.

Albert Edward was killed in battle; his mother took his place at the mill.

But the war did not cease; though friend and foe alike were almost drowned in blood it seemed as powerful as eternity, and in time Tony Vassall too went to battle and was killed. The country gave Patience a widow's pension, as well as a touching inducement to marry again; she died of grief. Many people died in those days, it was not strange at all. Nathan and his wife got so rich that after the war they died of over-eating, and their daughter Olive came into a vast fortune and a Trustee.

The Trustee went on lending the Braddle money to the country, the country went on sending large sums of interest to Olive (which was the country's tribute to her because of her parents' unforgotten, and indeed unforgettable, kindness), while Braddle went on with its work of enabling the country to do this. For when the war came to an end the country told Braddle that those who had not given their lives must now turn to and really work, work harder than before the war, much, much harder, or the tribute could not be paid and the heart of Braddle would therefore cease to beat. Braddle folk saw that this was true, only too true, and they did as they were told.

The Vassall girl, Nancy, married a man who had done deeds of valour in the war. He was a mill hand like her father, and they had two sons, Daniel and Albert Edward. Olive married a grand man, though it is true he was not very grand to look at. He had a small sharp nose, but that did not matter very much because when you looked at him in profile his bouncing red cheeks quite hid the small sharp nose, as completely as two hills hide a little barn in a valley. Olive lived in a grand mansion with numerous servants who helped her to rear a little family of one, a girl named Mercy, who also had a small sharp nose and round red cheeks.

Every year after the survivors' return from the war Olive gave a supper to her workpeople and their families, hundreds of them; for six hours there would be feasting and toys, music and dancing. Every year Olive would make a little speech to them all, reminding them all of their duty to Braddle and Braddle's duty to the country, although, indeed, she did not remind them of the country's tribute to Olive. That was perhaps a theme unfitting to touch upon, it would have been boastful and quite unbecoming.

'These are grave times for our country,' Olive would declare, year after year; 'her responsibilities are enormous, we must all put our shoulders to the wheel.'

Every year one of the workmen would make a little speech in reply, thanking Olive for enabling the heart of Braddle to continue its beats, calling down the spiritual blessings of heaven and the golden blessings of the world upon Olive's golden head. One year the honour of replying fell to the husband of Nancy, and he was more than usually eloquent for on that very day their two sons had commenced to doff bobbins at the mill. No one applauded louder than Nancy's little Dan or Nancy's Albert Edward, unless it was Nancy herself. Olive was always much moved on these occasions. She felt that she did not really know these people, that she would never know them; she wanted to go on seeing them, being with them, and living with rapture in their workaday world. But she did not do this.

'How beautiful it all is!' she would sigh to her daughter, Mercy, who accompanied her. 'I am so happy. All these dear people are being cared for by us, just simply us. God's scheme of creation – you see – the Almighty – we are his agents — we must always remember that. It goes on for years, years upon years it goes on. It will go on, of course, yes, for ever; the heart of Braddle will not cease to beat. The old ones die, the young grow old, the children mature and marry and keep the mill going. When I am dead . . .'

'Mamma, mamma!'

'O yes, indeed, one day! Then *you* will have to look after all these things, Mercy, and you will talk to them – just like me. Yes, to own the mill is a grave and difficult thing, only those who own them know how grave and difficult; it calls forth all one's deepest and rarest qualities; but it is a divine position, a noble responsibility. And the people really love me – I think.'

The Higgler

I

On a cold April afternoon a higgler was driving across Shag Moor in a two-wheeled cart.

H. WITLOW
Dealer in Poultry
DINNOP

was painted on the hood; the horse was of mean appearance but notorious ancestry. A high upland common was this moor, two miles from end to end, and full of furze and bracken. There were no trees and not a house, nothing but a line of telegraph poles following the road, sweeping with rigidity from north to south; nailed upon one of them a small scarlet notice to stonethrowers was prominent as a wound. On so high and wide a region as Shag Moor the wind always blew, or if it did not quite blow there was a cool activity in the air. The furze was always green and growing, and, taking no account of seasons, often golden. Here in summer solitude lounged and snoozed; at other times, as now, it shivered and looked sinister.

Higglers in general are ugly and shrewd, old and hard, crafty and callous, but Harvey Witlow, though shrewd, was not ugly; he was hard but not old, crafty but not at all unkind. If you had eggs to sell he would buy them, by the score he would, or by the long hundred. Other odds and ends he would buy or do, paying good bright silver, bartering a bag of apples, carrying your little pig to market, or fetching a tree from the nurseries. But the season was backward, eggs were scarce, trade was bad – by crumps, it was indeed! – and as he crossed the moor Harvey could not help discussing the situation with himself. 'If things don't change, and change for the better and change soon, I can't last and I can't endure it; I'll be damned and done, and I'll have to sell,' he said, prodding the animal with the butt of his whip, 'this cob. And,' he said, as if in afterthought, prodding the foot-board, 'this cart, and go back to the land. And I'll have lost my fifty pounds. Well, that's what war does for you. It does it for you, sir,' he announced sharply to the vacant moor, 'and it does it for me. Fifty pounds! I was better off in the war. I was better off working for farmers – much. But it's no good chattering about it, it's the trick of life; when you get so far, then you can go and order your funeral. Get along, Dodger!'

The horse responded briskly for a few moments.

'I tell ye,' said Harvey adjuring the ambient air, 'you can go and order your funeral. Get along, Dodger!'

Again Dodger got along.

'Then there's Sophy, what about Sophy and me?'

He was not engaged to Sophy Daws, not exactly, but he was keeping company with her. He was not pledged or affianced, he was just keeping company with her. But Sophy, as he knew, not only desired a marriage with Mr Witlow, she expected it, and expected it soon. So did her parents, her friends, and everybody in the village, including the postman who didn't live in it but wished he did, and the parson who did live in it but wished he didn't.

'Well, that's damned and done, fair damned and done now, unless things take a turn, and soon, so it's no good chattering about it.'

And just then and there things did take a turn. He had never been across the moor before; he was prospecting for trade. At the end of Shag Moor he saw standing back on the common, fifty yards from the road, a neat square house set in a little farm. Twenty acres, perhaps. The house was girded by some white palings; beside it was a snug orchard in a hedge covered with blackthorn bloom. It was very green and pleasant in front of the house. The turf was cleared and closely cropped, some ewes were grazing and under the blackthorn, out of the wind, lay half a dozen lambs, but what chiefly moved the imagination of Harvey Witlow was a field on the far side of the house. It had a small rick-yard with a few small stacks in it; everything here seemed on the small scale, but snug, very snug; and in that field and yard were hundreds of fowls, hundreds, of good breed, and mostly white. Leaving his horse to sniff the greensward, the higgler entered a white wicket gateway and passed to the back of the house, noting as he did so a yellow wagon inscribed ELIZABETH SADGROVE. PRATTLE CORNER.

At the kitchen door he was confronted by a tall gaunt woman of middle age with a teapot in her hands.

'Afternoon, ma'am. Have you anything to sell?' began Harvey Witlow, tilting his hat with a confident affable air. The tall woman was cleanly dressed, a superior person; her hair was grey. She gazed at him.

'It's cold,' he continued. She looked at him as uncomprehendingly as a mouse might look at a gravestone.

'I'll buy any mottal thing, ma'am. Except trouble; I'm full up wi' that already. Eggs? Fowls?'

'I've not seen you before,' commented Mrs Sadgrove a little bleakly, in a deep husky voice.

'No, 'tis the first time as ever I drove in this part. To tell you the truth, ma'am, I'm new to the business. Six months. I was in the war a year ago. Now I'm trying to knock up a connection. Difficult work. Things are very quiet.'

Mrs Sadgrove silently removed the lid of the teapot, inspected the interior of the pot with an intent glance, and then replaced the lid as if she had seen a black beetle there.

'Ah, well,' sighed the higgler. 'You've a neat little farm here, ma'am.'

'It's quiet enough,' said she.

'Sure it is, ma'am. Very lonely.'

'And it's difficult work too.' Mrs Sadgrove almost smiled.

'Sure it is, ma'am; but you does it well, I can see.

Oh, you've some nice little ricks of corn, eh! I does well enough at the dealing now and again, but it's teasy work and mostly I don't earn enough to keep my horse in shoe leather.'

'I've a few eggs, perhaps,' said she.

'I could do with a score or two, ma'am, if you could let me have 'em.'

'You'll have to come all my way if I do.'

'Name your own price, ma'am, if you don't mind trading with me.'

'Mind! Your money's as good as my own, isn't it?'

'It must be, ma'am. That's meaning no disrespects to you,' the young higgler assured her hastily, and was thereupon invited to enter the kitchen.

A stone floor with two or three mats; open hearth with burning logs; a big dresser painted brown, carrying a row of white cups on brass hooks and shelves of plates overlapping each other like the scales of fish. A dark settle half hid a flight of stairs with a small gate at the top. Under the window a black sofa, deeply indented, invited you a little repellingly, and in the middle of the room stood a large table, exquisitely scrubbed, with one end of it laid for tea. Evidently a living-room as well as kitchen. A girl, making toast at the fire, turned as the higgler entered. Beautiful she was: red hair, a complexion like the inside of a nut, blue eyes, and the hands of a lady. He saw it all at once, jacket of bright green wool, black dress, grey stockings and shoes, and forgot his errand, her mother, his fifty pounds, Sophy – momentarily he forgot everything. The girl strangely stared at him. He was tall, clean-shaven, with a loop of black hair curling handsomely over one side of his brow.

'Good afternoon,' said Harvey Witlow, as softly as if he had entered a church.

'Some eggs, Mary,' Mrs Sadgrove explained. The girl laid down her toasting-fork. She was less tall than her mother, whom she resembled only enough for the relationship to be noted. Silently she crossed the kitchen and opened a door that led into a dairy. Two pans of milk were creaming on a bench there and on the flags were two great baskets filled with eggs.

'How many are there?' asked Mrs Sadgrove, and the girl replied: 'Fifteen score, I think.'

'Take the lot, higgler?'

'Yes, ma'am,' he cried eagerly, and ran out to his cart and fetched a number of trays. In them he packed the eggs as the girl handed them to him from the baskets. Mrs Sadgrove left them together. For a time the higgler was silent.

'No,' at length he murmured, 'I've never been this road before.'

There was no reply from Mary. Sometimes their fingers touched, and often, as they bent over the eggs, her bright hair almost brushed his face.

'It is a loneish spot,' he ventured again.

'Yes,' said Mary Sadgrove.

When the eggs were all transferred her mother came in again.

'Would you buy a few pullets, higgler?'

'Any number, ma'am,' he declared quickly. Any number; by crumps, the tide was turning! He followed the mother into the yard, and there again she left him, waiting. He mused about the girl and wondered about the trade. If they offered him ten thousand chickens, he'd buy them, somehow, he would! She had stopped in the kitchen. Just in there she was, just behind him, a few feet away. Over the low wall of the yard a fat black pony was strolling in a field of bright greensward. In the yard, watching him, was a young gander, and on a stone staddle beside it lay a dead thrush on its back, its legs stiff in the air. The girl stayed in the kitchen; she was moving about, though, he could hear her; perhaps she was spying at him through the window. Twenty million eggs he would buy if Mrs Sadgrove had got them. She was gone a long time. It was very quiet. The gander began to comb its white breast with its beak. Its three-toed feet were a most tender pink, shaped like wide diamonds, and at each of the three forward points there was a toe like a small blanched nut. It lifted one foot, folding the webs, and hid it under its wing and sank into a resigned meditation on one leg. It had a blue eye that was meek – it had two, but you could only see one at a time – a meek blue eye, set in a pink rim that gave it a dissolute air, and its beak had raw red nostrils as if it suffered from the damp. Altogether a beautiful bird. And in some absurd way it resembled Mrs Sadgrove.

'Would you sell that young gollan, ma'am?' Harvey inquired when the mother returned.

Yes, she would sell him, and she also sold him two dozen pullets. Harvey packed the fowls in a crate.

'Come on,' he cried cuddling the squawking gander in his arms, 'you needn't be afraid of me, I never kills anything afore Saturdays.'

He roped it by its leg to a hook inside his cart. Then he took out his bag of money, paid Mrs Sadgrove her dues, said 'Good day, ma'am, good day,' and drove off without seeing another sign or stitch of that fine young girl.

'Get along, Dodger, get along wi' you.' They went bowling along for nearly an hour, and then he could see the landmark on Dan'el Green's Hill, a windmill that never turned though it looked a fine competent piece of architecture, just beyond Dinnop.

Soon he reached his cottage and was chaffing his mother, a hearty buxom dame, who stayed at home and higgled with any chance callers. At this business she was perhaps more enlightened than her son. It was almost a misfortune to get into her clutches.

'How much you give for this?' he cried, eyeing with humorous contempt an object in a coop that was neither flesh nor rude red herring.

'Oh crumps,' he declared, when she told him, 'I am damned and done!'

"Go on with you, that's a good bird, I tell you, with a full heart, as will lay in a month.'

'I doubt it's a hen at all,' he protested. 'Oh, what a ravenous beak! Damned and done I am.'

Mrs Witlow's voice began indignantly to rise.

'Oh, well,' mused her son, 'it's thrifty perhaps. It ain't quite right, but it's not so wrong as to make a fuss about, especially as I be pretty sharp set. And if it's hens you want,' he continued triumphantly, dropping the crate of huddled fowls before her, 'there's hens for you; and a gander! There's a gander for you, if it's a gander you want.'

Leaving them all in his cottage yard he went and stalled the horse and cart at the inn, for he had no stable of his own. After supper he told his mother about the Sadgroves of Prattle Corner. 'Prettiest girl you ever seen, but the shyest mottal alive. Hair like a squirrel, lovely.'

'An't you got to go over and see Sophy tonight?' inquired his mother, lighting the lamp.

'Oh Lord, if I an't clean forgot that! Well, I'm tired, shan't go tonight. See her tomorrow.'

II

Mrs Sadgrove had been a widow for ten years – and she was glad of it. Prattle Corner was her property, she owned it and farmed it with the aid of a little old man and a large lad. The older this old man grew, and the less wages he received (for Elizabeth Sadgrove was reputed a 'grinder'), the more ardently he worked; the older the lad grew the less he laboured and the more he swore. She was thriving. She was worth money was Mrs Sadgrove. Ah! And her daughter Mary, it was clear, had received an education fit for a lord's lady; she had been at a seminary for gentlefolk's females until she was seventeen. Well, whether or no, a clock must run as you time it; but it wronged her for the work of a farm, it spoiled her, it completely deranged her for the work of a farm; and this was a pity and foolish, because some day the farm was coming to her as didn't know hay from a bull's foot.

All this, and more, the young higgler quickly learned,

and plenty more he soon divined. Business began to flourish
with him now; his despair was gone, he was established, he
could look forward, to whatever it was he wanted to look
forward, with equanimity and such pleasurable anticipation
as the chances and charges of life might engender. Every
week, and twice a week, he would call at the farm, and though
these occasions had their superior business inducements
they often borrowed a less formal tone and intention.

'Take a cup of tea, higgler?' Mrs Sadgrove would abruptly
invite him; and he would drink tea and discourse with her
for half an hour on barndoor ornithology, on harness, and
markets, the treatment of swine, the wear and tear of gear.
Mary, always present, was always silent, seldom uttering
a word to the higgler; yet a certain grace emanated from her
to him, an interest, a light, a favour, circumscribed indeed
by some modesty, shyness, some inhibition, that neither of
them had the wit or the opportunity to overcome.

One evening he pulled up at the white palings of Prattle
Corner. It was a calm evening in May, the sun was on its
downgoing, chaffinches and wrens sung ceaselessly. Mary
in the orchard was heavily veiled; he could see her over the
hedge, holding a brush in her gloved hands, and a bee
skep. A swarm was clustered like a great gnarl on the limb
of an apple tree. Bloom was thickly covering the twigs. She
made several timid attempts to brush the bees into the skep,
but they resented this.

'They knows if you be afraid of 'em,' bawled Harvey;
'I better come and give you a hand.'

When he took the skep and brush from her she stood
like one helpless, released by fate from a task ill-under-
stood and gracelessly waived. But he liked her shyness, her
almost uncouth immobility.

'Never mind about that,' said Harvey, as she unfastened
her veil, scattering the white petals that had collected
upon it; 'when they kicks they hurts, but I've been stung
so often that I'm 'nocolated against 'em. They knows if
you be afraid of 'em.'

Wearing neither veil nor gloves he went confidently to the tree, and collected the swarm without mishap.

'Don't want to show no fear of them,' said Harvey. 'Nor of anything else, come to that,' he added with a guffaw, 'nor anybody.'

At that she blushed and thanked him very softly, and she did look straight and clearly at him.

Never anything beyond a blush and a thank you. When, in the kitchen or the parlour, Mrs Sadgrove sometimes left them alone together Harvey would try a lot of talk, blarneying talk or sensible talk, or talk about events in the world that was neither the one nor the other. No good. The girl's responses were ever brief and confused. Why was this? Again and again he asked himself that question. Was there anything the matter with her? Nothing that you could see; she was a bright and beautiful being. And it was not contempt, either, for despite her fright, her voicelessness, her timid eyes, he divined her friendly feeling for himself; and he would discourse to his own mother about her and her mother:

'They are well-up people, you know, well off, plenty of money and nothing to do with it. The farm's their own, freehold. A whole row of cottages she's got, too, in Smoorton Comfrey, so I heard; good cottages, well let. She's worth a few thousands, I warrant. Mary's beautiful. I took a fancy to that girl the first moment I see her. But she's very highly cultivated – and, of course, there's Sophy.'

To this enigmatic statement Mrs Witlow offered no response; but mothers are inscrutable beings to their sons, always.

Once he bought some trees of cherries from Mrs Sadgrove, and went on a July morning to pick the fruit. Under the trees Mary was walking slowly to and fro, twirling a clapper to scare away the birds. He stood watching her from the gateway. Among the bejewelled trees she passed, turning the rattle with a listless air, as if beating time to a sad music that only she could hear. The man knew that he was deeply fond of her. He passed into the orchard, bade her good morning, and, lifting his ladder into one of the trees nearest the hedge, began to pluck cherries. Mary moved slimly in her white frock up and down a shady avenue in the orchard waving the clapper. The brightness of sun and sky was almost harsh; there was a little wind that feebly lifted the despondent leaves. He had doffed his coat; his shirt was white and clean. The lock of dark hair drooped over one side of his forehead; his face was brown and pleasant, his bare arms brown and powerful. From his high perch among the leaves Witlow watched for the girl to draw near to him in her perambulation. Knavish birds would scatter at her approach, only to drop again into the trees she had passed. His soul had an immensity of longing for her, but she never spoke a word to him. She would come from the shade of the little avenue, through the dumb trees that could only bend to greet her, into the sunlight whose dazzle gilded her own triumphant bloom. Fine! Fine! And always as she passed his mind refused to register a single thought he could offer her, or else his tongue would refuse to utter it. But his glance never left her face until she had passed out of sight again, and then he would lean against the ladder in the tree, staring down at the ground, seeing nothing or less than nothing, except a field mouse climbing to the top of a coventry bush in the hedge below him, nipping off one thick leaf and descending with the leaf in its mouth. Sometimes Mary rested at the other end of the avenue; the clapper would be silent and she would not appear for – oh, hours! She never rested near the trees Witlow was denuding. The mouse went on ascending and descending, and Witlow filled his basket, and shifted his stand, and wondered.

At noon he got down and sat on the hedge bank to eat a snack of lunch. Mary had gone indoors for hers, and he was alone for awhile. Capriciously enough, his thoughts dwelt upon Sophy Daws. Sophy was a fine girl, too; not such a lady as Mary Sadgrove – oh lord, no! her father was a gamekeeper! – but she was jolly and ample. She had been a little captious lately, said he was neglecting her. That wasn't true;

hadn't he been busy? Besides, he wasn't bound to her in any sort of way, and of course he couldn't afford any marriage yet awhile. Sophy hadn't got any money, never had any. What she did with her wages – she was a parlourmaid – was a teaser! Harvey grunted a little, and said 'Well!' And that is all he said, and all he thought, about Sophy Daws, then, for he could hear Mary's clapper begin again in a corner of the orchard. He went back to his work. There at the foot of the tree were the baskets full of cherries, and those yet to be filled.

'Phew, but that's hot!' commented the man, 'I'm as dry as a rattle.'

A few cherries had spilled from one basket and lay on the ground. The little furry mouse had found them and was industriously nibbling at one. The higgler nonchalantly stamped his foot upon it, and kept it so for a moment or two. Then he looked at the dead mouse. A tangle of entrails had gushed from its whiskered muzzle.

He resumed his work and the clapper rattled on throughout the afternoon, for there were other cherry trees that other buyers would come to strip in a day or two. At four o'clock he was finished. Never a word had he spoken with Mary, or she with him. When he went over to the house to pay Mrs Sadgrove Mary stopped in the orchard scaring the birds.

'Take a cup of tea, Mr Witlow,' said Mrs Sadgrove; and then she surprisingly added, 'Where's Mary?'

'Still a-frightening the birds, and pretty well tired of that, I should think, ma'am.'

The mother had poured out three cups of tea.

'Shall I go and call her in?' he asked, rising.

'You might,' said she.

In the orchard the clappering had ceased. He walked all round, and in among the trees, but saw no sign of Mary; nor on the common, nor in the yard. But when he went back to the house Mary was there already, chatting at the table with her mother. She did not greet him, though she ceased talking to her mother as he sat down. After drinking his tea he went off briskly to load the baskets into the cart. As he climbed up to drive off Mrs Sadgrove came out and stood beside the horse.

'You're off now?' said she.

'Yes, ma'am; all loaded, and thank you.'

She glanced vaguely along the road he had to travel. The afternoon was as clear as wine, the greensward itself dazzled him; lonely Shag Moor stretched away, humped with sweet yellow furze and pilastered with its telegraph poles. No life there, no life at all. Harvey sat on his driving board, musingly brushing the flank of his horse with the trailing whip.

'Ever round this way on Sundays?' inquired the woman, peering up at him.

'Well, not in a manner of speaking, I'm not, ma'am,' he answered her.

The widow laid her hand on the horse's back, patting vaguely. The horse pricked up its ears, as if it were listening.

'If you are, at all, ever, you must look in and have a bit of dinner with us.'

'I will, ma'am, I will.'

'Next Sunday?' she went on.

'I will, ma'am, yes, I will,' he repeated, 'and thank you.'

'One o'clock?' The widow smiled up at him.

'At one o'clock, ma'am; next Sunday; I will, and thank you,' he said.

She stood away from the horse and waved her hand. The first tangible thought that floated mutely out of the higgler's mind as he drove away was: 'I'm damned if I ain't a-going it, Sophy!'

He told his mother of Mrs Sadgrove's invitation with an air of curbed triumph. 'Come round – she says. Yes – I says – I 'ull. That's right – she says – so do.'

III

On the Sunday morn he dressed himself gallantly. It was again a sweet unclouded day. The church bell at Dinnop had begun to ring. From his window, as he fastened his most ornate tie, Harvey could observe his neighbour's two small children in the next garden, a boy and girl clad for church-going and each carrying a clerical book. The tiny boy placed his sister in front of a henroost and, opening his book, began to pace to and fro before her, shrilly intoning: 'Jesus is the shepherd, ring the bell. Oh lord, ring the bell, am I a good boy? Amen. Oh lord, ring the bell.' The little girl bowed her head piously over her book. The lad then picked up from the ground a dish which had contained the dog's food, and presented it momentarily before the lilac bush, the rabbit in a hutch, the axe fixed in a chopping block, and then before his sister. Without lifting her peering gaze from her book she meekly dropped two pebbles in the plate, and the boy passed on, lightly moaning, to the clothes-line post and a cock scooping in some dust.

'Ah, the little impets!' cried Harvey Witlow. 'Here, Toby! Here, Margaret!' He took two pennies from his pocket and lobbed them from the window to the astonished children. As they stooped to pick up the coins Harvey heard the hoarse voice of neighbour Nathan, their father, bawl from his kitchen: 'Come on in, and shut that bloody door, d'y'ear!'

Harnessing his moody horse to the gig Harvey was soon bowling away to Shag Moor, and as he drove along he sang loudly. He had a pink rose in his buttonhole. Mrs Sadgrove received him almost affably, and though Mary was more shy than ever before, Harvey had determined to make an impression. During the dinner he fired off his bucolic jokes, and pleasant tattle of a more respectful and sober nature; but after dinner Mary sat like Patience, not upon a monument, but as if upon a rocking-horse, shy and fearful, and her mother made no effort to inspire her as the higgler did, unsuccessful though he was. They went to the pens to look at the pigs, and as they leaned against the low walls and poked the maudlin inhabitants, Harvey began, 'Reminds me, when I was in the war . . .'

'Were you in the war?' interrupted Mrs Sadgrove.

'Oh, yes, I was in that war, ah, and there was a pig. . . . Danger? Oh lord, bless me, it was a bit dangerous, but you never knew where it was or what it 'ud be at next; it was like the sword of Damockels. There was a bullet once come 'ithin a foot of my head, and it went through a board an inch thick, slap through that board.' Both women gazed at him apprehendingly. 'Why, I might 'a been killed, you know,' said Harvey, cocking his eye musingly at the weather-vane on the barn. 'We was in billets at St Gratien, and one day a chasseur came up – a French yoossar, you know – and he began talking to our sergeant. That was Hubert Luxter, the butcher: died a month or two ago of measles. But this yoossar couldn't speak English at all, and none of us chaps could make sense of him. I never could understand that lingo somehow, never; and though there was half a dozen of us chaps there, none of us were man enough for it neither. "Nil compree," we says, "non compos." I told him straight, "You ought to learn English," I said, "it's much easier than your kind of bally chatter." So he kept shaping up as if he was holding a rifle, and then he'd say "Fusee – bang!" and then he'd say "cushion" – kept on saying "cushion". Then he gets a bit of chalk and draws on the wall something that looks like a horrible dog, and says "cushion" again.'

'Pig,' interjected Mary Sadgrove softly.

'Yes, yes!' ejaculated Harvey, 'so 'twas! Do you know any French lingo?'

'Oh, yes,' declared her mother, 'Mary knows it very well.'

'Ah,' sighed the higgler, 'I don't, although I been to France. And I couldn't do it now, not for luck nor love. You learnt it, I suppose. Well, this yoossar wants to borrow my rifle, but of course I can't lend him. So he taps on this horrible pig he'd drawn, and then he taps on his own head, and rolls his eyes about dreadful! "Mad?" I says. And that was it, that was it. He'd got a pig on his little farm there what had gone mad, and he wanted us to come and shoot it; he was on leave and he hadn't got any ammunition. So Hubert Luxter he says, "Come on, some of you," and we all goes with the yoossar and shot the pig for him. Ah, that was a pig! And when it died it jumped a somersault just like a rabbit. It had got the mange, and was mad as anything I ever see in my life; it was full of madness. Couldn't hit him at all at first, and it kicked up bobs-a-dying. "Ready, present, fire!" Hubert Luxter says, and bang goes the six of us, and every time we missed him he spotted us and we had to run for our lives.'

As Harvey looked up he caught a glance of the girl fixed on him. She dropped her gaze at once and, turning away, walked off to the house.

'Come and take a look at the meadow,' said Mrs Sadgrove to him, and they went into the soft smooth meadow where the black pony was grazing. Very bright and green it was, and very blue the sky. He sniffed at the pink rose in his buttonhole, and determined that come what might he would give it to Mary if he could get a nice quiet chance to offer it. And just then, while he and Mrs Sadgrove were strolling alone in the soft smooth meadow, quite alone, she suddenly, startlingly, asked him: 'Are you courting anybody?'

'Beg pardon, ma'am?' he exclaimed.

'You haven't got a sweetheart, have you?' she asked, most deliberately.

Harvey grinned sheepishly: 'Ha, ha, ha,' and then he said, 'no.'

'I want to see my daughter married,' the widow went on significantly.

'Miss Mary!' he cried.

'Yes,' said she; and something in the higgler's veins began to pound rapidly. His breast might have been a revolving cage and his heart a demon squirrel. 'I can't live for ever,' said Mrs Sadgrove, almost with levity, 'in fact, not for long, and so I'd like to see her settled soon with some decent understanding young man, one that could carry on here, and not make a mess of things.'

'But, but,' stuttered the understanding young man, 'I'm no scholar, and she's a lady. I'm a poor chap, rough, and no scholar, ma'am. But mind you . . .'

'That doesn't matter at all,' the widow interrupted, 'not as things are. You want a scholar for learning, but for the land . . .'

'Ah, that's right, Mrs Sadgrove, but . . .'

'I want to see her settled. This farm, you know, with the stock and things are worth nigh upon three thousand pounds.'

'You want a farmer for farming, that's true, Mrs Sadgrove, but when you come to marriage, well, with her learning and French and all that . . .'

'A sensible woman will take a man rather than a box of tricks any day of the week,' the widow retorted. 'Education may be a fine thing, but it often costs a lot of foolish money.'

'It do, it do. You want to see her settled?'

'I want to see her settled and secure. When she is twenty-five she comes into five hundred pounds of her own right.'

The distracted higgler hummed and haa'ed in his bewilderment as if he had just been offered the purchase of a dubious duck. 'How old is she, ma'am?' he at last huskily inquired.

'Two-and-twenty nearly. She's a good healthy girl, for I've never spent a pound on a doctor for her, and very quiet she is, and very sensible; but she's got a strong will of her own, though you might not think it or believe it.'

'She's a fine creature, Mrs Sadgrove, and I'm very fond of her. I don't mind owning up to that, very fond of her I am.'

'Well, think it over, take your time, and see what you think. There's no hurry, I hope, please God.'

9

'I shan't want much time,' he declared with a laugh, 'but I doubt I'm the fair right sort for her.'

'Oh, fair days, fair doings!' said she inscrutably, 'I'm not a long liver, I'm afraid.'

'God forbid, ma'am!' His ejaculation was intoned with deep gravity.

'No, I'm not a long-living woman.' She surveyed him with her calm eyes, and he returned her gaze. Hers was a long sallow face, with heavy lips. Sometimes she would stretch her features (as if to keep them from petrifying) in an elastic grin, and display her dazzling teeth; the lips would curl thickly, no longer crimson, but blue. He wondered if there were any sign of a doom registered upon her gaunt face. She might die, and die soon.

'You couldn't do better than think it over, then, eh?' she had a queer frown as she regarded him.

'I couldn't do worse than not, Mrs Sadgrove,' he said gaily.

They left it at that. He had no reason for hurrying away, and he couldn't have explained his desire to do so, but he hurried away. Driving along past the end of the moor, and peering back at the lonely farm where they dwelled amid the thick furze snoozing in the heat, he remembered that he had not asked if Mary was willing to marry him! Perhaps the widow took her agreement for granted. That would be good fortune, for otherwise how the devil was he to get round a girl who had never spoken half a dozen words to him! And never would! She was a lady, a girl of fortune, knew her French; but there it was, the girl's own mother was asking him to wed her. Strange, very strange! He dimly feared something, but he did not know what it was he feared. He had still got the pink rose in his buttonhole.

IV

At first his mother was incredulous; when he told her of the astonishing proposal she declared he was a joker; but she was soon as convinced of his sincerity as she was amazed at his hesitation. And even vexed: 'Was there anything the matter with this Mary?'

'No, no, no! She's quiet, very quiet indeed, I tell you, but a fine young woman, and a beautiful young woman. Oh, she's all right, right as rain, right as a trivet, right as ninepence. But there's a catch in it somewheres, I fear. I can't see through it yet, but I shall afore long, or I'd have the girl, like a shot I would. 'Tain't the girl, mother, it's the money, if you understand me.'

'Well, I don't understand you, certainly I don't. What about Sophy?'

'Oh lord!' He scratched his head ruefully.

'You wouldn't think of giving this the go-by for Sophy, Harvey, would you? A girl as you ain't even engaged to, Harvey, would you?'

'We don't want to chatter about that,' declared her son. 'I got to think it over, and it's going to tie my wool, I can tell you, for there's a bit of craft somewheres, I'll take my oath. If there ain't, there ought to be!'

Over the alluring project his decision wavered for days, until his mother became mortified at his inexplicable vacillation.

'I tell you,' he cried, 'I can't make tops or bottoms of it all. I like the girl well enough, but I like Sophy, too, and it's no good beating about the bush. I like Sophy, she's the girl I love; but Mary's a fine creature, and money like that wants looking at before you throw it away, love or no love. Three thousand pounds! I'd be a made man.'

And as if in sheer spite to his mother; as if a bushel of money lay on the doorstep for him to kick over whenever the fancy seized him; in short (as Mrs Witlow very clearly intimated) as if in contempt of Providence he began to pursue Sophy Daws with a new fervour, and walked with that young girl more than he was accustomed to, more than ever before; in fact, as his mother bemoaned, more than he had need to. It was unreasonable, it was a shame, a foolishness; it wasn't decent and it wasn't safe.

On his weekly visits to the farm his mind still wavered. Mrs Sadgrove let him alone; she was very good, she did not pester him with questions and entreaties. There was Mary with her white dress and her red hair and her silence; a girl with a great fortune, walking about the yard, or sitting in the room, and casting not a glance upon him. Not that he would have known it if she did, for now he was just as shy of her. Mrs Sadgrove often left them alone, but when they were alone he could not dish up a word for the pretty maid; he was dumb as a statue. If either she or her mother had lifted so much as a finger then there would have been an end to his hesitations or suspicions, for in Mary's presence the fine glory of the girl seized him incontinently; he was again full of a longing to press her lips, to lay down his doubts, to touch her bosom – though he could not think she would ever allow that! Not an atom of doubt about *her* ever visited him; she was unaware of her mother's queer project. Rather, if she became aware he was sure it would be the end of him. Too beautiful she was, too learned, and too rich. Decidedly it was his native cunning, and no want of love, that inhibited him. Folks with property did not often come along and bid you help yourself. Not very often! And throw in a grand bright girl, just for good measure as you might say. Not very often!

For weeks the higgler made his customary calls, and each time the outcome was the same; no more, no less. 'Some dodge,' he mused, 'something the girl don't know and the mother does.' Were they going bankrupt, or were they mortgaged up to the neck, or was there anything the matter with the girl, or was it just the mother wanted to get hold of him? He knew his own value if he didn't know his own mind, and his value couldn't match that girl any more than his mind could. So what *did* they want him for? Whatever it was Harvey Witlow was ready for it whenever he was in Mary's presence, but once away from her his own craftiness asserted itself: it was a snare, they were trying to make a mock of him!

But nothing could prevent his own mother mocking him, and her treatment of Sophy was so unbearable that if the heart of that dusky beauty had not been proof against all impediments, Harvey might have had to whistle for her favour. But whenever he was with Sophy he had only one heart, undivided and true, and certain as time itself.

'I love Sophy best. It's true enough I love Mary, too, but I love Sophy better. I know it; Sophy's the girl I must wed. It might not be so if I weren't all dashed and doddered about the money; I don't know. But I do know that Mary's innocent of all this craftiness; it's her mother trying to mogue me into it.'

Later he would be wishing he could only forget Sophy and do it. Without the hindrance of conscience he could do it, catch or no catch.

He went on calling at the farm, with nothing said or settled, until October. Then Harvey made up his mind, and without a word to the Sadgroves he went and married Sophy Daws and gave up calling at the farm altogether. This gave him some feeling of dishonesty, some qualm, and a vague unhappiness; likewise he feared the cold hostility of Mrs Sadgrove. She would be terribly vexed. As for Mary, he was nothing to her, poor girl; it was a shame. The last time he drove that way he did not call at the farm. Autumn was advancing, and the apples were down, the bracken dying, the furze out of bloom, and the farm on the moor looked more and more lonely, and most cold, though it lodged a flame-haired silent woman, fit for a nobleman, whom they wanted to mate with a common higgler. Crafty, you know, too crafty!

v

The marriage was a gay little occasion, but they did not go away for a honeymoon. Sophy's grandmother from a distant village, Cassandra Fundy, who had a deafness and a speckled skin, brought her third husband, Amos, whom the family had never seen before. Not a very wise man, indeed he was a common man, stooping like a decayed tree, he was so old. But he shaved every day and his hairless skull was yellow. Cassandra, who was yellow too, had long since turned into a fool; she did not shave, though she ought to have done. She was like to die soon, but everybody said old Amos would live to be a hundred; it was expected of him, and he, too, was determined.

The guests declared that a storm was threatening, but Amos Fundy denied it and scorned it.

'Thunder p'raps, but 'twill clear; 'tis only de pride o' der morning.'

'Don't you be a fool,' remarked his wife enigmatically, 'you'll die soon enough.'

'You must behold der moon,' continued the octogenarian; 'de closer it is to der wheel, de closer der rain; de furder away it is, de furder der rain.'

'You could pour that man's brains into a thimble,' declared Cassandra of her spouse, 'and they wouldn't fill it – he's deaf.'

Fundy was right; the day did clear. The marriage was made and the guests returned with the man and his bride to their home. But Fundy was also wrong, for storm came soon after and rain set in. The guests stayed on for tea, and then, as it was no better, they feasted and stayed till night. And Harvey began to think they never would go, but of course they couldn't and so there they were. Sophy was looking wonderful in white stockings and shiny shoes and a red frock with a tiny white apron. A big girl she seemed, with her shaken dark hair and flushed face. Grandmother Fundy spoke seriously, but not secretly to her.

'I've had my fourteen touch of children,' said Grandmother Fundy. 'Yes, they were flung on the mercy of God – poor little devils. I've followed most of 'em to the churchyard. You go slow, Sophia.'

'Yes, granny.'

'Why,' continued Cassandra, embracing the whole company, as it were, with her disclosure, 'my mother had me by some gentleman!'

The announcement aroused no response except sympathetic, and perhaps encouraging, nods from the women.

'She had me by some gentleman – she ought to ha' had a twal' month, she did!'

'Wasn't she ever married?' Sophy inquired of her grandmother.

'Married? Yes, course she was,' replied the old dame, 'of course. But marriage ain't everything. Twice she was, but not to he, she wasn't.'

'Not to the gentleman?'

'No! Oh, no! He'd got money – bushels! Marriage ain't much, not with these gentry.'

'Ho, ho, that's a tidy come-up!' laughed Harvey.

'Who was that gentleman?' Sophia's interest was deeply engaged. But Cassandra Fundy was silent, pondering like a china image. Her gaze was towards the mantelpiece, where there were four lamps – but only one usable – and two clocks – but only one going – and a coloured greeting card a foot long with large letters KEEP SMILING adorned with lithographic honeysuckle.

'She's hard of hearing,' interpolated grandfather Amos, 'very hard, gets worse. She've a horn at home, big as that . . .' His eyes roved the room for an object of comparison, and he seized upon the fire shovel that lay in the fender. 'Big as that shovel. Crown silver it is, and solid, a beautiful horn, but' – he brandished the shovel before them – 'her won't use 'en.'

'Granny, who was that gentleman?' shouted Sophy. 'Did you know him?'

'No! no!' declared the indignant dame. 'I dunno ever his name, nor I don't want to. He took hisself off to Ameriky, and now he's in the land of heaven. I never seen him. If I had, I'd a given it to him properly; oh, my dear, not blayguarding him, you know, but just plain language! Where's your seven commandments?'

At last the rain abated. Peeping into the dark garden you could see the fugitive moonlight hung in a million raindrops in the black twigs of all sorts of bushes and trees, while along the cantle of the porch a line of raindrops hung, even and regular, as if they were nailheads made of glass. So all the guests departed, in one long staggering, struggling, giggling and guffawing body, into the village street. The bride and her man stood in the porch, watching and waving hands. Sophy was momentarily grieving: what a lot of trouble and fuss when you announced that henceforward you were going to sleep with a man because you loved him true! She had said goodbye to her grandmother Cassandra, to her father and her little sister. She had hung on her mother's breast, sighing an almost intolerable farewell to innocence – never treasured until it is gone, and thenceforward a pretty sorrow cherished more deeply than wider joys.

Into Harvey's mind, as they stood there at last alone, momentarily stole an image of a bright-haired girl, lovely, silent, sad, whom he felt he had deeply wronged. And he was sorry. He had escaped the snare, but if there had been no snare he might this night have been sleeping with a different bride. And it would have been just as well. Sophy looked but a girl with her blown hair and wet face. She was wiping her tears on the tiny apron. But she had the breasts of a woman and decoying eyes.

'Sophy, Sophy!' breathed Harvey, wooing her in the darkness.

'It blows and it rains, and it rains and it blows,' chattered the crumpled bride, 'and I'm all so bescambled I can't tell wet from windy.'

'Come, my love,' whispered the bridegroom, 'come in, to home.'

VI

Four or five months later the higgler's affairs had again taken a rude turn. Marriage, alas, was not all it might be;

his wife and his mother quarrelled unendingly. Sometimes he sided with one and sometimes with the other. He could not yet afford to install his mother in a separate cottage, and therefore even Sophy had to admit that her mother-in-law had a right to be living there with them, the home being hers. Harvey hadn't bought much of it; and though he was welcome to it all now, and it would be exclusively his as soon as she died, still, it was her furniture, and you couldn't drive any woman (even your mother) off her own property. Sophy, who wanted a home of her own, was vexed and moody, and antagonistic to her man. Business, too, had gone down sadly of late. He had thrown up the Shag Moor round months ago; he could not bring himself to go there again, and he had not been able to square up the loss by any substantial new connections. On top of it all his horse died. It stumbled on a hill one day and fell, and it couldn't get up, or it wouldn't – at any rate, it didn't. Harvey thrashed it and coaxed it, then he cursed it and kicked it; after that he sent for a veterinary man, and the veterinary man ordered it to be shot. And it was shot. A great blow to Harvey Witlow was that. He had no money to buy another horse; money was tight with him, very tight; and so he had to hire at fabulous cost a decrepit nag that ate like a good one. It ate – well, it would have astonished you to see what that creature disposed of, with hay the price it was, and corn gone up to heaven nearly. In fact Harvey found that he couldn't stand the racket much longer, and as he could not possibly buy another it looked very much as if he was in queer street once more, unless he could borrow the money from some friendly person. Of course there were plenty of friendly persons, but they had no money, just as there were many persons who had the money but were not what you might call friendly; and so the higgler began to reiterate twenty times a day, and forty times a day, that he was entirely and absolutely damned and done. Things were thus very bad with him, they were at their worst – for he had a wife to keep now, as well as a mother, and a horse that ate like Satan, and worked like a gnat – when it suddenly came into his mind that Mrs Sadgrove was reputed to have a lot of money, and had no call to be unfriendly to him. He had his grave doubts about the size of her purse, but there could be no harm in trying so long as you approached her in a right reasonable manner.

For a week or two he held off from this appeal, but the grim spectre of destitution gave him no rest, and so, near the close of a wild March day he took his desperate courage and his cart and the decrepit nag to Shag Moor. Wild it was, though dry, and the wind against them, a vast turmoil of icy air strident and baffling. The nag threw up its head and declined to trot. Evening was but an hour away, the fury of the wind did not retard it, nor the clouds hasten it. Low down the sun was quitting the wrack of storm, exposing a jolly orb of magnifying fire that shone flush under eaves and through the casements of cottages, casting a pattern of lattice and tossing boughs upon the interior walls, lovelier than dreamed-of pictures. The heads of mothers and old dames were also imaged there, recognizable in their black shadows; and little children held up their hands between window and wall to make five-fingered shapes upon the golden screen. To drive on the moor then was to drive into blasts more dire. Darkness began to fall, and bitter cold it was. No birds to be seen, neither beast nor man; empty of everything it was except sound and a marvel of dying light, and Harvey Witlow of Dinnop with a sour old nag driving from end to end of it. At Prattle Corner dusk was already abroad: there was just one shaft of light that broached a sharp-angled stack in the rickyard, an ark of darkness, along whose top the gads and wooden pins and tilted straws were miraculously fringed in the last glare. Hitching his nag to the palings he knocked at the door, and knew in the gloom that it was Mary who opened it and stood peering forth at him.

'Good evening,' he said, touching his hat.

'Oh!' the girl uttered a cry, 'Higgler! What do you

come for?' It was the longest sentence she had ever spoken to him; a sad frightened voice.

'I thought,' he began, 'I'd call – and see Mrs Sadgrove. I wondered . . .'

'Mother's dead,' said the girl. She drew the door farther back, as if inviting him, and he entered. The door was shut behind him, and they were alone in darkness, together. The girl was deeply grieving. Trembling, he asked the question: 'What is it you tell me, Mary?'

'Mother's dead,' repeated the girl, 'all day, all day, all day.' They were close to each other, but he could not see her. All round the house the wind roved lamentingly, shuddering at doors and windows. 'She died in the night. The doctor was to have come, but he has not come all day,' Mary whispered, 'all day, all day. I don't understand; I have waited for him, and he has not come. She died, she was dead in her bed this morning, and I've been alone all day, all day, and I don't know what is to be done.'

'I'll go for the doctor,' he said hastily, but she took him by the hand and drew him into the kitchen. There was no candle lit; a fire was burning there, richly glowing embers, that laid a gaunt shadow of the table across a corner of the ceiling. Every dish on the dresser gleamed, the stone floor was rosy, and each smooth curve on the dark settle was shining like ice. Without invitation he sat down.

'No,' said the girl, in a tremulous voice, 'you must help me.' She lit a candle: her face was white as the moon, her lips were sharply red, and her eyes were wild. 'Come,' she said, and he followed her behind the settle and up the stairs to a room where there was a disordered bed, and what might be a body lying under the quilt. The higgler stood still staring at the form under the quilt. The girl, too, was still and staring. Wind dashed upon the ivy at the window and hallooed like a grieving multitude. A crumpled gown hid the body's head, but thrust from under it, almost as if to greet him, was her naked lean arm, the palm of the hand lying uppermost. At the foot of the bed was a large washing bowl, with sponge and towels.

'You've been laying her out! Yourself!' exclaimed Witlow. The pale girl set down the candle on a chest of drawers. 'Help me now,' she said, and moving to the bed she lifted the crumpled gown from off the face of the dead woman, at the same time smoothing the quilt closely up to the body's chin. 'I cannot put the gown on, because of her arm, it has gone stiff.' She shuddered, and stood holding the gown as if offering it to the man. He lifted that dead naked arm and tried to place it down at the body's side, but it rested and he let go his hold. The arm swung back to its former outstretched position, as if it still lived and resented that pressure. The girl retreated from the bed with a timorous cry.

'Get me a bandage,' he said, 'or something we can tear up.'

She gave him some pieces of linen.

'I'll finish this for you,' he brusquely whispered, 'you get along downstairs and take a swig of brandy. Got any brandy?'

She did not move. He put his arm around her and gently urged her to the door.

'Brandy,' he repeated, 'and light your candles.'

He watched her go heavily down the stairs before he shut the door. Returning to the bed he lifted the quilt. The dead body was naked and smelt of soap. Dropping the quilt he lifted the outstretched arm again, like cold wax to the touch and unpliant as a sturdy sapling, and tried once more to bend it to the body's side. As he did so the bedroom door blew open with a crash. It was only a draught of the wind, and a loose latch – Mary had opened a door downstairs, perhaps – but it awed him, as if some invisible looker were there resenting his presence. He went and closed the door, the latch had a loose hasp, and tiptoeing nervously back he seized the dreadful arm with a sudden brutal energy, and bent it by thrusting his knee violently into the hollow of the elbow. Hurriedly he slipped the gown over the head and inserted the arm in the sleeve. A strange impulse of modesty stayed him for a moment: should he call the girl and let her complete the robing of the naked body under the quilt? That preposterous pause seemed to add a new anger to the wind, and again the door sprang open. He delayed no longer, but letting it remain open, he uncovered the dead woman. As he lifted the chill body the long outstretched arm moved and tilted like the boom of a sail, but crushing it to its side he bound the limb fast with the strips of linen. So Mrs Sadgrove was made ready for her coffin. Drawing the quilt back to her neck, with a gush of relief he glanced about the room. It was a very ordinary bedroom: bed, washstand, chest of drawers, chair, and two pictures – one of deeply religious import, and the other a little pink print, in a gilded frame, of a bouncing nude nymph recumbent upon a cloud. It was queer: a lot of people, people whom you wouldn't think it of, had that sort of picture in their bedrooms.

Mary was now coming up the stairs again, with a glass half full of liquid. She brought it to him.

'No, you drink it,' he urged, and Mary sipped the brandy.

'I've finished – I've finished,' he said as he watched her, 'she's quite comfortable now.'

The girl looked her silent thanks at him, again holding out the glass. 'No, sup it yourself,' he said; but as she stood in the dim light, regarding him with her strange gaze, and still offering the drink, he took it from her, drained it at a gulp and put the glass upon the chest, beside the candle. 'She's quite comfortable now. I'm very grieved, Mary,' he said with awkward kindness, 'about all this trouble that's come on you.'

She was motionless as a wax image, as if she had died in her steps, her hand still extended as when he took the glass from it. So piercing was her gaze that his own drifted from her face and took in again the objects in the room: the washstand, the candle on the chest, the little pink picture. The wind beat upon the ivy outside the window as if a monstrous whip were lashing its slaves.

'You must notify the registrar,' he began again, 'but you must see the doctor first.'

'I've waited for him all day,' Mary whispered, 'all day. The nurse will come again soon. She went home to rest in the night.' She turned towards the bed. 'She has only been ill a week.'

'Yes?' he lamely said. 'Dear me, it is sudden.'

'I must see the doctor,' she continued.

'I'll drive you over to him in my gig.' He was eager to do that.

'I don't know,' said Mary slowly.

'Yes, I'll do that, soon's you're ready. Mary,' he fumbled with his speech, 'I'm not wanting to pry into your affairs, or any thing as don't concern me, but how are you going to get along now? Have you got any relations?'

'No,' the girl shook her head, 'no.'

'That's bad. What was you thinking of doing? How has she left you – things were in a baddish way, weren't they?'

'Oh, no,' Mary looked up quickly. 'She has left me very well off. I shall go on with the farm; there's the old man and the boy – they've gone to a wedding today; I shall go on with it. She was so thoughtful for me, and I would not care to leave all this, I love it.'

'But you can't do it by yourself, alone?'

'No. I'm to get a man to superintend, a working bailiff,' she said.

'Oh!' And again they were silent. The girl went to the bed and lifted the covering. She saw the bound arm and then drew the quilt tenderly over the dead face. Witlow picked up his hat and found himself staring again at the pink picture. Mary took the candle preparatory to descending the stairs. Suddenly the higgler turned to her and ventured: 'Did you know as she once asked me to marry you?' he blurted.

Her eyes turned from him, but he guessed – he could feel that she *had* known.

'I've often wondered why,' he murmured, 'why she wanted that.'

'She didn't,' said the girl.

That gave pause to the man; he felt stupid at once, and roved his fingers in a silly way along the roughened nap of his hat.

'Well, she asked me to,' he bluntly protested.

'She knew,' Mary's voice was no louder than a sigh, 'that you were courting another girl, the one you married.'

'But, but,' stuttered the honest higgler, 'if she knew that why did she want for me to marry you?'

'She didn't,' said Mary again; and again, in the pause, he did silly things to his hat. How shy this girl was, how lovely in her modesty and grief!

'I can't make tops or bottoms of it,' he said; 'but she asked me, as sure as God's my maker.'

'I know. It was me, I wanted it.'

'You!' he cried, 'you wanted to marry me!'

The girl bowed her head, lovely in her grief and modesty. 'She was against it, but I made her ask you.'

'And I hadn't an idea that you cast a thought on me,' he murmured. 'I feared it was a sort of trick she was playing on me. I didn't understand, I had no idea that you knew about it even. And so I didn't ever ask you.'

'Oh, why not, why not? I was fond of you then,' whispered she. 'Mother tried to persuade me against it, but I was fond of you – then.'

He was in a queer distress and confusion: 'Oh, if you'd only tipped me a word, or given me a sort of look,' he sighed. 'Oh, Mary!'

She said no more, but went downstairs. He followed her and immediately fetched the lamps from his gig. As he lit the candles: 'How strange,' Mary said, 'that you should come back just as I most needed help. I am very grateful.'

'Mary, I'll drive you to the doctor's now.'

She shook her head; she was smiling.

'Then I'll stay till the nurse comes.'

'No, you must go. Go at once.'

He picked up the two lamps, and turning at the door said, 'I'll come again tomorrow.' Then the wind rushed into the room: 'Goodbye,' she cried, shutting the door quickly behind him.

He drove away into deep darkness, the wind howling his thoughts strange and bitter. He had thrown away a love, a love that was dumb and hid itself. By God, he had thrown away a fortune, too! And he had forgotten all about his real errand until now, forgotten all about the loan! Well, let it go; give it up. He would give up higgling; he would take on some other job; a bailiff, a working bailiff, that was the job that would suit him, a working bailiff. Of course there was Sophy; but still – Sophy!

The Bogey Man

Long, long ago there lived with her godmother a fair and pleasant girl named Sheila, who had queer gifts; her godmother was the best of godmothers, but had queer habits, and as they lived in a house with a peculiar chimney all their neighbours, the maltster, the cooper, the miller, the tanner, the reeve, indeed all the important people, thought them peculiar persons. Sheila and her godmother did not mind this, because they did not know of it; and if they had known of it they would not have minded very much, because it was true.

One time, in early spring, the godmother fell sick of a quinsy, and as she lay in her bed her throat so swelled that the necklace of crystal beads she had worn for years tightened upon her and burst. She gathered up the beads and laid them beside her.

'I wish,' she said to Sheila, 'I had a box to put these beads in.'

The girl looked high and she looked low.

'Is there no box?' urged the old woman. 'Find me a box,' but there was no box there, nor the means to one, for poverty was on them.

'God bless all,' the godmother sighed, 'but I wish I had a box to put these beads in.'

Sheila went to the wabster's to get a stone of flax, and on the window-sill of that man's house there lay a tiny black box. It was a beautiful box, black like ebony, it was exactly the kind of box to put beads in.

'Have you found a box for my beads?' the godmother asked when she returned.

'No, I have not,' said Sheila.

'God bless all,' sighed the old woman, 'but what shall I do for my beads? I wish I had a box for my beads.'

All day Sheila sat spinning the flax, but the next morning she went to the chandler's to buy some salt, and upon the chandler's counter lay a tiny black box, exactly like the one she had seen the day before. Exactly. Strange and very strange. It was just big enough to put two starlings' eggs in and no more; so beautiful that Sheila's heart and eyes and fingers were tormented, but there was no help for that. There was nothing to spare for trinketry. She took home the salt.

'A box, a box; did you find me a box?' the old godmother began again.

'No, indeed, dear godmother; but see, I will put your beads in this gallipot.'

'O dear no,' the godmother cried, 'O dear, dear no. Fungus and rust! Is there not one little box to be had in the whole world for a sick woman who wants to live in peace?'

Day long Sheila sat spinning below while her godmother lay sighing in the room above, but the next morning she went to the miller's to buy linseed, and upon a bench outside the miller's door lay a little black box. The same, yes, the same; Sheila was sure it was that same box she had seen before in the other places. It was a miracle, it was tempting, destiny was in it, she demurred no longer, so while the miller's back was turned she snatched up the box secretly, and bore it home with the linseed.

'Yes, indeed, godmother, I have a beautiful box for you.' Sheila gave the box into the old woman's hand, and said the miller had given it to her.

'Humph,' said the old woman, 'it is small.' But she put the beads into the box and set it on a shelf beside her and straightaway began to get better.

There was flax to be spun all day and every day, so Sheila spun and spun the flax. When she took up her godmother's porridge in the morning she looked at the little shelf and saw the beads lying outside the box.

'O godmother, why do you not keep your beads in the little box I brought you?'

'What?' said the old lady.

'Your beads,' Sheila said, 'do you see, they are not in the box?'

The godmother stared, for there they were. 'Fungus and rust!' she said, 'when I am dead I don't care what becomes of my beads.'

'You must keep them in the box now or they will be scattered,' said Sheila. 'It is a nice box.' And she opened the box and restored the beads to it.

The next morning she took up the porridge as she was used to do.

'O,' she cried, as she gave the bowl to her godmother, 'but you must keep your beads in the box I brought for you.'

'What?' said the old lady.

'Look, you have left them loose on the shelf again!'

'I have not touched box or beads, neither, not at all, I have not.'

'They are not in the box now.'

'God bless all,' cried Sheila's godmother, 'but as sure as heaven is heaven I have not stretched a finger to those beads! What can it mean?'

'I will put them back,' and Sheila put them back.

The next morning it was so again, the beads lay in a tidy heap outside the box. So Sheila was for secretly taking the box away from the shelf and putting it on the chimney shelf in the room below. But it was all one; each morning and every morning the beads lay outside the box, and Sheila knew now that the thing was bedevilled. She had stolen it, and that, though her godmother was ill a score of times over and they poor as pigeons, that was wrong to do. Godmother was getting better, but there was a shadow in the house now, a shadow that could not be seen but could be felt like a chill-cold air. It hovered just behind Sheila's shoulder and would not leave her. It was not a ghost, it was just a shadow; a shadow so vague and swift that she could never see it, not even in the candlelight. Turn as she would it was never to be seen, but she knew it was there. At times she had the feeling that it was a small shadow, and then she minded it no more than she minded a mouse; unpleasant, but nothing to arouse fear or passion. There were other times when it was like a cloud larger than the world, towering above the cottage, blotting out the light from heaven and the reason from her mind.

Sheila was a fair and honest girl, there was only one thing to be done. Without a word of all this to her godmother she conveyed the little box back to the miller's bench one day and left it secretly there. When she got home her godmother called to her.

'Sheila, Sheila, where are my beads?'

Sheila went to the chimney shelf to fetch the beads. The girl stared with trembling fear, a bee could have knocked her down – the black box was there again.

'Sheila, Sheila.'

'Yes, godmother, yes,' and she took up the box. It rattled with the beads, the beads were in it. She took them upstairs to fasten upon the old woman's neck, and they fitted her as well as ever they did. And very joyful Sheila was, for her godmother was almost well again. But the next morning as Sheila lit the fire she heard her voice: 'Sheila! Where are my beads, Sheila?'

The girl ran up to the old woman's bed. Yes, the beads were gone. They searched in the bed and about the room but the beads were not there.

'O, where are my beads?' moaned the old woman. 'They were on my neck as sure as sure and I have not touched them.'

Downstairs again hurried Sheila to peep in the little black box, and there were the beads lying in it. She took them and fastened them on her godmother's neck and they fitted her as well as ever they did.

Well, what was to be done about the box now? In its

presence the cottage was full of fear and wickedness. Sheila could not bear it, so at noon she took the box firmly in her hand and conveyed it away, hurrying through the meadows along a green and silent path of grass until she came to a lake side. The water was still as glass until she flung the box into it; there the box rippled for a few moments before it sunk among the reeds. Sheila hastened home and when she got there the chimney shelf was empty and the beads were safe upon her godmother's neck.

'I am feeling so well,' said the old woman. 'I shall soon get up and spin again.'

Throughout the bright afternoon Sheila sat spinning, singing as easily as a bird, for the house was sweet and dear as it had ever been and there was no shadow at her shoulder and no fear in her heart. At evening who should come along but Gentle John, a youth who loved Sheila. He had been angling, he had caught a large pike, he had brought it for her. Sheila kissed him and thanked him and he went whistling away.

'O, what a fish, what a beautiful fish!' exclaimed the godmother. 'Baste it and broil it, Sheila, dear child. What a fish it is!'

Sheila cut the pike open and there in its belly lay the little black box.

'Ach, beast, you little, little beast!' groaned Sheila. 'O dear, this comes of my wickedness; but if water won't drown you the fire must burn you.' So saying she flung the box into the fire and cooked the fish upon it, shedding many bitter tears as she did this, for the room had grown full of shadow again and her fears were all about her. Before she went to bed the box she had thrown in the fire had come out of the fire when she was not looking and lay upon the chimney shelf once more. Throughout the night Sheila could not rest, knowing there was only one thing to be done, and that was to restore the box to the miller and confess her sin. So on the morrow early she took the box with her and knocked at the mill door.

'Ah, Sheila, my child, how is your good godmother today?'

The miller was a vast and sturdy man whose beard was black, so black that the words he spoke seemed to issue in blackness too. Kindly he was, though, with thick scarlet lips, and tufted eyebrows curling upwards in the shape of a bird's wing, dusty with meal. Sheila meekly held out the box to him, and he took it. His arms were bushy with black hairs, and dusty.

Said Sheila: 'I stole it.'

'Stole it! O, Sheila, O! For why did you steal it? You know you must not steal.'

Said Sheila, 'I wanted it for godmother's beads.'

'Wanted it! But you know you must not. When did you take it?'

Sheila told him.

Said the miller, 'But you must not steal. That will not do at all.' Blacker and blacker the words sounded rolling from the bearded lips. 'Whose box is this?'

'I stole it from you.'

'Me! But no,' said the miller, 'that is not so, it is not mine.'

'Yes, yes,' Sheila told him.

Said the miller, 'It is not, I tell you. You see, if it was mine it would belong to me, but it does not belong to me and it is not mine.'

'Yes, yes,' repeated the girl, 'it was lying there,' and she pointed to the bench beside the door, an old bench of warped oak, but with new white legs of willow.

'It is a neat little box. Do you know what I would do with it were it mine?' said the miller, trying to open it. He could not open it and he shook it against his ear. 'What is in it?'

'Nothing,' said Sheila.

'O yes, there is something in it. Listen!' He shook it against Sheila's ear, and there was something in it. 'Well, no; I have never seen this box afore.'

'Indeed, indeed,' cried Sheila. 'I stole it from you. You must take it back.'

Said the miller, 'No, no, you must not say that. I do not like this.' He crossed himself, 'As God is my hap I have never seen this box before; it is not mine, take it away,' and he gave it to Sheila quickly.

'Keep it, keep it,' she begged.

'No, no,' the miller sternly replied. 'Be off! Take it away. You know you must not steal. I would not have it for the world. It does not belong to me, it is not mine, I tell you.'

Sheila blushed for the shame of it, 'Forgive me the stealing,' said she.

'Well, I cannot say as to that. 'Tis no box of mine, and if it belongs not to me how can it be stole from me, and how can I forgive you for stealing what is not mine? I could no more do that than I could crawl into heaven backwards. I would if I could, but you see . . . Why are you crying? That is no use now.'

Sheila could bear no more, so she ran away, while the miller bawled angrily after her.

'You know you must not steal, don't you, eh, don't you!'

Sheila ran into the fields and ran until she could run no more. The budding trees were bare, the grass was scanty, the earth cold, but bravely shone the sun, so she flung herself down under a squinancy tree, still clutching the mysterious box. Out upon it! What could she do with it? She could not use it, or destroy it, or restore it; she could not escape it. She had done wrong, but she wronged nobody; though the deed was bad it was done for a good sake. And now she had owned her fault – for that was the way of grace and blessedness – but it brought her to nothing but derision. Escape was vain, all peace was gone. Out upon it! What could she do?

A bright day it was, and so full of hardship. An ass grazed close by – Sheila wondered if it would eat the box for her. High up in the air two jackdaws were fighting – she wondered if they would carry the box away for her. Something rattled within when she shook it, and the lid moved, so she put the thing down upon the grass and, kneeling before it, lifted the lid.

Curled up inside the box was a little smiling old man, no bigger than a thimble. Immediately he cocked his legs over the side of the box and stood bowing to Sheila.

'Good day to you,' he said, and his voice was the sound that shrivels in the grass when the wind is gusty.

The tiny thing! Beside him was a dandelion, and the flower towered above him like a palm tree, but he was all alive in a slaty jacket and yellow breeches and shoes with crystal buckles. Long bright hair he had and a cap of green velvet; his cheeks were like apples and his beard was flowing gold.

'O, sir,' murmured Sheila, still on her knees, 'please forgive me.'

'Forgive you! O, la, la, la!' cunningly cried the droll, and strutting like an actor. 'Forgiveness is easy, is it not? O yes, it is nothing. You are a young woman full of pride – O yes! – but that is nothing. And full of penitence, and that is nothing, too. Pride is nothing, penitence nothing, forgiveness nothing, but even a bargain in farthings must be paid to be made, and I am a plain business man. What costs nothing brings no balm, and you would not like that, you would not like that, now would you?'

'No, sir.'

'Why not?' asked the droll.

'Because I stole the miller's box.'

'The miller's box! Hoity toity, nothing of the kind, the box belongs to me, it is my property, shelter, and home, it is altogether and entirely mine. I am Shiloh.'

'Who, sir?' said the trembling girl. 'I do not know . . .'

'My name is Shiloh.'

'You see, sir, I never heard that name before.'

The dwarf was astonished: 'What!'

'No, I have not heard of you before, sir.'

'Humph,' he said, with a disagreeable air, 'the universe

does its work very quietly. O dear, how tired I am!' And his little mouth yawned so much that he stood a-tiptoe.

'Why don't you go to sleep then, sir,' remarked Sheila, thinking that if only she could get him into the box again and fasten it some way she would keep him prisoner.

'Sleep! Yes, that is what I am fit for. I have not slept for seven hundred years.'

Sheila looked at him very sternly, for of course that was a lie.

'Seven hundred years.' He repeated the yawn.

'I don't see how that can be,' Sheila said.

'But it *is* so.' The droll was easily angered. 'Do not contradict. Seven hundred years awake and seven hundred years asleep; then awake, then asleep again; you understand that, don't you? You are not a fool, are you? I am quite grown up, I have lived a long while, I've been asleep six times. I knew the king of all, who lived before the Jews.'

'O no, no,' protested Sheila, and she could not refrain from giggling.

'Stop it, stop it!' screamed the little droll. So furious was he that he clenched the trunk of the dandelion in his two arms and wrestled with it as if it were a deadly enemy; but he could not move the dandelion, so he climbed angrily to the top of it and then slid back again with a loud whistling noise.

'What king was that you knew, sir?' Sheila gently asked when he was calmer.

'I forget,' replied Shiloh.

'But you cannot forget a king,' Sheila said. 'You must not.'

'Don't bother me, please. I was asleep a long time after.'

'Yes, but you were awake a long time, too.'

'That is so, that is true,' Shiloh agreed. 'His name was Tick ... Tick ... no, Tigley Plisher, I think that was it. And dozens of others ... Snatchrib, do you know of him? No! Important monarchs they were. Excuse me, I must forgive you, and I must pay you well. You see, I must pay well for the forgiveness I give, otherwise it is worth nothing, neither to you nor I. I will make you rich, I will coddle you in silk and beaver. You would like to be beautiful, perhaps?'

At that Sheila picked him up with her finger and thumb as you might a grasshopper, dropped him in the box again, slapped down the lid and held her white forefinger tightly upon it.

'O wicked, wicked, little man. What shall I do with him now?' thought she. She could think of nothing, so she sprang up and ran away, leaving the box under the squinancy tree; but before she had gone very far she heard a strange cry like the wind rising behind her. Looking breathlessly back, all the way back to the squinancy tree, she could see nothing alarming. True, the box was gone, but nothing moved or was to be seen in that field except the ass grazing.

'Hoi!' She heard the cry again, it came from the earth below, the dwarf was standing between her feet, carrying the box on his shoulder. 'No use to run! No use to run! No use to run!' he called up at her, and sliding the box to the ground he sat upon it, kicking it with his heels in a way that made Sheila more angry than ever.

Shiloh said, 'Sit down,' and when she had sunk down facing him he drew up his little feet and sat cross-legged on the black box, nursing his knees.

'Listen, listen quietly, and I will tell you everything. I am Shiloh; you stole my box . . .'

'I gave it back, I do not want it, I hate it.'

'. . . stole my box,' pursued Shiloh, rapping the box angrily with his tiny knuckles, 'and you must bear the mischief of it.'

Said Sheila, 'Pray, sir, do forgive me.'

'Of course, of course, certainly,' he replied, 'but listen quietly, for I must tell you more, much more. As you see, I do not belong to this world; I am secret and alien in it and have no power to forgive a mortal until a compact has been made between us.'

Sheila's tears began to fall, 'O, sir, what must I do?'

Said Shiloh: 'Listen quietly and you will understand. I must offer, and you must take, a rich gift; that is the one sign and condition of our bond. You may choose what gift you will. Then I shall belong to you, and when I belong to you I am bound to do your slightest wish or your mightiest bidding. First of all you would command me to forgive you, and I would do so gladly, that all should be well between us.'

But Sheila was not such a ninny as the little demon supposed, and although she feared that she was now miserably netted in a mysterious and disturbing adventure she sharply and firmly said 'No' to the droll.

'What!' Shiloh passionately cried. 'Listen, is it that fool Gentle John? I warn you, if he wins your love from me I shall be furious. Now, now, what must I give you, Sheila? Say, and I am your immortal friend.' Silently he waited, then yawned, 'O, how tired I am!'

'Go to sleep then,' shouted Sheila indignantly, and springing to her feet once more she ran to her home.

'Godmother, how are you today, godmother?'

'I am not well, my child, I am not well; I fear my end is come,' and the old woman plucked off her nightcap and dashed it upon the floor. Sheila gave her a cupful of the same warm broth, made of apes' bones and caterpillars' blood, which had cured the saddler's apprentice of the rake's rash, and soon godmother sank into a sweet sleep. Sheila then went down to spin, and she spun very pensively for the rest of the day. Towards evening Shiloh suddenly appeared upon the arm of her spinning wheel, and bowed his deep bow.

'I am Shiloh,' he began again, 'whose box you stole.'

'You know I restored it to you,' Sheila said very earnestly.

'Why, I declare,' – Shiloh grinned cunningly – 'it is still upon your chimney-shelf!'

And so it was. Sheila snatched it up and placed it before the imp.

'Take it away. We do not want it here.'

'Very well,' said Shiloh. 'Poof!' he said, and gave the box a tap with his tiny finger. 'Poof!' and the box was gone. 'But I do not forgive you, Sheila, as yet. O no. But tell me,' he went on pleasantly, 'what gift you have chosen?'

'None, nothing at all.' Sheila was firm about it. 'I would not accept a grain of earth. You are not what you pretend to be, and I fear you will do nothing but evil.'

'And you, you are all you pretend to be, virtuous and good,' sneered Shiloh, 'and I fear you stole a box from me.'

Sheila stayed silent.

'You wrong me indeed and deeply,' he continued sadly, 'you who could befriend me for ever. When I was born I was no bigger than I am now, but I grew and grew until I became as tall as a tree.' Shiloh stood tilted upon his toes, with his arms outspread as if he would touch the sky. 'After that I began to grow small again, small and smaller until I am but the wafer you see me. Now I must sleep for seven hundred years and renew my life, but unless I am bidden to sleep by a mortal, I shall live and decline and dwindle until I am nothing. But the cosmos is agreeable and eternity is kind, and you can aid me, here you can acquit yourself, here you may even serve mankind, for were I the very soul of evil yet I must become your slave if you take my gift. You may bid me to sleep and I must sleep seven centuries through and there would be no evil in the world.'

Shiloh had sunk down into a despondent posture, his voice was wavering and low.

'But why, why must I first take a gift from you?' asked Sheila.

The droll looked eager once more. 'I serve a master who is helpless without mortal aid, whose being is but cloud and fantasy, his voice but the roar of the wind in a cobweb, his light the moon in a moth's eye. But with mortal aid he can o'er-leap eternity. The reward he gives could never be earned by human kind – what earthly merit could possibly deserve everlasting bliss? Yet I offer a tangible gift, and your belief obtains it, in proof of my master's greatness. I will give you a chamber pot made all of gold. It was once Cleopatra's. Grand and glistening it is; it rings like a marriage bell and rolls like thunder.'

Said Sheila gravely, 'There is only one truth, the truth of heaven.'

'O, the truth!' yawned Shiloh, 'ah, is it here, or there, or anywhere?'

'I would not take a grain of earth from you,' repeated Sheila.

'Then I shall never forgive you,' Shiloh threatened, 'and you must bear the mischief for ever. O, la, la, la,' he sighed, 'once you were a beautiful maid, you have become ugly already.'

Sheila did not answer him, she just tossed her head and smiled and thought: if it came to that, he was not very handsome himself.

'Ho, ho, yes,' continued Shiloh, chafing his hands that were like the paws of mice, 'ugly you are, and ugly you shall remain.'

And still Sheila smiled, knowing it was all untrue. Shiloh was deeply offended, for nothing angered him one-half as much as Sheila's doubts of him. It is very true, alas, that in all our purposes, fickle, faithful, malicious, or merely wayward, we desire undeviating faith, though it may yield us nothing but arguments for private mockery. The tiny man leaped like a flea in one mad raging jump from the spinning wheel to the table that stood against the wall by the window. He stumbled in a cleft of the table, but picked himself up and began to run. Right across the table he fled, his tiny legs going fast on the trot like the spokes in a wheel, until at last he reached the wall. There he took a piece of chalk from his pocket and after turning to be sure that Sheila was watching, he began to draw upon the wall a picture of a snail. Quickly he drew a snail with horns and its shell upon its back, and when the picture was done he tickled the snail with his fingers, whispered words to it, and thereupon the snail came alive and began to move upon the wall. Sheila saw it. And Shiloh seized the two bold horns and straddled himself across the slow snail's glistening shoulders. 'Kep! Kep!' he cried, guiding the snail in a circle upon the wall, and while it travelled so Shiloh leaned with his chalk and drew a white ring as large as a dish. *Needs must when the devil drives*, and Sheila saw that a snail can be very rapid at times and she thought it odd until Shiloh explained that every snail in its eager youth is swift as the thunderstone, is really congealed lightning, and that it goes slowly only to prevent itself leaping distractedly over the corners of the world. 'Of course they soon grow out of that,' said Shiloh, yawning, 'they are not young for long.' Meanwhile the snail roved back and forth across the interior space of the ring and where-ever it went Shiloh whitened with his chalk, until in the end there was a round white disc left upon the wall, glistening with the shine the snail had smeared in its track. Then Shiloh jumped down upon the table, puffing and blowing and brushing little clouds of chalk from his jacket.

'Look now!' he cried. Sheila could see into the disc as if it were a looking-glass, and O, she had changed indeed, she was ugly as death itself, her own likeness frightened her. The dwarf had vanished. Nothing was left of the snail but a small clot on the table that looked like melting honey. Sheila rubbed and scratched at the white disc until her fingers bled, but it was fixed.

Well, she was now more than ever determined not to accept a gift from the tiny thing, he was a demon seeking to enslave her to some purpose that could only be evil.

Day after day Shiloh came and pestered her and she could not dismiss him. Where he lived or wandered was unknown to her, but that he never slept was clear, for he was always yawning.

In he came. 'Good morning, Sheila. Is your godmother so well?'

And Sheila sighed, 'No, she is sick, and sick again, and the chill-cold days break her spirit. Poor godmother!'

'Ahum! She would laugh at fine sunny weather. Shall I send a rare hot midsummer day? I can do that, you know.'

'No,' said Sheila, 'she does not care for hot days, she might catch a sunstroke.'

'A windy day?' he suggested, 'she wants bracing air. Shall I send a gale? I can do that, you know.'

'No,' said Sheila, 'it might blow the house down.'

'Tut! A fall of snow, then? That is often beautiful.'

'No,' said Sheila. 'She might die of freezing.'

'Aren't you the little twisting-bee!' he cried in anger. 'I am Shiloh, whose box you stole. Your godmother's sickness lies in your own keeping, you can heal her in a moment. Make me your slave, and I must do your will.'

'You can do this,' Sheila said, 'without my taking a gift from you; you are wise and skilled. O do it, sir, and I will bless your name for ever.'

'Pooh! what is the good of that?' said he. 'No, I serve a master, the King of Kings, but we are emptiness itself without your mortal alloy. Do as I bid and I will serve you like a queen. And if you fear me you have only to put me to sleep and I shall sleep for seven hundred years.'

'No,' said the tempted girl slowly, 'not even for godmother can I do this; you are full of evil. Lies, lies! Why do you lie so?'

'O,' Shiloh said, 'because I am weary, and dissimulation is stimulation.'

'I don't understand that.'

'Well, it *is* so.' He yawned and yawned. 'Besides, I am the Other Side of things. All you think good may be bad, all you think bad may be good.'

'And I don't understand *that*.'

Shiloh replied: 'Strong meat for men and lily buds for maids; did Ajax feed on apples?'

'I beg your pardon, sir,' said Sheila.

Again Shiloh yawned. Then quietly and most beautifully a bell tinkled one sweet golden note in the room, an echo of enchantment fluting a brief air, a star of sound fallen from a cloud into a cloud. It seemed to have come from the white disc on the wall.

'Go look,' said Shiloh, pointing towards the disc, and Sheila looked there and saw herself again pure and fair, beautiful as before. Said the droll, 'There, I give you that looking-glass, it is yours.'

'No, no, no,' whispered Sheila, but as she spoke her image in the glass changed again into a rude and wretched thing, and Shiloh was gone.

From day to day now Sheila's maddening plight increased. Had she not owned the theft? Had she not given back the box? Yet she was not free, not free; far from free and shackled from top to toe. Godmother's illness, too, was due to her wickedness, and now even her recovery lay in the peril of her young soul. Her ugliness had become a fact, it was not a mere jest of the looking-glass; the neighbours' children mocked her, and Gentle John came no more but followed after other young maids of the village. Beauty would come back to her – so would Gentle John – if she took the imp's gift, but that would plunge her into everlasting woe. A terrible thing godmother's quinsy had been since it burst that necklace and the beads must have a box and Sheila is tempted and the devil gets loose on the world again! He had been chained for years and years, as everybody knew, chained in a bottomless pit, but here he was again – it was surely him. It was on a rainy March eve he came next, the wind blew loud in the forest, and the dry limbs were falling down.

'Who is your master?' asked Sheila. 'Do you mean that Tigley man?'

'No,' the imp cried, 'no, O no, not at all. My master is the king of all.'

'King! King of all! Why, what does he do?' exclaimed Sheila. For a space the droll answered not a word. Then he began, 'Listen, listen quietly, I will tell you. He . . .' Shiloh paused, then held one hand to his lips in cautious utterance; his eyes glanced sidelong, uneasily. 'He can ask all the questions no one is clever enough to answer, and he can answer all the questions no one is clever enough to ask.'

Sheila said dubiously, 'What questions?'

Said Shiloh, 'It is no use to tell you . . . besides . . .'

'What are the answers then?'

'There are no answers to such questions.'

'Then why does he ask them?'

'Because they cannot be answered, of course.'

'Nonsense.' Sheila was annoyed. 'I do not believe you. No questions, no answers – pooh! There is no such person at all.'

'Hush, hush, Sheila! I could show you my master. Hush! I could show you, terrible and gigantic beyond belief. I could, I could.'

Then said Sheila, 'Show me.'

The little thing shuddered as he sat cross-legged. 'No. But yes, I will, I will show you, I will show you. Hush! Take the rushlight in your hand and hold the flame of it level with this table.'

So Sheila took the rushlight and did that.

'Hush!' said Shiloh again, 'I will show you'; and he rose and tiptoed solemnly close up to the flame, so that his shadow was thrown large upon the wall, his funny hat, his beard and hair, his jacket and breeches and shoes, as large as a little boy.

'There,' he whispered. 'Do you not see?'

'Ha, ha!' laughed Sheila. 'Why, Shiloh, that is yourself, it is your own shadow.'

'Hush!' said he, 'hush! Be silent! It is the king of all, king of everlasting bliss and everlasting horror. Yes, it is so.'

But Sheila could not contain her scorn. 'That is not a king at all, you deceive me again and again; it is yourself, your own shadow. Look now!' She took the rushlight and hid the flame beneath the table. The life almost bubbled from her heart. Light was hidden, but the shadow of the imp remained upon the wall. Slowly it turned and walked along the wall, and as it moved there was a glow under its feet as if they trod upon fire. Just as it was fading from her sight Sheila saw the head of the shadow lift in a deep yawn.

It was long before her fears were calmed, for a wild storm warred without, and there was a wild doom within whirling around her trembling soul. She sought frenziedly for the tiny imp, but he was gone; if he had appeared then Sheila would surely have crushed him under her foot as a beetle is crushed – perhaps that would free her. But the dark mood passed with the darkness, and when day dawned crisp and clear Sheila had forgotten her anger and thought of Shiloh with only pitying kindness.

Later as she sat near the window eating porridge Shiloh suddenly peered over the rim of her dish. 'Hullo!' He drew himself up by his two arms to sit on the edge of the dish, and dangling his legs he watched Sheila consume each spoonful.

'Take care, or you will slide into my porridge,' Sheila said, 'and I could easily eat you.' He only laughed and combed his beard with his fingers.

'I will show you something. Open the window, Sheila, and I will show you.'

So Sheila opened the window. It was a bright and tuneful morning, the spring birds sang joyously and the sky was bundled up with glittering cloud. A hazel tree grew outside the window, and on every twig a catkin hung, all gold, and on the end of every catkin a single drop of the night's rain hung, all crystal, except that a drop here and there was coloured as if made of the dew of rainbows and the light of streams.

'Lift me up into that tree, Sheila.' Sheila held down her hand and when Shiloh had clambered upon one of her fingers she carefully put him out upon a thin branch of the nut tree. Then he swung himself along the branches, as gay as a tom-tit, reaching after the long thick catkins one at a time and hugging them to his breast while he put his hand carefully down to catch the raindrop in his palm. It filled his palm and he rolled it so for a space as a boy rolls a ball; then he threw it in at the window to Sheila, and it would fall upon the table sharp and brittle, rolling like a bead and glittering like a gem. Most were white, but he gathered some of green and blue and yellow and red.

'Help me down, Sheila.' She helped him down and stood him on the table among the solid drops; they were so large to him that he walked among them as a shepherd among his sheep. Said Shiloh, 'These would make fine beads; what pretty beads they would make to be sure!' Then Sheila saw that each raindrop had a thread hole in it.

'I will make a thread for them,' he cried. 'Bend down.' He snatched two or three strands of hair from Sheila's golden head, and trudged along the table with the hairs dangling across his shoulder. Then he laid them down beside the beads. Very big and fine they were, and he twisted and rolled them between his hands until a single shining thread was made.

'Beautiful beads!'

'Yes, indeed,' Sheila said gaily as she watched him.

'Beautiful beads, beautiful beads!' he kept on saying as he threaded them swiftly upon the glistening hair. They were all threaded.

'I wonder if they will fit you?'

Shiloh began then to haul at one end of the rope of beads, 'Come up, come up!' like a man hauling a boat upon a beach; the beads themselves rattled along the board with the sound of moving shingle. Sheila bent her head once more to the table and looped the beads around her neck, but Shiloh still kept one end of them in his hand.

'Give me the other end,' said he, and Sheila did so. They fitted closely around her soft neck. 'Ah . . . !' sighed the little imp. Sheila stood up, but he clung to the ends of the necklace and hung at her throat like a locket. His left hand held one end of the beads and his right hand the other.

'That will do,' said Sheila, bending down for him to step upon the table.

'That will do,' she said again, for he did not release his hold.

'Do you hear me!' She shook the necklace, but Shiloh did not hear, he did not let go; his little fists were wound tightly into the ends of the coil, and he was fast asleep, at last asleep, for ever on Sheila's neck. His silence frightened the girl and she tried to snatch the tiny man from his clasp on the necklace, but to her horror she found he was no longer warm and living, he was hard and cold; he had, indeed, all on the moment of sleep turned into gold. She tried to slip the necklace over her head but it was not loose enough. In a frenzy she tore at the beads and tried to snatch them apart, but the coil of hair was so strongly woven that it neither broke nor gave, and the knife could not cut it. She had been trapped, the demon had given her his gift and O, she was lost for ever. Sly, remorseless devil; this was the sleep he had desired.

'Choong!' went the sweet one bell-note that seemed to pour from the looking-glass. Sheila was startled from her struggle to break the necklace. She stared like an image, then the sudden quiet swirled and stung her, and she crept to the looking-glass and peered. Once again she was beautiful as of old. She was more beautiful, it was sweet comfort to see, and she stared so long at the fine reflection that her fears began to leave her. What was done could not be undone. It was beyond her strength. It was not by her will. She had been tricked. Turning from the lovely glass she saw upon the chimney shelf again the little black box that had been her downfall. Perhaps . . . perhaps the real, the living Shiloh, was hiding in it? Sheila opened the box. It was full of golden guineas. And there was her godmother descending the stairs: 'I am quite well again, Sheila, I am as well as ever I was!'

All this was long, long ago, but Sheila lives and blooms like a never-fading flower; she does not grow old or unhappy, and she believes that she will live for seven hundred years. And what will happen then? Ah well, there is time enough for grief, for though her godmother died in the extreme of

age the tiny black box is always full of guineas, and Sheila
is the loveliest of women. But she does not wed. Why is this?
And why, when she goes to a ball, does she always hang a
silver penny over the figure of Shiloh sleeping on her neck?
That is neither here nor there. All the wedded men of the
world, when they see her, wish they had not married or been
taken in marriage, and all the unwedded ones declare that
they will never marry or be taken in marriage but by her
alone. And they vow fond eternal fealties to Sheila.

The Truant Hart

Monty Barlass was a farmer and a publican. Fifty easy-going years had grown him good and left him active, for he had a wife that suited him and his occupation was grand. Petty farming made him hale, and the small additional task of running The Dover Inn kept him affable.

At five o'clock one summer's morning he hoisted the window blind of his bedroom and looked forth. Overnight it had come a storm, but now it was fine everywhere, though the wind was still at full. In front of him Peck Common with its three or four acres of bland turf was crisp and genial. The four ash trees were streaming with sound and casting long frail shadows over the pool of spring water in the middle. Half a dozen tile-and-flint cottages tucked themselves snug and shy between fat hedges on the far side of the common. Everything was beautiful. His wife stirred in the bed beside him.

'How are you?' he inquired.

'I'm not so very grand, thank you,' she said. So he turned and hoisted up the blind of a window in the side wall and gazed at his barn and his shelters. Timmy Dogtrees, the boy, was already there. A horse looked over the half-door of its stall. Some calves were trailing from the sloshy croft to nibble at a defenceless stack of beans. The old sow wandered into the heifers' shed where it was dry, but they ejected her. Hens, dumpy as muffs or spindly as hawks, were bobbing about, the ducks mused in the puddles, and little porkers trotted hither and yon. Windily the trees tossed their shining foliage.

'How are you?' he said again to to his wife, but she was

fast asleep now, so he pulled on his breeches and went downstairs and there, having hustled into his boots, he thought of taking a peep at his garden, over behind the barn. Monty opened the yard door and stepped over a lolling dog, shouting 'Hoi' to the calves that feared him, 'Hoosh' to the pigs that didn't, and nearly spread-eagling a kitten as he avoided the hens that wanted to pick something from his boots.

O, what a spectacle of desolation met his sight in the garden! Misery, mortification and madness! A long grove of kidney beans, pride of the summer and flushed with unusual pods, lay in wanton ruin, smitten and prostrate; the potato crop – its haulms had been strong as bushes and level as water – was no longer a crop, it was a bed of gall. Surely an elephant had gambolled upon it. Cabbages were torn and gashed; in short, the whole garden had been ravished and put to grief by someone or something or other. But what? No gate was open, there was no gap in the hedge and beyond the hedge itself there was only a great beech wood stretching a mile or more. Not another farm for a very long way. How could a cow get in there? Whose cow? And get out again! Damage? Somebody would have to pay for the damage, and pay good and all for the damage. But who? He inquired of Timmy Dogtrees. But that boy never was any good for anything in this mortal world. Not a thing. The only thing he was any good for ... By the skimmer of Satan, the tomato plants were all smashed too! A score of tomato plants! A hundredweight of tomatoes – two hundredweight!

At breakfast Monty stormed and Monty swore, but Mrs Barlass said *she* hadn't done it. She said it again at noon, too, because Monty was swearing again. Such a form of exchange Monty never excelled in; it left him conversationally confuted, dumb.

'But if I had my way ...' continued Mrs Barlass.

'Ah, what would you do, ma'am?' There was relief in sarcasm.

'I'd watch out for them.'

'Watch out! And what would you? And why, and where, and who, and how? Find out! Here's my damage and I can't odds it. I shall never find that out, I do not suppose.'

Mrs Barlass – the handsome woman she was, with brooches and plump pink fingers! – was then called out to the bar to attend a butcher who had blown his nose very deliberately and distinctly there, but Mrs Barlass wanted nothing of him that day, so, 'Good morning, ma'am' he said.

'Good morning, butcher.'

'I'll call again, Saturday.'

'Yes.'

'All being well.'

'Yes.'

'Good morning, ma'am.'

In came Willie Waugh for a pint or so before she could return to her dinner, and when Monty heard who it was he took Waugh into the garden and showed him the destruction, the greens, the beans, the potatoes, tomatoes, celery and peas, the whole agglomeration of riot and savagery.

Willie Waugh was a sturdy, somewhat dissolute-looking man – but the lord knows it you cannot condemn a man for his appearance, even when he does call a spade a spade. An old conical hat he had on, and an old comical coat with sleeves too long for him, and sometimes his cottage was called The Poacher's Rest.

Willie tilted his conical hat and scratched his grey hair.

'That's a tidy come-up!' he said.

'A cow, I reckon?' Mr Barlass suggested.

Willie shook his head. 'No. I'll tell you. A deer done that. Two or three perhaps.'

'What do you say: deer?'

'There's often some of 'em knocking about the 'ood, escaped from Lord Camovers's park. That's a deer, Monty, right enough. See, it lep in over the hedge by that elm tree' – Willie waved his pipe about as he pointed out the signs – 'and that's the way it went back, too.'

Well, so Monty went off to interview Lord Camovers's keeper, and the keeper said he could not do anything, but that if Monty ever did see a deer in his garden he was to be sure and shoot it. Mr Barlass told Willie Waugh of this.

'Righto! We'll lay for him, Monty; we'll lay for him tonight, eh?' said Willie.

So that night, a beautiful soft smooth night, Monty took his gun and Willie took his, and they crept out into the garden.

'If you sees him, Monty, let him have it under the forelegs.'

They made themselves snug behind two or three trusses of hay, where they could watch the elm tree and be comfortable, with a big jar of beer, devilish near a gallon, and some bread and cheese. But they dared not speak and they dared not smoke and so, by and by, although it was two or three coats colder, Monty heaved up a sigh and began to snore. Willie nudged him awake. 'Lord, that won't do, Monty!' And he gave him a sup of beer. A lovely night it was, past one o'clock, with stars in the contented heavens, and everything quiet except for the mice in the hedge, and not too dark except for the forest, and that was as black as ever and ever amen. And there was Monty snoring again.

'Give over!' hissed Willie Waugh; 'that deer'd hear you in kingdom come.'

Monty roused up again for awhile, and Willie lay with his gun cocked, listening like a man whose hope of eternity depended on his ears. And what did he hear? Nothing. At least, nothing but Monty snoring long trajectory snores, or whirligig snores, snores of anguish and fury and joy, high and low, a terrific diapason.

'So help me Solomon!' groaned Willie. 'I'm off.' And home he went, leaving Monty snoring to the dawn.

The next night they tried again, but it was all the same; Monty was overcome and Willie had to leave him to it. Willie was incensed, and the day after that, when he went across to see Monty, he said so.

'I'm surprised at you! No deer'd come 'ithin a hundred

mile . . . S'elp me, why you . . . not of a snore like that; O my, you gave it a good 'un . . . not 'less he was mad. He'd skip like the hindlegs of a flea. Now if you waunts to ketch a deer this-a-ways I tell you what we've to do. Have you got any wire? Lots of it?'

Yes, Monty had got bushels of wire: 'What sort?'

'Any plain stranded wire?'

'I got some fencing wire.'

'Thass it; thass the very hammer.'

'But what are you thinking of, Willie Waugh?'

'Ha, ho! There's more in my jelly-knot than any lawyer ever knew! I waunt about half a chain of it.'

'What you want it for?'

'Or ever will know, Monty!'

'What are you going to do with it?'

'You wouldn't believe it if I was to tell you, Monty.'

'Well, I'm damned if I believes it if you don't.'

Then Willie told him he was going to set a snare for that deer, just the same as he would set a wire for a rabbit, only bigger. Monty swore. It was foolish. It couldn't be done.

'Give me the wire,' said Willie Waugh.

And he gave him the wire and Willie made a loop of this strong wire, the same as he would for a rabbit, but much larger, and set it nice and artful over the hedge by the elm tree, just where he fancied the deer would leap, and bound the end of it round the elm tree, with plenty of play on it, too, twenty feet or more.

'He won't have it,' commented Monty.

'He will,' said Willie, 'you see!'

They set the snare towards evening and really, Monty began to think, it looked good and reasonable.

'You can snore the lumps out of a flock bed tonight, Monty. O my . . . s'elp me, well . . . no more of that canter in the garden. And in the morning, please God, we shall see.'

So that's how they left it.

Well, Willie Waugh got up early in the morning, very

early he got up and took his gun and walked across to The Drover. He couldn't hear anything when he got to the garden, but he cocked his gun, crept warily to the hedge, and peeped over. And believe it, or believe it not, you, but there was a great stag deer lying there among the greenery. Stone dead it was, with the wire taut round its skull.

'Poor creature!' murmured Waugh. It had dashed both its antlers off; it must have gone mad when it felt the thong, for it had been rushing at the tree, gouging great pieces of the bark. Its horns lay there, and the garden was in a worse cantription than before. But when Willie called and told Monty, Monty was very glad, and he said Willie could have the deer for himself and take it away and make what he could on it.

The day was a Friday, and Willie had a job of work to do so he could not take the deer away then, but next day he and Monty and Timmy heaved it up into Willie's cart, and away drove Willie to a town half a dozen miles off for to sell it to a butcher. But the butcher would not buy it. Willie went to another, but he would not buy it either. Not a butcher in that town would buy the deer off Willie Waugh.

'O dear!' said Willie to the last of them. 'That's a tidy come-up. Look here, will you skin it and dress it for me, so as I can sell the joints the best I can?'

Yes, the butcher said he could do that for him; but he could not do it that day, being Saturday and a busy day for him; and he could not do it on a Sunday because it was not fitting; but if Willie would leave the carcass with him he would prepare it and have it ready by Monday midday.

'That 'ull do, that 'ull do well.' And Willie drove homewards, thinking over the names of all the folk he could sell a piece to, and calculating that he could make nearly enough out of it to buy the pony a set of harness.

Monday comes, and he drives again to the butcher. By ginger, that was a hot day! He threw off his coat as he jogged along, and he had a pint at The Golden Ball and another at

The Load of Faggots. The butcher took him into his killing shed and showed him the carcass of the deer, beautifully dressed, a fine beast; so fat that you could not see its kidneys. But it was a very queer colour all over. Very queer. Already it was black, extraordinarily black.

'Yes,' explained the butcher, 'that's where you were wrong. You should have pouched him and let his innards out. Directly he was dead. That's where you were wrong. Always have the innards out first thing.'

'He smells queer,' commented Willie, as they were laying the deer in the cart.

'O, it's good honest meat,' the butcher assured him. Willie covered it up with a clean sack, paid the butcher his dues and set towards home again. It was so hot that he could not keep from sweating, nohow, and the flies were most cruel; in fact, when he got down at The Dog and Partridge there was a great cloud of flies following the cart, a regular cloud. The landlady of The Dog and Partridge came out to inspect the carcass, but what with its colour, its smell, and the flies, she declared that she really could not fancy a portion of it. The same at The Load of Faggots, and the same at The Golden Ball. Nobody fancied it, and by the time he arrived at Peck Common, Willie Waugh was of like mind himself, although he was always very hearty with his food.

'It's gone already,' he exclaimed despondently. The flies were like ten hives of bees mad swarming on his cart. 'It's too far gone.' They could not put up with it in the house. His wife said, 'O dear, no.' 'I shall have to bury it,' sighed Willie, and he tipped the carcass out on the common and covered it with straw and piled faggots upon it. He told his wife to cut off the best portions and boil it for the hens, and for days he offered lumps of it free to his neighbours for the same purpose, but they fought shy of it even for that. Dogs had been chivvying the remains, and every person that poked his nose into the air of that common observed that there was something about that would be better elsewhere. All except Mother Dogtrees, Timmy's great-aunt. She helped herself to a fairish portion, indeed you might say that she had a very nice forequarter of that deer.

'Come again, Rose, and don't spare it,' said Willie Waugh to her, 'you get on with it.'

Rose Dogtrees had a grateful soul, and she wanted to offset Willie's kindness with a trifle of her own. So one evening when he came across from The Drover after dark he found Mrs Dogtrees waiting at his home for him. Being a very neat-handed cook she had baked a nice little pie for supper and had brought it along for him and his wife.

'Heigh up!' he cried. 'There was no call for you to do that, Rose. It's very kind of you. Sit down and eat along of us.' And he pulled a large bottle of beer from his pocket. They cut the pie in three. It was a sin to cut such a wonder of a pie, so smart it was, so sweet it was, with a crusty rose on top and four diamond leaves, and cunning little notches all round the edge. They cut the pie in three and fell to.

'By cram, this is lovely!' cried Willie. 'Crust as light as love, and the meat's like cream.'

'It is, truly,' said Mrs Waugh. Her name was Ivy. She was a Baxter from Smoorton Comfrey. 'It is indeed.'

'Ha, you like it!' cackled old Mother Dogtrees.

'I could eat this for a fortnight, ma'am, and much obliged to you.'

'No thanks to me,' replied the old woman. 'It's your own meat in it.'

'My meat?' said Willie.

'Your venison.'

'My venison?' echoed Willie.

'Yes, that old deer. You give me a piece last week.'

'But that deer!' He was almost awestruck. 'But God bless us, Rose, it lay out on the common for a week! Thass so. I couldn't face it, and no more I couldn't stand it! Why God bless us' – he swallowed a few more ounces – 'it's beautiful! And we been a chucking it to the fowls!'

'More fool you!'

'Thass right. Ho, ho! That's right, Rose.'

'Why, it's kings' meat!'

'Thass right. And I never tasted anything so beautiful in my life,' cried Willie, 'never! But I tell ye – I knew he was a good 'un. You couldn't see his kidneys for fat. There now. And we bin a giving it to the hens.'

'I never give mine,' laughed Rose.

'Ah, well, there . . . save me Solomon . . . has it all gone, mother?' he asked his wife.

Yes, it was all gone now, every bit of it. Might have brought him pounds even now if only people hadn't been so foolish and he so hasty. Pounds! That pony's harness was very weak and withering. Still, the hens had fattened. And Monty might stand him something when he heard the fatal news.

'Fill up glasses,' he said, 'yours too, Rose.' Willie Waugh lifted his own glass. 'Well, I'm not a chapel-going feller, never was. I never said a prayer in my life (did I, Ivy?); but here's to God Almighty who allus sends us a good harvest . . .'

'Amen,' whispered Mrs Dogtrees.

'. . . and my daily drop,' added he.

O, Willie Waugh was a rough chap; he liked hearty food, and he called a spade a spade; that was his hobby.

The Man from the Caravan

A sharp dry radiant evening, the April moon seraphically beaming upon Brindon town. A long thin shadow from the church steeple lay across the square pointing like a dart to the statue of the seventeenth-century flockmaster who had built all those almshouses for seven ancient men and six ancient women – God bless the odd one – and the flockmaster's shadow pointed in its turn to the fountain which had a round trough for horses, a dip for dogs, a tiny stoop for children, and was so small altogether that it had no shadow worth mentioning and so ended the line like a large fullstop. Though the shops were shut and the town lamps were not lit it was easy to perceive names and signs, it was light enough to read small posters, for there was Marion Clark standing with her bicycle reading all about a dance at the Alexander Rooms. Tonight! Tonight! Young laughing people across the square were hurrying into the ballroom adjacent to the inn, in front of which stood a pillar surmounted by a dumpy white bear carrying a bunch of gilded grapes in its teeth. Marion could see the bear, it was looking at her, could see it as plain as she could see her own shoes. They were black and she was dressed in mourning black that vaguely suggested widowhood; she was young, and the moonlight bloomed upon her pale face that mingled weariness, or a little petulance, with its fragile beauty.

Turning from the contemplation of so much impending jollity she was about to cycle home to Teckle, two miles away, when a hand clutched her arm: 'Ha! ha!' and a tall elderly man in a heavy black coat that reached to his boots, and huge gloves that reached to his elbows, said: 'Steady, now! Is it Marion? Yes, good evening!'

'Colonel! How do you do?' He had a grey moustache guarded by two terrific wrinkles, and a voice like a pilot.

'My soul, but this is lucky you know, does one good. Off to Teckle?'

'Yes, Colonel, I am just going home.'

'So am I. Let's shy your bicycle in the car, shall we? Hooray! It's just over there.'

He took the bicycle and they crossed the square together.

'My soul, this moonlight! Isn't it? Ah, yes, does one good.'

The colonel's car stood outside the Alexander Rooms, people were arriving two and two.

How kind and splendid Colonel Badger had always been to her since she had met him three months ago! That was when her dear husband had been killed in a motor accident and the colonel who had commanded her husband's regiment – the forty something – during the war, the colonel himself had actually attended the funeral, although her husband had only been a sergeant, and had looked after things in such a beautiful way. Even as the coffin was being lowered into the grave Marion had actually seen a tear fall from his eyes. That was true chivalry, and it touched Marion's heart. Moreover, the colonel continued to look after things in a beautiful way, for of course her husband's death had impoverished her, hopelessly. He had been a district agent in a petroleum company, and the compensation she had been awarded for the tragic accident was only a hundred and twenty a year, so she could not continue to live in a town or in the style his income had afforded. How cruel it all was, it was not right, everything had been against her, there was nothing inevitable about it at all, it was just the perversity of – of fate. The crucifix she had once used she had discarded, hidden it away; she was too bitter with God. When she had to move from the town it was the colonel who had found a cottage for her in his own village where he was Lord of the Manor and so forth. Now she was a sort of protégée of his and he often invited her, sometimes her sister as well, to tea at his great house where she met his wife who suffered from St Vitus's dance and had to be perambulated in a go-cart. How she got up and down stairs Marion did not know. The poor lady always wore most astonishing hats indoors, and she rolled her eyes and mumbled incomprehensible things and kept dropping her teacup to the floor, but the dear, devoted colonel always ignored the smashes and had relays of cups ready for her. They were the best china sort, too. Of course they ought to have been metal cups, but Marion never liked to suggest that.

While the colonel was settling the bicycle in the car Marion stood on the pavement gazing through the open doorway of the dance hall. How fascinating the music sounded. How happy all those couples must be!

'A dance,' she exclaimed as the colonel finished. 'Isn't it lively!'

'O! That's good. A dance! Er . . . shall we look at it for a moment or two?'

He peered at the clock in the car, then gazed at the rich moon on high.

'Ah, glorious, does one good. Come on,' he growled, and stalked into the hall with Marion.

'How much?' he asked fiercely of the doorkeeper, and whatever it was he bought two tickets.

The hall was large, but as yet there were only about twenty couples dancing. The ladies were elegantly dressed, but the men, who looked like clerks and shopkeepers, were not so, and in all of them the enjoyment seemed a little strained.

'Now what the deuce is all this? Don't know any of these people, do you?' And the colonel went on talking very agreeably to Marion until at last he went across to a gentleman who seemed to have charge of the dancing.

'My friend is anxious to dance,' said he to him, 'but I myself do not dance. What can you do about that?'

The gentleman, who had a monocle and stiff upright hair, and kept on saying '*Pardonnez moi*,' followed Colonel Badger back to Marion who, doffing her coat and hat, was wafted away into a dance with the monocled man, and for an hour or more afterwards was lightly reeling on the arm of some perfectly idiotic male who said the idiotically perfect things to her, while Colonel Badger sat and watched and yawned, or went out to look at the motor-car, then back to the buffet to eat snacks that he thought were arid, sip drinks that he felt were sickening him, and smoked cigarettes that bedevilled his brain. And all the while Marion was gay and enchanted with life.

'I say, you know,' the Colonel said at last, 'we ought to be going.'

So Marion put on her things again and they left the hall. Much higher hung the moon now, the shadows were shorter and slanted diagonally across the square. Neither of them spoke on the homeward journey, but Marion was in a happier mood than she had been for a long time. Living remotely in the country made widowhood even less supportable, for there were simply no distractions and so many occasions for nursing a grief that she was sure would never leave her. She was growing old; she was nearly twenty-six and had been married five years; a mother, too, with a darling little son, Joe, and now she was a widow, and mature as any duchess in her pride and dignity. Yes, she was. But the dreary prospect! A long phalanx of years stretching diminishingly, like stiff wooden soldiers that you knocked down accidentally one at a time until there were no more left. Marion's hair was dark and short, it waved in lovely masses over her brow and neck and ears. Indolent grace pervaded all her charms; she was slender, with a sort of Egyptian slimness; but her nerves were so strained – it was a penalty you had to pay for conscious superiority – that she was often peevish and bitter; when she laughed it was with an almost silent hysteria, a joyless convulsion that rocked her whole body. Whenever she remembered her dead husband she wept, but she did not often think of him. After all, it was she who suffered, he was beyond her reach, beyond all, and the burden was hers to bear. So she thought most often of a sorrow that was herself, and that too with pity and a flow of tears. Alas, she was one of those million romantic-souled women who suffer profoundly from the discordant impact of their surroundings and even their own families; who sometimes imagine that their own mothers must have had a love affair with a nobleman, a viscount or a baronet at least, and that they themselves are the distinguished result of that infidelity. Discontent, laziness, a desire for dominance, a preoccupation with the idea of unchastity, fill the minds of these unhappy women, who are usually petted by their families, contemplate suicide, and spend hours in bewailing the misfortune that their real father – the rich and titled unknown – has somehow eluded their grasp.

The motor stopped at a small thatched cottage standing sideways to the road, looking into its own garden that was next door and had white wooden palings. Behind this fence grew a file of six gooseberry bushes with spurs as stiff as forks, and two slim trees, a plum and a pear, which would soon be covered with the delicious delicate bloom that in some way nurtured tough and forbidding fruits; tulips, sunflowers, lilies would bloom there in their glory later on. Now, in the moonlight, the garden was bare enough, though its nudity was gracious.

Marion stepped down, 'Thank you for such a jolly evening; it has been most splendid.'

The colonel hauled out her bicycle and stood it inside the gateway. Then he took Marion's hand and held it a long time; that was stupid of him.

'Everything going all right?' he asked tenderly.

'O yes,' replied Marion, 'yes.'

'Little son all right?'

'Yes.'

'Nice little chap.'

'O, he's such a joy, the comfort of my life.'

'Splendid!' said Colonel Badger. 'Yes, don't coop yourself up, you know. Come out and break away from things. It will all come right, if you let it. Come up to tea tomorrow?'

'O dear, but I can't. I . . . We've got a tiresome visitor coming.'

'Humph! yes,' sighed the colonel, gazing at heaven. 'It's cold, but ach! what moonlight, what moonlight! 'Pon my soul, but it does you good. Well, see you sometime?'

'O yes.'

'Soon?'

Curse the man! She dragged her hand away. 'O quite soon. Good night, Colonel.'

Br-r-r-r! Poof! And he was gone.

Behind the yellow curtains in the latticed panes shone a pink light. The door opened straight into Marion's sitting-room. Supper was on the table, a square oak table with a cloth thrown diagonally upon it. The floor was tiled and covered here and there with rush mats. There was an open hearth with logs burning upon it. A black beam nestled in the ceiling, the walls were russet brown, there were several white doors, and a settee near the fire was covered with a glaring pattern of green chintz. Much of the furniture still had a wedding-present sort of look about it. On the settee Rose lay dozing. To comfort Marion in her bereavement Rose Ransome, her unmarried sister, had thrown up her job – she was a typist – and had come to live with Marion for a few months, but already the patient Rose was afflicted by the melancholy of Marion and the monotony of Teckle. Each day was a hard-boiled-egg of a day that you had to make up your mind to swallow unflinchingly.

'I've been to a dance with the colonel, Rose!'

Rose sat up, yawning madly. 'Want any supper?'

'And I danced with a most fascinating man.'

Her eyes were briskly beaming as she told Rose all about it: the colonel, the dance, the fascinating man.

'And he's coming here tomorrow!'

'What for?'

'Tea.' Marion then sat down to a supper of cold bacon and beer.

'His name is Rosslyn Teague, he writes novels and lives

in a caravan. Gracious, look at me eating, Rose; I've an appetite like a donkey. It's near Brindon now, and I've heard of his books. I saw something in the paper about him the other day, but I can't remember what.'

'Don't shout so.' Rose was sleepy and Marion's voice was shrill. 'You'll wake Joe up.'

'The darling! Is he all right?'

'Of course he is.'

II

The man duly came to tea. Rosslyn Teague was one of those men about whom you can define nothing; he was neither tall nor short, fat nor thin, young nor old, handsome nor ugly. A small dark moustache and large teeth were what first impressed Rose; his eyes were a little ironical, so was the tilt of the fawn hat he wore. He had a brown belted raincoat, a walking-stick, his trousers were turned up at the bottom and his socks were speckled blue. As he passed through the low doorway he knocked his head against the lintel. Marion wailed, 'It's such a tiny, tiny house, too tiny, but beggars can't be choosers and besides . . .' She chattered on, 'We are poor, but I do assure you we are honest.'

'Honesty,' said the man Teague in a deepish voice as he cast off his coat and handed it to Rose, 'flatters no one. Ha, ha, ha! God's sorrow on it, it's an anachronism.' And soon he was sitting on the settee, warming his hands at the fire as if . . . well, as if he owned the place. That was the nice thing about Rosslyn Teague, you could not help being familiar with him, somehow, straightway. He was a comfort. Of course they talked, as Marion intended they should, about books, for Marion was a great reader; she had to be, what else could one do when the people you had in sheer desperation to consort with were so uncouth, so unintelligent, mean and pitiless, absolute carrion? She loved reading about passion and talking about passion. Best of all she liked stories of powerful devastating men – it did not matter who wrote them – or of fascinating women who reduced their lovers to a state of abject madness. And Thackeray! O, the adorable Becky!

Rose prepared tea and, having served it to Teague and Marion who sat at the table, she sat on the settee with the little boy Joe reclining against her. Tall, blackhaired, she was altogether quietly lovely, of richer build than her sister, a year or two younger.

'But I hate your Thackeray,' Teague was saying; 'he's such a bore. Dickens now . . .'

'O, I hate your Dickens,' retorted Marion; 'he's one continual sob; he's planted such horrible onions all over his books.'

'Pooh!' grinned Teague.

'Bah!' said Marion. 'But you know, I've never read a book of yours. Shameful, isn't it? Would you lend me one?'

'Me too,' Rose cried.

'O, Rose never reads.' There was a breath of contempt in Marion's tone.

'No,' Teague mused, rather disconcertingly. 'No, she need not. She is herself a poem, a picture, a harmony.'

Silently the girls sipped their tea. Little Joe, nestling on Rose's lap, patted her handsome bosom and whispered, 'Pudding!'

'I'll give you each a book of mine,' resumed Teague, 'if you like. I'll bring them over.'

When he stayed on to supper Marion apologized for the scrappiness of the meal, but Teague swore it was divine, and indeed he ate a great deal and drank a quantity of beer. It was a pleasant time. At his departure the two sisters stood in the doorway bidding him Good night. He took Marion's hand, 'Good night, Marion,' he said, and she said 'Good night, Ross.' They were standing close together and he kissed her. Marion kissed him too. He turned to her sister, 'And Rose?' Rose turned her lips away from him, but he embraced and kissed her, as it seemed to Marion, far more fervently. Then he was gone.

'Bah!' snapped Marion as the door closed upon him.

Rose was silent.

'Say something!'

Rose only turned to the table and began to move the dishes.

'Every girl he meets!' – Marion rubbed her lips with her handkerchief – 'Faugh!'

'Well . . .' Rose was temporizing. 'Why did you kiss him back?'

'O, shut up!'

'What's a kiss? I thought him nice; he wanted to cheer you, he saw that you were miserable.'

'You're not miserable. You haven't a single passion, your thoughts are like cotton-wool.'

Two afternoons later they strolled over to visit him and on the way were overtaken by Colonel Badger in his car, who gave them a lift as far as the field in which the caravan stood. There was a farmhouse near by and a dead walnut tree.

'*Ah, le bon Dieu!*' cried Teague, as they approached. He was clad in brown cord breeches with grey gaiters, a grey shirt, and there was a yellow muffler round his neck. 'Hail, and enter!' They went up the little ladder and entered a dainty fairy place, green without and blue within, handsome cushions on a bench, stove no bigger than a hat box, all sorts of ingenious devices, and even small pictures on the walls. The pictures were of the sort one does not often see in private dwelling-places, does not want to see there, but Marion understood that such things are agreeable to artistic natures. While Teague was gone down the steps to fill a kettle Rose stared at them and commented and giggled. 'Don't,' Marion admonished her. Marion understood such things, she had been married, and even if she had not been married, she would have understood.

'Who was the cavalier in the car?' inquired Teague when he had put the kettle on the stove. Cigarettes for them? Marion explained that he was the dear sweet old friend, the colonel, she had already told him of.

'Huh! he's such a fussy old fool,' protested Rose scoffingly, 'a perfect old loon, fuss, fuss, fuss. Look at the way he hooshed us about the funeral, as if we were a lot of soldiers or sheep! Lord, he did; shoving us into the right pews and snuffling and sneezing all over everybody – he'd got a beast of a cold. O dear, when he bent over the grave, there was a drip on the end of his nose – it fell down with such a whack.'

'Rose! Please! Don't!'

'Now he makes eyes at her,' pursued Rose, turning to Teague.

Marion sighed forlornly; it was unbearable.

'I can't stand him,' insisted Rose; and she made fun of his wife, his house, his speech, and to Marion's astonishment Teague seemed to enjoy such vulgarity. Would no one ever understand the delicacy of her superior nature?

They left the caravan soon after tea and Teague walked a part of the way home with them, leading them just through the farm-yard where a man straddled on a bank of dung was pumping water into an ox trough; the stalls were littered with dead bracken, hens were couched under the mangers, and pigs were foraying for offal.

'Good evening,' said Teague to the man. 'A squall coming?'

'Ah,' the man sighed.

Yes, the evening clouds were extraordinary, Marion mused as they paced along the road; the white, delicate, sunlit ones, and that huge, black, sprawling monster with thunder groping in it like a storm in the bowels of Tophet.

'Ah,' she declared, 'love is like that.'

'Then save me from love!' ejaculated Teague. 'Your visions! your thoughts! O dear, what a mind you have!'

Marion looked at him in dismay. 'Why, why do you always abuse and deride me?'

'But I don't.' He was very gay about it. 'I don't deride, I adore you.'

He kissed them both then and there and went back to his caravan. The sisters fetched little Joe from the neighbour who had temporarily taken charge of him, and for the rest of the evening they were morose. They stayed up late, Marion was not tired, it was hateful to go to bed.

When Teague came again – for of course he came and was to come often – he was merry and boisterous, and played games with little Joe and wrestled with Rose for the possession of him. After tea he produced two of his books, one called *Time and Trouble* and the other *Clementine's Desire*.

'Which will you have?' he asked Rose.

'I don't mind,' said she.

Marion picked up both books and fluttering over the leaves of each in turn said: 'I shall have *Clementine*. And do write something in it, won't you?'

He sat down and with the flourish of a man signing the pay-roll of an army wrote *Rosslyn Teague* on the fly-leaf. Marion took the book to the settee and lying there began to read it rapidly, while Rose and Teague with the child between them played draughts at the table.

Presently Rose murmured, 'Write something in my book.'

'Yes? What shall I write?'

'What you like,' said Rose.

'Anything I like?'

'Yes,' said Rose.

He opened the copy of *Time and Trouble*, and wrote:

To Rose, With Love, from Ross.

'O!' cried she, and she put out her hand and pressed his.

'What has he written?' inquired Marion languidly.

'Look!' Rose offered her the book.

'Read it out,' Marion demanded.

'No, you look,' repeated her sister.

'I don't want to see it,' Marion said, and resumed her reading. Rose shut the book and left it on the table. It was time for little Joe to go to bed, so she took him upstairs, undressed him, and stayed with him until he was asleep in his bed. Marion went to the table, picked up the book called *Time and Trouble* and read the inscription.

To Rose, With Love, from Ross.

She flung the book down and seized Teague fiercely by the arm.

'Sit over here,' she commanded, half dragging him to the settee, and sitting down beside him. 'I will not have you philandering and fooling with Rose. I will not. Do you hear? Why do you flatter her and turn her head like . . . like this? It's disgraceful and mean; she's a fool. Can't you see?'

'I see she is rather beautiful,' Teague said.

'What! Do you think so? Perhaps . . . if only her face had been oval.'

'But it *is* oval.'

'No, it is round. Mine is oval.'

'No, but yours is round.'

'O, how can you?' Marion turned her head in disgust. 'Now, remember, I won't have it. She is in my care. Do you hear?' she queried hotly.

'Yes, I hear. It's true, what you say; you're quite right. But . . . but you, you are young and blooming, too.'

'There's a difference, I've been married, and so have you. It is different.'

'Indeed! What difference? Do you mean I may "philander" with you?' Teague asked it calmly, as if he had been asking the time.

'She's young, with all the innocent bloom on her, and altogether too easily swayed. Difference, why it is obvious!'

'To whom, Marion?'

'Anybody; most of all to a man of intelligence and – I don't doubt – experiences.'

'Not to a moralist like me. May I philander with you?'

'A moralist! You! Be quiet. You have no morals, you're a genius.'

Teague was amused, if only diffidently so.

'But you are,' she murmured.

'O Marion! Don't put that on me. May I philander with you? May I?'

'No, you may not.'

'Ah!' Teague flung his arms around her. 'I shall love you better than anything.'

'I know you're a rascal, Ross, a brute, a beast, a phi-landerer,' said Marion Clark; but she was an acquisitive woman, and so, with the tears just drying on her widow's cheeks, she bent over him, called him her sweetheart and pinned a flower in his coat. They could hear Rose, still up-stairs, murmuring the infant to sleep.

'Will you come to see me?' whispered Teague. 'Alone?'

'Don't you like my sister then?' Marion asked, quite loudly.

'Come alone,' he insisted, more softly than before.

'You're not to be trusted. No. And my situation – you see? It would be improper, people would think evil of me.'

'I should not.'

'My dear!' she murmured. 'But you're not to be trusted – and I could not trust myself.'

Marion closed her eyes against his breast, tingling with turbulent shame. No, not yet. O, perhaps, yes; some day, yes, soon; indeed soon. He told her all his tender thoughts of her, urging his fond desire, and when the urgency offended her he was offended too. Rose came down at last. Then they were sitting coolly apart.

'Lay the table, Rose; Ross is staying to supper.'

III

Marion would not go to the caravan, so Teague came to Marion – almost every evening as she had begged him to. To honour these occasions she would buy a bottle of burgundy or some other wine, and it was astonishing how easily Teague consumed it, for the sisters scarcely sipped a drop. Every evening he would visit them, and Marion, noting his fond-ness for wine, always provided some, as well as dainty dishes for supper. In a month her household bills had mounted up to a terrifying figure, incredibly startling but incontestable;

her small income could not possibly support such an expenditure. O, it was cruel, embittering, horrible! Some economies were possible, some personal luxuries were resigned, and though the cost was still alarming, the young widow went on paying the price of her pride. Teague seemed to be blissfully unaware of her small resources; it is true he often came with a bottle of wine concealed in his pocket, but Marion could not restrain her desire to feed him well when he came – and he came often – because she was sure he did not live properly in that caravan, on bread and cheese and tins of corned beef. How pathetic the man was – his little kettle! his little stove! But at night she was haunted by the cost of that suave dementing wine; she could not do without the man, in his absence she was as restless as a bee in a window; he was all her solace, all her joy – but his appetite was ruining her. What could she do? Ah, pride and love! All she did for him did not advance their intimacy one jot, they were where they started, indeed he seemed to be receding and she dared not abate her outlay. Worst of all she had a sour absurd suspicion that he was playing fast and loose on some secret occasions with Rose, though she could not detect them. O, Rose was subtle as a snake, but Marion would not let her out of her sight. The sisters bickered, there was enmity between them, but one caress from Ross would soothe all Marion's jealous fears and she would be happy and careless even of her debts. What the outcome would be she could not guess. Teague tried no more to persuade her to meet him, they were never alone together for more than a few minutes – Rose! Rose! – but at night she would lie in a fever of love: 'O why not pay your passion the tribute of all its claims?' But she could not; perhaps Rose was more courageous? If Ross still praised her sister, her beauty, industry, patience, Marion could always deride Rose's intelligence.

'O, she is empty-headed, no brains, she reads the stupidest books . . . '

'She reads mine!' interrupted Teague.

'Only because she knows you, she does not appreciate

them, she has no taste, I wish she had. I try my best with
her but she hasn't a single passion, her thoughts are like
cotton-wool. What can you make of a girl who speaks of
Ruskin's *Stones of Venus*? Sickening!'

'Ha! ha! ha!' laughed Teague, and Marion laughed, too.

'Ho! ho!' roared Teague.

'Don't, Ross!' Really, he seemed to like Rose the more
for such deplorable foolery. It was no consolation that he
laughed just as much at Marion, he was always in opposition
to her, and they often quarrelled, not obtusely but with a
half-disguised raillery.

'Why do you two nag so?' Rose suddenly asked one day.
'You are like two cockerels. You're not fair to her, Ross; she
is clever and has such a sweet nature.'

'Thank you, Rose,' cried Marion; 'but I'm quite able to
defend myself – when the necessity arises.'

And then one lovely June evening she had gone off with
the colonel to supper at his house. She knew Ross was coming to the cottage, she had invited him; indeed he would
come whether or no, but before he arrived the colonel had
come in his car and whisked her off. For a while she enjoyed
the thought of Ross's chagrin, but the pleasure soon wilted.
Rose had stopped at home to mind the infant; in her eager-
ness to wound him she had overlooked the consequence that
Ross and Rose would be alone a whole evening together, a
happiness she herself had never secured. O, with what fury
she repented of her hastiness, loathing her own stupidity
more and more as the evening crawled and crept. Her mind
darkened in its shocking imaginations: Rose smiling at Ross;
Ross – she dared not think. It almost made her shriek at the
colonel's persistence in detaining her so late, so dangerously,
booming and baaing about his cursed china, his filthy books,
his prints, and his gramophone with the millions of records
that made her sick – nowhere in the world was there such an
awkward oaf-like maniac.

When she did get home Ross was gone, and oh, she was
filled with as much bitterness and sorrow and jealousy and

misgivings as if he were gone for ever and she was never to
see him again. And there was another long bill from the
shopkeeper awaiting her. It was impossible to go on thus,
utterly tragically impossible! She adored him, her love, he
was marvellous; but she could not win him, and all the
bitterness of defeat flared out against her sister. Rose sat
knitting: Rose was stupid. She was bigger, healthier,
stronger, there was a sweet bloom upon her. And she ate
like a horse. Like a horse, thought Marion savagely as she
fingered that deplorable bill. God, what burdens I have to
bear, how unjust and cruel everything is! If she would only
go I could manage; I could save everything, I could be
happy, at ease; yes, I would be alone with him.

'What did you do all the evening?' she inquired lightly,
smiling.

'O, nothing much,' answered Rose.

'You told him where I was gone?'

'Yes – didn't you want me to?'

'Was he angry?'

'No.'

'What did he say?'

'Nothing.'

'Rose – is that true? What did you do all the evening?'

'We talked and had supper and talked.'

'Is that all – only talked? Humph! What an opportunity
wasted!'

'What?' There was an acrid tone in Rose's voice.

Marion punched the hat pin into her hat and dashed it on
the settee. 'Bah! I don't trust him, no, I wouldn't trust him,'
she bitterly exclaimed, 'nor you either, I wouldn't trust you.'

Rose was silent, malignantly silent.

'Don't pretend,' continued Marion.

Rose burst out: 'You're jealous. Why did you go with the
colonel? You trust him.'

'O, the blasted idiot! It's easy to talk of jealousy, and deceit
is easy. O, it is very, very easy. Why did Ross go?'

'You must ask him. If you want him,' added Rose, coolly

sneering, 'why don't you have him; why don't you go with him, and not keep hinting things of me! Why don't you go with him 'stead of vacillating about like a sheep! He'll have you – if he's that sort.'

'That sort! Yes, I do, I do want him, I do; I'm sick of other girls having the man I want, bad or no. This is a man I love and you are stealing him, you are in the way, can't you see! Leave us alone, clear off, go back where you came from!'

'I will,' said Rose instantly. 'It's time I did; I can't stay with you any longer; I'd made up my mind. I've got to go, and I'll go tomorrow.'

'O, no, no, no, Rose! I'm harassed, I'm mad and half ruined. Look at that bill.'

'I'm going tomorrow,' said Rose emphatically. 'I've got to go. I must go.'

And in the morning Rose departed. Marion tearfully bade her good-bye and the motor-bus took her to the station.

Then Marion waited all day, she waited for the evening and the evening came. There was a piercing lustre in the light, as if the hastening sun shone with vanity. Each stalk of grass glistened like a hair, every curve in the surrounding pastures was touched by a shadow and every shadow was emphatic. So bright the air, and so alluring the little garden with its plot of grass, its ambush of shrubs, its lilac and stalks of roses and bower of orchard shade. But Marion shivered, her spirit was sick. In the doorway at last it grew cold, and the floor was gruff under her footsteps. Ross had not come, and he did not come.

The next evening, she put the child to bed and hurried over to the caravan. It was gone. O, it was gone, and Rose was gone!

There was treachery in that sister, horrible; her fears had been right after all; and Ross was gone, following Rose the fraud, Rose the impostor, without a sign, no sign but this emptiness, though he knew she would die for him. But it was Rose's perfidy that stung, not his. Never, never, never would she again meet or receive that sly, faithless, ignoble creature, not if she were dying. Let her die, she would be glad, she would befriend her no more. After all these months of keeping her, feeding her; cherishing her, almost to the point of ruin – O, the deadly ingratitude! Let her not write to her; she would not answer a single letter, not one, not even if she were dying; she would burn them all unopened. By God, she would burn Rose too! It was almost dark when she wandered home. Pale moths fluttered against her face; the stars were faint in the sky, not so clear as the gentle glitter in the grass where glowworms hung. At home the house seemed filled with desolation. Weeping, she beat her hands together. What could she do in a world so remorselessly empty. 'O you must pray and entreat God, my friend.' She took a candle up to her bedroom and sought in the chest for the hidden crucifix on its chain of jet. The child, wide-eyed, watched her as she tumbled the things about.

'Mum,' he said.

'Go to sleep, now, go to sleep,' she said wearily. Thoughts of Ross and Rose swirled through her mind. Where were they, what were they doing, now, at this moment? She could not cease to bewail the wicked nature of her sister.

'Mum,' the startled child called, 'there's a daddy-long-legs here.'

'Go to sleep,' gasped the distracted woman, 'or I'll make it eat you.'

But then she flung herself beside him, gathered him to her thin breasts and begged him to forgive her. When she had sung him to sleep she tossed the crucifix back into the chest and crept downstairs. There was Ross's book upon the shelf, and beside it, yes, the book he had given to Rose; Rose had forgotten it! Faugh! Marion read the inscription:

To Rose, With Love, from Ross.

and tore out the horrible page; she destroyed it. There was her own book, the one he had given her. All he had written on the page was *Rosslyn Teague*, so bare, so formal. There was an image in her mind of what should have been written there, tender and sweet. Marion got out the pen and the inkstand. Sitting at the table she wrote and scratched and altered that cold inscription, imitating as carefully as she could the beloved handwriting, until the page fairly glowed.

To Marion (it read now)
With fondest love from
Ross.
O lyric love, half angel and half bird,
And all a wonder and a wild desire.

Lifting the book to her lips she kissed the page. 'I know, I know, I know he loved me, but why did he go with her? O, how vain it all is,' mourned the weeping woman. 'I'm dethroned before I was crowned.'

And she could not cease bewailing the wicked nature of her sister.

The Funnel

Henry Lapwing was a small pallid boy who grew into a small pallid person with thick red lips and very dark eyes. When he began to be a man a black moustache presumed to grow on him, and he let it grow. It bore, you might say, a charmed life, for the hair of his head began then to decline, until at thirty there was a bare baldness on him as big as a little saucer; at forty it was the shape of a little shovel. That is how he was now, Henry Lapwing, a timid man, not afraid of anything actual like pain or misfortune or people, but afraid, just simply, of life itself, something he could not name. Railway clerks, especially those of the lower grades, are often like that. He was, too, an unreflective man; it was enough to have survived so many years; most of his experiences were forgotten as soon as their momentary turbulence, pleasant or otherwise, had subsided; he had almost entirely forgotten his childhood. There was just one time he could remember of those far-off days, a summer morning when he was six or seven years old; he was rambling in a country lane, very sunny it was, he could smell something. Then he came upon two men lounging in a ditch, and beside them squatted a bear, a large black bear! Both men must have been Swiss – they had such fine sweeping moustaches and pink faces, and they were wearing comical velvet hats. One was playing on a clarionet, the other was feeding the bear with a piece of bread and jam. It had a chain on its muzzle. It was very sunny and he could smell the bear. Such claws it had!

And that is all about the bear. He had not been afraid of it, he had never been afraid of anything, but at school he was so stupid that if a boy playfully knocked him over Henry would remain on the ground and say 'Don't!' so pathetically that his assailant would cease to annoy him. And so when he grew up and engaged in the most serious hazard of life by marrying a high-spirited Irish girl who soon treated him in a similar way, Henry merely said 'Don't!' Instead of stamping upon his meek, pale face his wife permitted him to live – but not with her, not any longer. They had no children – Bridget could not forgive him that; and he had no ambitions. Bridget was full of ambition, and she had no child. She would not, she said, put up with it any longer. She would have, she said, no more to do with him. Bridget her name was, and she bade him leave her and seek his lot elsewhere. It did not fall to Henry to contest her dispensation – she was a substantial Hibernian – and he went that same night; it had all happened over supper, very unpleasant and very inconvenient. Henry forsook her and went seeking, and though he never found what you might call a fortune he did invent a funnel, a very peculiar adjustable funnel, a funnel which . . . but that was a long while after this affair.

The first emotion that engaged Henry after he had secured lodgings with a man who was a plumber by day and a Socialist by night (his wife and numerous children being neither the one nor the other), the very first emotion that engaged Henry was an anxiety about Bridget's fidelity. Henry had no jealous qualms at all, and he knew Bridget had none, but he also knew that Bridget hadn't any means, that she was alone, that she was attractive (ten years younger than himself), that she pined for a child – well, I ask you? How she proposed to live he did not know, and indeed he was far from caring, except for just one thing – that she should 'keep straight'. That was essential to him. Pride, I suppose it was.

A night or two after their separation he went round to their old home. It was a very little house in a very long street, 72 Turnbull Street; there were seventy-one more houses exactly like it, and seventy-two others, taking it all in all, not so very dissimilar – just a gross of them. At the end of the street, behind a hedge and some trees, was an open space often occupied by a 'fair' with a couple of rounda- bouts, some swings, and a coconut-shy. It was there now; he could see the glare of the naphtha lamps and hear the interminable melancholy drone of the organ pleading to an audience too meagre for mirth and too poor for patronage. In front of every Turnbull house there grew a railed garden with evergreens and a concrete path; each had a window upstairs, a window and a door below, and No. 72 had the gas-lamp facing it, so there was never a candle required at bedtime – not if you left the blind up.

Henry paced up and down the path a few moments before knocking; an autumn night it was, the leaves of the evergreens were quite chill, and the wind blew. When Bridget answered his knock she exclaimed:

'O,' very slowly; 'Henry!'

'I come for my overcoat,' said he.

'Well, come in for your overcoat, you.'

In the kitchen she helped him on with his overcoat, but then he sat down. The kitchen looked exactly the same, it had not altered at all. Nor had Bridget, the red-haired, big-bosomed creature. Handsome as a marigold.

'How are you getting on?'

'I'm well,' said she; and she looked very well with her hands on her fine hips: it was in the days when women had small waists and wore tight bodices. A smile of contemptuous contentment she gave, 'I'm well.'

Henry told her where he had gone to dwell now, and so on.

'How,' he then asked her, 'are you going to manage?'

'I'll manage,' Bridget declared.

'What are you going to do?'

'O, I'll manage,' said she.

'Keeping the house on?'

'God help you, what else can I do? But I don't want you in it.'

'I dunno,' said he. 'I suppose you'll want money?'

'No,' Bridget said, 'none of yours, and I don't want you.'

'I'll have to share my salary with you,' said Henry.

'I'll not be wanting that.'

'But . . . you must have money!'

'Wouldn't I earn it?'

'How?' Henry did not look at Bridget while he interrogated her. All he desired to convey was the notion that he did not want on his conscience the crime of having sent a woman to the devil. There was nothing offensive in that. But he could not explain, not to Bridget, why he thought that was her inevitable destination; it was not the kind of thing for a follower of Christianity. Besides she was growing furious again.

'You want to keep a holt on me, do you! Well, then, I'll not have it. It's my independence I want, not you or your money at all, do you see that!'

Half of the furniture had been provided by Bridget, a good half, but some was his, and so, although he did not want it, he wondered.

'How are you going to earn money?'

'I've my plans.'

What a cunning woman she was, but Henry was not to be fobbed off.

'Are you going out to a job?'

'I am not.'

'What job can you do here?'

'Why! Is it to do with you at all?'

Henry was silent. 'Eh?' asked Bridget.

He took the plunge and said meaningly: 'O, I know it is easy for a woman to get money, it's easy for a woman to go wrong.'

'Go wrong!' she shouted. 'Why, what's on you, you dirty rot-sock? If you weren't the fool of the world you'd know I'm be going to let lodgings to the young girls at the factory, good and decent, if you're wanting to know. I'll get three or four, may be; there's a score I could have if I liked, but three or four will do me neat and nice. An' that's how I'll keep the grace of God on my bones, if you're wanting to know, and no dirty capers. Yah, why'd I bother about what you think!'

No, no, Henry declared, he was only animated by kind intentions.

'Kind! Yah, I know you! It's to wash your little wushy soul in your own spittle, that's all.'

'And,' he ventured mildly, 'you may not be as lucky as you think for. You might have an illness, or be swindled, there's that. And you won't work for ever, there's old age.'

'Age!' O, but it was ridiculous talking of age to a brisk woman in her early prime.

'Yes, or I might die too,' he went on.

'You'll never live to match Methuselah.'

'Some people live longer than others,' sighed Henry; 'I don't know for why. And this money will be a nest-egg. I'm fixed on that, you must have it. I'm fixed on that.'

'Not a graineen. You may take your nest-egg,' said Bridget, 'and pay old Scratch. So don't sit there picking your nose, be off now – or must I take the poker to ye?'

That was not necessary.

Well, for the satisfaction of Henry's soul it did not matter what Bridget said about the allowance, or what she did with it; the debt would be paid, and the payment would absolve him. Folly? O, it was indeed! But Folly is a prison where no charter of deliverance ever comes. So every week he sent her the money, and at last Bridget, tired of ineffectual protests, put the money in a bank. It was a strain, a great strain, but the notable thing about Lapwing was that nothing could really daunt him, he could adapt himself to the turn of fortune when fortune took a bad turn. He had lost Bridget, lost home, resigned half his income, but his boots were always well heeled and his collar was clean for the most of the week. You could notice no difference in him, but there was no denying it was a great sacrifice, it pulled him down, it almost annihilated him, and all his thoughts turned on ways of acquiring some wealth in some easy fashion – lotteries, competitions, gambling, and the like. All these methods were utterly beyond his means, but there was an astonishing

section of things, so he heard, which would fetch you a
hundred pounds if you could accomplish any one of them.
If you could, for instance, smoke a whole cigar without
damaging the ash, you would get a hundred pounds for that
(from some American). Or if you found and produced without damage a kingfisher's nest, you would get a hundred
pounds (from the British Museum). Or a million omnibus
tickets would fetch you a hundred pounds (from some
hospital – only the tickets must all be different). The world
was full of such violent enigmatic beliefs. And there were
certain sorts of foreign stamps. In his boyhood Henry had
collected foreign stamps; he kept them, he had still got them,
they were in a little book with a brown embossed cover and
yellow leaves. Now and again he looked at them, wondering
what he could do about them. He did nothing.

Not from one year's end to the other did he set eyes on
Bridget; he was as friendless a man as you could wish – as
they say – to meet in a day's march. Each week he wrapped
the half of his money in an envelope and dropped it into her
letter-box. Whether she was doing well or ill he did not
know; he fancied she was thriving, and to be sure she was
still living in No. 72 Turnbull Street. At odd times, on
Saturday afternoons, he would go to watch a football match
which the Locomotive Club played against some other
station, but even then he would be alone; no one accompanied, and no one accosted him as he stood on the field with
his little legs wide apart, his hands in his trouser-pockets, his
pince-nez cunningly perched, his face frowning. Sometimes
his wan cheeks would fluster into a pink, his fists would
grind in his pockets, and forgetting his isolation he would
shout quite loudly: 'Where are your eyes, referee? Can't you
see, damn you? What are you up to?' And although neither
the referee nor the players regarded him at all, the spectators
would observe him and imagine him to be the very devil of a
judge of a true football match, and they too would begin to
bellow at the referee.

Two years after he had left Bridget, Henry went one

morning to the barber's. The barber was a Swiss, he reminded Henry of the men with the bear he had seen when a child, he was just such another – barring the hat and the bear and the clarinet – and that was the reason why Henry patronized his saloon. As he entered, the barber was replenishing a paraffin lamp with oil, and the oil overflowed because he could not see beyond the funnel he was using.

'Blast it,' muttered the barber. 'Good morning.'

Henry said good morning and hung up his hat.

The barber wiped his hands upon his apron and hung up the lamp.

'Hair cut?' demanded the Swiss.

'Yes,' said Henry meditatively, and the barber began to crop the little hair Henry did not want. As he sat there Henry invented in his mind a funnel that would prevent any such mishaps; invented it complete, it was most ingenious, an inspiration, he saw the solution at once, plainly, as plainly as he smelt paraffin that seemed to be oozing from his hair.

'Shampoo?'

'What?' asked the dreaming inventor.

The Swiss put his thick forefinger on a showcard: SHAMPOO, 5d. 'Good for debauchery,' he declared acridly, staring at Henry in the mirror, 'and profligacy.'

Henry was baffled. 'I'm all right,' he whispered.

'If your head aches,' the barber continued, 'shampoo is very beneficial.'

'It don't ache,' Henry said. 'I don't drink, and I don't have anything to do with women.'

For the first time the barber now smiled at him, compassionately too.

'Aw, what they say? A nature's nobleman; full of virtue – and other vices.'

'How much?' asked Henry, standing up and adjusting his pince-nez. He paid the barber his two pence and went hurriedly off to work.

Among sheaves of waybills and consignment notes he

spent a harassing forenoon; there was always some mer-
chandise missing or damaged or delayed; such things were
his special province: a depot only two stations down the
line had mislaid a ton and a half of marmalade, and a
woman whose perambulator had been smashed in transit
could not have stormed at Lapwing more violently if her
baby had been smashed too. Nevertheless he managed to
scratch numerous drawings of funnels upon odd pieces of
paper, funnels and funnels, the new Idea, the Lapwing
Adjustable Funnel. During the next few weeks he not
merely tinkered with funnels, he lived and moved and had
his being with funnels; then slept with them and dreamed
of them, indeed he dreamed of one that was supremely
useful in cases of debauchery and profligacy: you poured
in virtue and it never overflowed; you poured in vice and
it came out virtue. At last the thing was perfect; it worked:
worked with any liquid. He tried it with milk, tried it with
paraffin, with soup, cocoa, and cod-liver oil – nothing could
overflow. It only remained to get the thing manufactured
and marketed.

What a difficulty that was! Here was a man with an im-
plement of perfection, there was a public burning to experience its benefits. But Lapwing was a canny person; he
was not so unwise as to show his invention to any living soul
until he was protected from all chance of the beautiful idea
being stolen from him, and that meant a large sum for patent
fees. For a time the problem stupefied him; indeed he was
almost tempted to poach on that half of his salary which he
always gave to Bridget, but in the midst of his bewilderment
the notion came to him that Bridget herself might be able to
help. It was not *impossible* for her to have that much money;
he would go to her and ask; if she failed him – well, no harm
was done, he would think of something else. So off he went
to Bridget.

Good Lord! she was astonishing; she had not aged an
hour. O, she was full and fine and flourishing, with eight or
nine girl lodgers; she had had to rent the next-door house

as well, she had to have a servant to help her; opulent she was, positively opulent!

'And what do you want?' she said when she saw him at her door.

'I want to show you something.'

'You're thin,' Bridget commented, 'aren't you well? Come in here.'

She took him into a very tidy parlour with a lot of new furniture in it.

'What do you want to show me?'

'My funnel,' replied Henry, producing it. 'And perhaps you could do me a favour.'

The upshot was that Bridget – not as a favour, not as a speculation, but solely to get rid of him and keep clear of him – handed him twenty pounds. She actually wrote him a cheque for it.

Before he went away she told him very kindly that she did not want him to go on sending that weekly money to her, it was not necessary, and it was almost a nuisance now. But Henry was adamant about that: O yes, he must go on doing that – it signified.

'But can't you see,' cried Bridget irritably, 'that I've no call for it? Look at me, look at my furniture and my business and my servant!'

'No.' Henry was immovable. 'Responsibility is responsibility; right is right all the world over.'

He went away with the twenty pounds and patented the funnel, and then it did not take long to find a firm which was so impressed by the possibilities of his invention that they, as it were, discreetly darted at Henry and his funnel. They offered a handsome sum for it outright, but Lapwing would not sell, he would only give them a licence to manufacture it on royalty terms. With this they had to be content and do their best. Catby, Meagle and Timms was the firm, and they did magnificently. Before a year was gone the funnel was produced in brass, iron, tin, copper, zinc, and aluminium; it was displayed in shop windows, advertised in newspapers, billed on the hoardings, The Lapwing Adjustable Funnel, and success was such that Henry soon received a cheque for £100 on account of royalties.

The receipt of this threw him into a desperate perspiration lasting for an hour, after which the first thing he did was to ask Catby, Meagle and Timms to prepare a model of the funnel entirely of silver, and despatch it with his compliments to Mrs Henry Lapwing, 72 Turnbull Street. Then he debated long on what best to do with that hundred pounds. Good God, what could he do with such a sum! It was so vast, so commanding, so pristine, it would be a sacrilege to break into it and spend a halfpenny of it! In the end he sent that, too, to Bridget, with a letter saying that it was her share of the proceeds of his invention; that he would now discontinue sending her the weekly sum. That was the most gratifying outcome to Henry, he need not any longer share his income with Bridget – at any rate for a long time to come. Nothing could exceed the gratification of that; it was just like having his income doubled; he would be well off, never so well off in his life as now. With a twinge of guilt he remembered that a short time before his weekly salary had been increased by half-a-crown, and he had not shared it with Bridget. Responsibility was a good thing, a steadying thing, as no one could deny, but it was also a difficult thing. Now, for a couple of years at least his responsibility to Bridget was already discharged, the burden fallen from his shoulders, and his own income, in a sense, was doubled. He had done a splendid thing for himself; whichever way he looked at it he came out with profit.

Coincident with this agreeable state of affairs Lapwing was transferred to another station forty miles down the line, and he left his old town in winter without a word to Bridget, without a regret. Henry had no imagination, he could never see faces in the fire, and he lived as aptly in the new town as he had lived in the old. There was only one slight disturbing result: on chill dark nights when the wind seemed to hang in the great trees, he could sometimes faintly hear among

their uproar a music, far off, very very far off, thin but just
audible, and he would lie in his bed striving to catch that
echoing delight, for it was but an echo whose source was
stupidly confused. The only music he could remember was
the music of the organ on the fair ground at the bottom of
Turnbull Street. A thousand times he had savoured its
dispiriting tunes; they were never changed, but he had listened to their melancholy clamour, especially on windy nights,
with a strange pleasure. Now again the flames of the naph-
thas would flicker in the gusty air, and he could recall how
he had heard in that most musical quiet when the organ
stopped, the scratching of rags of paper blowing along the
gritty road.

At the end of his first year in the new town he received
another cheque from Catby, Meagle and Timms; larger,
much larger than before. Three hundred and fifty pounds!
The walls of his world seemed to burn about him and break
in cinders, while a golden palace reared up into the sky.
But, alas, a letter from Catby himself contained tragic news.
It appeared that the enormous success of the Lapwing
Funnel had inspired many other inventors, and cheap imita-
tions were now flooding the market; in particular there was
a rival funnel which, being naturally automatic instead of
scientifically adjustable like the Lapwing, could be sold at
less than half the price of Henry's invention. Messrs Catby,
while congratulating themselves and Henry upon their
past success, now feared that unless he could devise a much
cheaper funnel there was little prospect of any more
royalties; in point of fact their sales had now practically
ceased.

'I'm glad,' murmured Henry when the shock had been
partially absorbed, 'damn glad I sent her that hundred
pounds. I'd 'a been in a pretty pickle soon if I hadn't,
shouldn't I?' Which reflection shows that Henry was contented with his lot, he had been beyond cares, he was enjoy-
ing life. So completely convinced was he of the rightness of
his earlier action that he could now do no other than send

the second cheque straight off to Bridget. By the time that was exhausted he would be somewhere within hail of retiring age, a pension, and then . . . ? Well, then he did not know; you could not get blood out of a stone, but at present it did not matter.

There was no reply from Bridget. For two years he had not seen her, for a whole year they had lived in different towns; he knew she was well, he was quite content, he was safe for seven or eight years at least.

How vain are all attempts to impose on destiny! Within a few months Lapwing became disastrously involved in a conspiracy to defraud the railway company. He had been made the innocent tool of a set of villains, riff-raff of the uniformed staff, who had swindled the company through his unconscious compliance. It was impossible to suspect him, but his superiors could not see their way to entrust their affairs any longer to one so easily duped. Lapwing was discharged.

He was stoical at first, but after a week or two of unemployment he perceived that he was ruined, irretrievably ruined. Well on into middle age and discharged for incompetence! Black indeed was the outlook. One could not go on inventing funnels – there were no more to invent. Just when his resources were almost gone, and his mind had begun to glance furtively at the idea of all the money he had sent Bridget, he received a letter from the servant at Turnbull Street informing him that Bridget was ill, and suggesting his immediate attendance. At once he packed his belongings, burned his boats, left the tragic town for good and returned to Turnbull Street, not with any resolution, but with a vague hope.

It was dark in the evening when he got there. The servant who opened the door recognized him and exclaimed:

'O, sir, she's gone!'

'Gone?' Henry stared dubiously.

'Half-past four', wailed the girl, bursting into tears. Then Henry realized that his wife was dead. As he stood dazed in the doorway a familiar sound began to woo his ears, the sound of the organ on the fair ground at the bottom of the street. Bright and lively it sounded!

'Would you like to see her?' inquired the girl, wiping her eyes.

He walked in and stood his bag in the passage. The girl brought a lighted candle and showed him up to Bridget's room. The door was shut; the girl paused, looked at Henry, and then knocked very quietly upon the door. She began to weep again and handed the candlestick to the man.

'In there,' she said, and watched him enter the room before she descended the stairs.

There was nobody in the room, nobody but himself and Bridget. She lay on the bed under a sheet. All the rites were done, a nurse had seen to it. Although he feared greatly, the man lifted the sheet. He dropped it quickly in place again. Well, that's how it was, she was dead, she could not wrangle with him any more. Upon the mantelpiece was a doctor's certificate.

'Pneumonia.' Henry perused it and put it in his pocket. Before leaving he surveyed the room; it was better furnished now, there were knick-knacks, and Bridget had had her photograph taken recently. Comfortable it looked. At the foot of the stairs the girl met him again, and taking the candle from him blew it out with a sigh.

'Would you like some supper, sir?'

'Yes,' said Henry, and she led him into the kitchen. There, while Henry ate, he listened to her account of Bridget's illness. He said at last:

'I've come to stop. We shall have to carry on, of course. What about the lodgers, are there many? You can manage, I suppose?'

'I'll try, sir. Seven,' the girl said.

'Seven! Do the best you can, that's right. I'll make it worth your while,' Henry declared.

There was no bedroom available for him, so he slept on a sofa in the parlour. He woke early next morning, but did not interfere with the household routine in any way.

The seven young lodger girls had their breakfast in the adjoining house. But after breakfast Henry began an inspection of things; in the parlour were two other new photographs of Bridget – what a stupid craze! And there was a bureau he had not seen before. Having found the keys he opened the bureau and in a drawer he discovered two bank books, one relating to a current account showing £120, and the other a deposit account of £600. On examining the latter he perceived that it was made up of just those sums he had sent Bridget since their separation. Lapwing's eyes grew misty and his brow moist; his hands shook and his heart seemed to rattle. She had been a wonderful, contriving woman, he acknowledged it.

Later in the morning he called at the registrar's office to record his wife's demise, visited a tailor to order a suit of mourning, and requested an undertaker to bury his dead; but so many other anxieties and the like occupied him to the day of the funeral that he quite forgot to order a wreath. However, there was a beauty subscribed for by the seven young lodgers, and a little bunch of flowers from the servant; everything was reasonable and right. When all was over his bag was taken up to the vacant bedroom, and at night he slept once again in the bed that had been Bridget's and his.

The following day he put the two bank books in his pocket and went to the bank. Lapwing explained his business to a young clerk who possessed a gentle, encouraging, aristocratic voice; the clerk took him to the manager; the manager sent him to a solicitor a few doors away; the solicitor intimated to Henry that Bridget had made a will, leaving the whole of her money, property and effects to a purser in the mercantile marine who appeared occasionally to dwell in Hucknall Torkard.

Bridget's solicitor talked so rapidly: it seemed to Henry that his heart was being torn from his breast and flung to the ground; it was being flogged. Something within him gulpingly murmured 'Don't!' but the only utterance that crossed his lips was, 'O, I see.'

'I must communicate with this gentleman at once,' said the solicitor, a tall, lean, stern man with a harsh voice and a lot of collar. 'I am the sole executor.' He went on talking and talking and talking. 'I hope we shall not inconvenience you, Mr Lapwing. The law must take its course, I fear; its operations are purely automatic.' His long white fingers dwelt heavily upon a glass paperweight and pressed it more firmly upon his papers. 'As a human being I could wish they were more . . . er . . . more . . . '

'Adjustable?' said Henry.

'Exactly, adjustable. But as a lawyer, no; you see, no.' Pulling his chair a little more closely under him, he sighed:

'Um . . . ah . . . yes . . . that's all,' and Henry got up to go.

'You had better,' cried the solicitor, 'leave those bank books with me.' Henry handed them to him.

'I'll send my clerk round to Turnbull Street this morning. You'll be there?'

'Yes,' said Henry.

'Good morning, Mr Lapwing,' and he suddenly smiled so charmingly.

But the widower did not meet the solicitor's clerk; he never went back to Turnbull Street. He just hurried off to the station, took a ticket to the deuce knows where, and was never seen or heard of again. And that was hasty of him, too hasty, for if he had stayed but a few days longer he would have learned that the purser had been drowned in the sea some little time before.

The Field of Mustard

On a windy afternoon in November they were gathering
kindling in the Black Wood, Dinah Lock, Amy Hardwick,
and Rose Olliver, three sere disvirgined women from
Pollock's Cross. Mrs Lock wore clothes of dull butcher's
blue, with a short jacket that affirmed her plumpness, but
Rose and Amy had on long grey ulsters. All of them were
about forty years old, and the wind and twigs had tousled
their gaunt locks, for none had a hat upon her head. They
did not go far beyond the margin of the wood, for the forest
ahead of them swept high over a hill and was gloomy; behind
them the slim trunks of beech, set in a sweet ruin of hoar and
scattered leaf, and green briar nimbly fluttering, made a sort
of palisade against the light of the open, which was grey, and
a wide field of mustard which was yellow. The three women
peered up into the trees for dead branches, and when they
found any Dinah Lock, the vivacious woman full of shrill
laughter, with a bosom as massive as her haunches, would
heave up a rope with an iron bolt tied to one end. The bolted
end would twine itself around the dead branch, the three
women would tug, and after a sharp crack the quarry would
fall; as often as not the women would topple over too. By and
by they met an old hedger with a round belly belted low, and
thin legs tied at each knee, who told them the time by his
ancient watch, a stout timepiece which the women sportively
admired.

'Come Christmas I'll have me a watch like that!' Mrs
Lock called out. The old man looked a little dazed as he
fumblingly replaced his chronometer. 'I will,' she continued,
'if the Lord spares me and the pig don't pine.'

'You . . . you don't know what you're talking about,' he said. 'That watch was my uncle's watch.'

'Who was he? I'd like one like it.'

'Was a sergeant-major in the lancers, fought under Sir Garnet Wolseley, and it was given to him.'

'What for?'

The hedger stopped and turned on them, 'Doing of his duty.'

'That all?' cried Dinah Lock. 'Well, I never got no watch for that a-much. Do you know what I see when I went to London? I see'd a watch in a bowl of water, it was glass, and there was a fish swimming round it . . . '

'I don't believe it.'

'There was a fish swimming round it . . . '

'I tell you I don't believe it . . . '

'And the little hand was going on like Clackford Mill. That's the sort of watch I'll have me; none of your Sir Garney Wolsey's!'

'He was a noble Christian man, that was.'

'Ah! I suppose he slept wid Jesus?' yawped Dinah.

'No, he didn't,' the old man disdainfully spluttered. 'He never did. What a God's the matter wid ye?' Dinah cackled with laughter. 'Pah!' he cried, going away, 'great fat thing! Can't tell your guts from your elbows.'

Fifty yards farther on he turned and shouted some obscenity back at them, but they did not heed him; they had begun to make three faggots of the wood they had collected, so he put his fingers to his nose at them and shambled out to the road.

By the time Rose and Dinah were ready, Amy Hardwick, a small slow silent woman, had not finished bundling her faggot together.

'Come on, Amy,' urged Rose.

'Come on,' Dinah said.

'All right, wait a minute,' she replied listlessly.

'O God, that's death!' cried Dinah Lock, and heaving a great faggot to her shoulders she trudged off, followed by

Rose with a like burden. Soon they were out of the wood, and crossing a highway they entered a footpath that strayed in a diagonal wriggle to the far corner of the field of mustard. In silence they journeyed until they came to that far corner, where there was a hedged bank. Here they flung their faggots down and sat upon them to wait for Amy Hardwick.

In front of them lay the field they had crossed, a sour scent rising faintly from its yellow blooms that quivered in the wind. Day was dull, the air chill, and the place most solitary. Beyond the field of mustard the eye could see little but forest. There were hills there, a vast curving trunk, but the Black Wood heaved itself effortlessly upon them and lay like a dark pall over the outline of a corpse. Huge and gloomy, the purple woods draped it all completely. A white necklace of a road curved below, where a score of telegraph poles, each crossed with a multitude of white florets, were dwarfed by the hugeness to effigies that resembled hyacinths. Dinah Lock gazed upon this scene whose melancholy, and not its grandeur, had suddenly invaded her; with elbows sunk in her fat thighs, and nursing her cheeks in her hands, she puffed the gloomy air, saying:

'O God, cradle and grave is all there is for we.'

'Where's Amy got to?' asked Rose.

'I could never make a companion of her, you know,' Dinah declared.

'Nor I,' said Rose, 'she's too sour and slow.'

'Her disposition's too serious. Of course, your friends are never what you want them to be, Rose. Sometimes they're better – most often they're worse. But it's such a mercy to have a friend at all; I like you, Rose; I wish you was a man.'

'I might just as well ha' been,' returned the other woman.

'Well, you'd ha' done better; but if you had a tidy little family like me you'd wish you hadn't got 'em.'

'And if you'd never had 'em you'd ha' wished you had.'

'Rose, that's the cussedness of nature, it makes a mock of you. I don't believe it's the Almighty at all, Rose. I'm sure it's the devil, Rose. Dear heart, my corn's a-giving me what-for; I wonder what that bodes?'

'It's restless weather,' said Rose. She was dark, tall, and not unbeautiful still, though her skin was harsh and her limbs angular. 'Get another month or two over – there's so many of these long dreary hours.'

'Ah, your time's too long, or it's too short, or it's just right but you're too old. Cradle and grave's my portion. Fat old thing he called me!'

Dinah's brown hair was ruffled across her pleasant face and she looked a little forlorn, but corpulence dispossessed her of tragedy. 'I be thin enough a-summertimes, for I lives light and sweats like a bridesmaid, but winters I'm fat as a hog.'

'What all have you to grumble at then?' asked Rose, who had slid to the ground and lay on her stomach staring up at her friend.

'My heart's young, Rose.'

'You've your husband.'

'He's no man at all since he was ill. A long time ill, he was. When he coughed, you know, his insides come up out of him like coffee grouts. Can you ever understand the meaning of that? Coffee! I'm growing old, but my heart's young.'

'So is mine, too: but you got a family, four children grown or growing.' Rose had snapped off a sprig of the mustard flower and was pressing and pulling the bloom in and out of her mouth. 'I've none, and never will have.' Suddenly she sat up, fumbled in her pocket, and produced her purse. She slipped the elastic band from it, and it gaped open. There were a few coins there and a scrap of paper folded. Rose took out the paper and smoothed it open under Dinah's curious gaze. 'I found something lying about at home the other day, and I cut this bit out of it.' In soft tones she began to read:

'The day was void, vapid; time itself seemed empty. Come evening it rained softly. I sat by my fire turning over the leaves of a book, and I was dejected, until I came upon a little old-fashioned engraving at the bottom of a page. It imaged a procession of some angelic children in a garden, little placidly-naked substantial babes, with tiny bird-wings. One carried a bow, others a horn of plenty, or a hamper of fruit, or a set of reedpipes. They were garlanded and full of grave joys. And at the sight of them a strange bliss flowed into me such as I had never known, and I thought this world was all a garden, though its light was hidden and its children not yet born.'

Rose did not fold the paper up; she crushed it in her hand and lay down again without a word.

'Huh, I tell you, Rose, a family's a torment. I never wanted mine. God love, Rose, I'd lay down my life for 'em; I'd cut myself into fourpenny pieces so they shouldn't come to harm; if one of 'em was to die I'd sorrow to my grave. But I know, I know, I know I never wanted 'em, they were not for me, I was just an excuse for their blundering into the world. Somehow I've been duped, and every woman born is duped so, one ways or another in the end. I had my sport with my man, but I ought never to have married. Now I'd love to begin all over again, and as God's my maker, if it weren't for those children, I'd be gone off out into the world again tomorrow, Rose. But I dunno what 'ud become o' me.'

The wind blew strongly athwart the yellow field, and the odour of mustard rushed upon the brooding women. Protestingly the breeze flung itself upon the forest; there was a gliding cry among the rocking pinions as of some lost wave seeking a forgotten shore. The angular faggot under Dinah Lock had begun to vex her; she too sunk to the ground and lay beside Rose Olliver, who asked:

'And what 'ud become of your old man?'

For a few moments Dinah Lock paused. She too took a sprig of the mustard and fondled it with her lips. 'He's no man now, the illness feebled him, and the virtue's gone; no man at all since two years, and bald as a piece of cheese –

I like a hairy man, like . . . do you remember Rufus Black-thorn, used to be gamekeeper here?'

Rose stopped playing with her flower. 'Yes, I knew Rufus Blackthorn.'

'A fine bold man that was! Never another like him here-abouts, not in England neither; not in the whole world – though I've heard some queer talk of those foreigners, Australians, Chinymen. Well!'

'Well?' said Rose.

'He was a devil.' Dinah Lock began to whisper. 'A perfect devil; I can't say no fairer than that. I wish I could, but I can't.'

'O come,' protested Rose, 'he was a kind man. He'd never see anybody want for a thing.'

'No,' there was playful scorn in Dinah's voice; 'he'd shut his eyes first!'

'Not to a woman he wouldn't, Dinah.'

'Ah! Well – perhaps – he was good to women.'

'I can tell you things as would surprise you,' murmured Rose.

'You! But – well – no, no. I could tell *you* things as you wouldn't believe. Me and Rufus! We was – O my – yes!'

'He *was* handsome.'

'O, a pretty man!' Dinah acceded warmly. 'Black as coal and bold as a fox. I'd been married nigh on ten years when he first set foot in these parts. I'd got three children then. He used to give me a saucy word whenever he saw me, for I liked him and he knew it. One Whitsun Monday I was home all alone, the children were gone somewheres, and Tom was away boozing. I was putting some plants in our garden – I loved a good flower in those days – I wish the world was all a garden, but now my Tom he digs 'em up, digs everything up proper and never puts 'em back. Why, we had a crocus, once! And as I was doing that planting someone walked by the garden in such a hurry. I looked up and there was Rufus, all dressed up to the nines, and something made me call out to him. "Where be you off to in that flaming hurry,"

I says. "Going to a wedding," says he. "Shall I come with 'ee?"
I says. "Ah yes," he says, very glad; "but hurry up, for I be
sharp set and all." So I run in-a-doors and popped on my
things and off we went to Jim Pickering's wedding over at
Clackford Mill. When Jim brought the bride home from
church that Rufus got hold of a gun and fired it off up
chimney, and down come soot, the bushels of it! All over the
room, and a chimney-pot burst and rattled down the tiles
into a p'rambulator. What a rumbullion that was! But
no one got angry – there was plenty of drink and we danced
all the afternoon. Then we come home together again
through the woods. O lord – I said to myself – I shan't
come out with you ever again, and that's what I said to
Rufus Blackthorn. But I did, you know! I woke up in bed
that night, and the moon shone on me dreadful – I thought
the place was afire. But there was Tom snoring, and I lay and
thought of me and Rufus in the wood, till I could have
jumped out into the moonlight, stark, and flown over the
chimney. I didn't sleep any more. And I saw Rufus the
next night, and the night after that, often, often. Whenever
I went out I left Tom the cupboardful – that's all he troubled
about. I was mad after Rufus, and while that caper was on I
couldn't love my husband. No.'

'No?' queried Rose.

'Well, I pretended I was ill, and I took my young Katey
to sleep with me, and give Tom her bed. He didn't seem to
mind, but after a while I found he was gallivanting after
other women. Course, I soon put a stopper on that. And
then – what do you think? Bless me if Rufus weren't up to
the same tricks? Deep as the sea, that man. Faithless, you
know, but such a bold one.'

Rose lay silent, plucking wisps of grass; there was a wry
smile on her face.

'Did ever he tell you the story of the man who was
drowned?' she asked at length. Dinah shook her head.
Rose continued. 'Before he came here he was keeper over
in that Oxfordshire, where the river goes right through the

woods, and he slept in a boathouse moored to the bank. Some gentleman was drowned near there, an accident it was, but they couldn't find the body. So they offered a reward of ten pound for it to be found . . .'

'Ten, ten pounds!'

'Yes. Well, all the watermen said the body wouldn't come up for ten days . . . '

'No more they do.'

'It didn't. And so late one night – it was moonlight – some men in a boat kept on hauling and poking round the house where Rufus was, and he heard 'em say 'It must be here, it must be here,' and Rufus shouts out to them, 'Course he's here! I got him in bed with me!'' '

'Aw!' chuckled Dinah.

'Yes, and next day he got the ten pounds, because he *had* found the body and hidden it away.'

'Feared nothing,' said Dinah, 'nothing at all; he'd have been rude to Satan. But he was very delicate with his hands, sewing and things like that. I used to say to him, "Come, let me mend your coat," or whatever it was, but he never would, always did such things of himself. "I don't allow no female to patch my clothes," he'd say, " 'cos they works with a red-hot needle and a burning thread." And he used to make fine little slippers out of reeds.'

'Yes,' Rose concurred, 'he made me a pair.'

'You!' Dinah cried. 'What – were you . . . ?'

Rose turned her head away. 'We was all cheap to him,' she said softly, 'cheap as old rags; we was like chaff before him.'

Dinah Lock lay still, very still, ruminating; but whether in old grief or new rancour Rose was not aware, and she probed no further. Both were quiet, voiceless, recalling the past delirium. They shivered, but did not rise. The wind increased in the forest, its hoarse breath sorrowed in the yellow field, and swift masses of cloud flowed and twirled in a sky without end and full of gloom.

'Hallo!' cried a voice, and there was Amy beside them,

with a faggot almost overwhelming her. 'Shan't stop now,' she said, 'for I've got this faggot perched just right, and I shouldn't ever get it up again. I found a shilling in the 'ood, you,' she continued shrilly and gleefully. 'Come along to my house after tea, and we'll have a quart of stout.'

'A shilling, Amy!' cried Rose.

'Yes,' called Mrs Hardwick, trudging steadily on. 'I tried to find the fellow to it, but no more luck. Come and wet it after tea!'

'Rose,' said Dinah, 'come on.' She and Rose with much circumstance heaved up their faggots and tottered after, but by then Amy was turned out of sight down the little lane to Pollock's Cross.

'Your children will be home,' said Rose as they went along, 'they'll be looking out for you.'

'Ah, they'll want their bellies filling!'

'It must be lovely a-winter's nights, you setting round your fire with 'em, telling tales, and brushing their hair.'

'Ain't you got a fire of your own indoors,' grumbled Dinah. 'Yes.'

'Well, why don't you set by it then!' Dinah's faggot caught the briars of a hedge that overhung, and she tilted round with a mild oath. A covey of partridges feeding beyond scurried away with ruckling cries. One foolish bird dashed into the telegraph wires and dropped dead.

'They're good children, Dinah, yours are. And they make you a valentine, and give you a ribbon on your birthday, I expect?'

'They're naught but a racket from cockcrow till the old man snores – and then it's worse!'

'Oh, but the creatures, Dinah!'

'You . . . you got your quiet trim house, and only your man to look after, a kind man, and you'll set with him in the evenings and play your dominoes or your draughts, and he'll look at you – the nice man – over the board and stroke your hand now and again.'

The wind hustled the two women closer together, and as

they stumbled under their burdens Dinah Lock stretched out a hand and touched the other woman's arm. 'I like you, Rose, I wish you was a man.'

Rose did not reply. Again they were quiet, voiceless, and thus in fading light they came to their homes. But how windy, dispossessed and ravaged, roved the darkening world! Clouds were borne frantically across the heavens, as if in a rout of battle, and the lovely earth seemed to sigh in grief at some calamity all unknown to men.

Polly Morgan

No, I suppose there are no such things as ghosts, not real ones, but I do know that it is possible to *believe* in one, just one fair fond illusion, a blessed exception made for you and no other, because that was the experience of my Aunt Agatha – and it may yet be mine. I was her favourite niece, I always spent my summers in her home.

Our family was a seafaring one, but she lived far from the sea on a long upland in the Chilterns. Copson was a dear and decent village; it began in an avenue of trees that ushered you from nowhere on those empty hills into a small common of turf and furze, a place of sun without shade, that the cuckoo loved; and then it trailed away along a lane to the open downs once more, where there was a windmill and a view over a vale. Almost the first thing you saw on entering Copson's quiet road was a CAUTION TO BEGGARS, but it might as well have been an invitation to them. They seemed to gravitate to Aunt Agatha's cottage and peep over the hedge at her in her garden amongst the violets or mignonette and the leafy things that hovered there, where as like as not she would be clipping her grass plot with a pair of dress-making scissors. They did not need to ask for anything, they just conducted a silent raid upon her charitable emotions.

That high heath seemed to have been founded in solitude. The fields flowed downwards from it on either side and your glance could follow only them and nothing else. A stone's-cast away there were no earthly features to meet the level gaze; on the right hand and the left there was nothing to be seen but the sky bending and breathing an admonition of silence. The score or so of scattered homes were obedient to that hush; the folk, though not unfriendly, were shy, and Aunt Agatha hadn't an intimacy with a soul in the place, knowing few of them save by name and none in the warmth of intercourse. And yet her heart was fervently with them in some aloof way.

One autumn morn, while cutting some chrysanthemum blooms in her garden, she heard the bell toll solemnly from the church on the far side of the common, signifying that someone was about to be buried. Who it was she did not know. By and by a cortège passed, a glass hearse containing a brown coffin that shone with brass and varnish. But not a flower or a mourner; beyond the official faces of the driver and the bearers walking beside the glass hearse there was no sign of grief or regret. Who could it be? Some poor creature who had died friendless? Her heart melted at those neglected obsequies, and hurrying indoors she changed into a black dress, took the sheaf of chrysanthemums and followed after the dead. By the time she reached the church door the service was over and the corpse was coming out to its burial. At the conclusion of the interment Aunt Agatha dropped her flowers into the grave, weeping.

It was not until then that she saw the name upon the coffin, Roland Bird, a farmer rich and eccentric who had dwelt not far off. But what ... what ... what could it mean? He had sons and daughters, stout hearty creatures. Where were they? And a stout hearty wife. Why were they all absent? They could not be ill, not all of them, surely? Thus to neglect him – was it possible they did not care, that nobody cared? There was not even one of his labouring men, or a neighbour, not one. She was deeply perturbed and went home sighing at the unkindness of human nature.

Aunt Agatha learned next day that the odd-minded farmer had solemnly and sternly enjoined that none should follow him to his grave and that no flowers should be thus foolishly wasted.

Well, my Aunt's violation of the dead man's wish had been – I know – as innocent as the act of a child, the impulsive offering of a heart most tender; but it was gossiped about, and in time a rumour grew like a maggot in a pippin that she must have been intimate with the queer farmer, a secret mistress or something vile like that. Poor dear Aunt had her qualms, but for some time she was unaware of this false gossip, such a rude interpretation of a simple deed, yet in the end it must have reached her. As for qualms, qualms was no word for her remorse. You see, the man's last solemn wish had been flouted, innocently enough, but to flout a dying prayer was irreparable, fatal as death itself, and Aunt Agatha was such a sweet maidenly old thing that her distress almost prostrated her. You could not, you could never, compound for such an unlucky mistake, it would go rolling on, rolling in endless waves through everlasting time. What the soul enjoins when its hand is on the latch of eternity is sacred, embodying hopes and aims that must have mystical warrant, though they seem slight and stupid to us. And she had ruined them, not callously but carelessly, as one kicks over an ant-hill.

When I went to stay with her in the following summer I heard of the strange upshot of the matter, partly from her and partly from her maid, a coarse creature named Fittle who was loquacious and careless but blindly devoted. The cottage has six rooms, with its windows all latticed, the steep roof all tiled, the walls smothered in creeper that turns from green to red, and it has a lovely tall chimney. What is there so ineffably right about a tall chimney that it makes a squat one look vulgar? Fittle had her grievance against the windows – they were hard to keep clean and leaked in the rain – but these artistic things all have their snares, everyone knows. Aunt's home was far too full of furniture, you could not step in it without pushing or writhing; it was brightened with exotic chintzes, and objects of brass and china bloomed uselessly on shelf and wall. But it was airily snug and smelt of flowering age; the limes breathed beside it, the furze burgeoned, and the cuckoo cried. Each year the place seemed to grow choicer and the little garden lovelier, except for that corner where a line of Fanny Fittle's intimate washing always made me impatient. Absurd, but at thirty one is so easily vexed.

Choicer and lovelier, I have said, and this year there was a change in my aunt, not at all retrograde but still a little mysterious. We had used to spend our evenings in games of chess or patience, or with music, but now as soon as twilight began my aunt would leave me and go to her own room to sup alone, and I would not see her again until the next morning. I took this to be a whim of approaching age, but her appearance belied the hint; she had indeed a new bloom, though it was not the bloom of youth; it was more a kind of spiritual grace. She was pale but dainty and trim, and kept up old fashions in her appearance, parting her grey-gold hair in the middle and folding-in on her neck. After noon she wore lace mittens and carried a fan. I was half her age, and brown, and neither delicate nor dainty. I wanted to read to her in bed, but she patted my hand with her fan and gently refused. 'No, dear Polly.' Her manner was so suave and tender that I could do nothing more, and I was much bothered until Fanny Fittle enlightened me. Then I was shocked; for a while I was frightened.

'She thinks she is haunted, Miss Morgan, but don't you believe it,' said Fittle to me. 'It's just a little fancy of hers and I have to pretend. It's all of a game with her.'

'A game?'

'Yes, can you understand it? A game with herself.'

'But what sort of game?'

'Well, as near as I can tell you, Miss, it's a game with a ghost, though I don't believe in 'em. Yes, and she likes it – an old lady of sixty! And the courage of a horse! But you can't credit her. How can you? I don't. It's not my place to do so, but I expostulated of it and she was quite short with me. There may be ghosts and ghosts, but you can't believe what you hear if you don't see it that way.'

In utter mystification I stared at the woman. She was

about my own age, with an angular ill-assorted body, all odds and ends of anatomy. I could see she was seriously perplexed by my aunt's foible.

'What do you mean – does she see anything?'

'Not that I know of, Miss,' Fittle replied. 'I don't see anything myself, and I don't see how she can, but she thinks she does.'

'Of course she doesn't see anything,' I said. 'Of course not! What is there to see? And when? And where?'

Fittle went on clearing my supper-table with a provoking deliberation.

'Of course, Miss, I don't know, but I do know there's something going on that I don't understand and can't get to the bottom of. And that upsets you; it would upset anyone. There's her supper, for instance; what does that signify?'

'Yes, Fanny. Why does she always have it alone, in her bedroom?'

'Well,' said Fittle, with an air, 'that's the question. *Does* she have it alone?' She hung in silence upon the significance of the inquiry, as if she knew an incredible answer. I could only shake my head, not denyingly, but to express my bewilderment.

'She may, or she may not,' the servant continued. 'But I can tell you something you perhaps don't know, Miss Morgan. I have to lay supper every evening for two people up there.' She pointed to the ceiling. I waited for her to go on.

'For two people, two of everything . . .'

I interrupted, 'That might be for a friend.'

'It's a friend that never comes then,' Fittle said.

'And a ghost couldn't eat anything,' I suggested, 'could it?'

Fanny countered with triumph, 'It never does eat anything – not that you'd notice. I can't tell for sure, because I'm not allowed to clear away the supper things at night, not until next morning. I'm never let into her room after I've taken up the supper; the door is always locked then.

I lay for two persons, but only one eats it. At least I can't say for certain, but there's only one plate ever used. She might clean the other one herself.'

It was no use pretending to myself that all this was just a vagary of Aunt's. I tried, without conviction, to convey that impression to Fanny Fittle. I was wasting words.

'Who is the ghost?' I asked, 'and when does it come?'

'It isn't a ghost at all really,' explained she, 'it's only an idea of hers, a fancy. She talks to herself a lot in there, but she talks in whispers so I can't hear the words.'

'When?'

'Often – whenever she likes.'

'But what is it supposed to be?' I urged impatiently. 'Is it a man, or a woman, or a child, or what is it? When did it begin? I've never heard any old tales of this house; have you?'

The servant went on meticulously folding up the white tablecloth, and without giving me a glance, said: 'No, Miss.'

'No what?'

'I mean I never heard any tales, and I don't know who it might be.'

'But you know when it started?'

'O, that? Yes. It started in the spring, two or three months ago.'

'What makes you think it's a ghost?'

'But I don't, Miss. I keep telling you I don't think it's a ghost at all. She's only pretending to herself, a sort of game, like children play.'

I did not accept that for one moment, it was too suggestive of senility, and Aunt Agatha was never more vividly alive.

'Doesn't do her any harm,' continued Fittle, 'only I thought I'd better tell you.'

'You don't think she is going – well, how can I put it? – silly, do you, Fittle?'

Fittle smiled with compassionate loyalty, 'O, no fear she ain't.' Dropping the cloth into a drawer she whisked off with the tray of dishes, and left me to the questioning blankness of the candle-lit room.

Before retiring to bed I went along to the kitchen. As I approached the door I could hear Fanny playing hymns on a mouth-organ, a hobby of hers which my aunt tolerated, perhaps even encouraged. Though Fanny hadn't a grain of religious feeling, her rhythmic fervour was mainly stimulated by evangelical compositions. I paused while she breathed 'Through the night of doubt and sorrow,' and then peeped in. The kitchen was lit by a paraffin lamp because Fittle disliked candles, and had a long shelf of brown jars full of pickles and jam, which strangely enough my aunt disliked.

'I wanted to ask you, Fanny: does she have her supper in her room when I am not here?'

'O yes. It's nothing to do with your being here, don't think that, Miss Polly.'

'And does she ever see "things" anywhere else, or is it always only upstairs?'

No, as far as Fanny knew, it was always upstairs.

I went off to my room and walked slowly past my aunt's door, but I heard nothing, no whispering; saw nothing, no ghosts. Fanny was an idiot. But I was glad to get safely into bed.

How can I write down the strangeness of the thing that came to inhabit there, that grew as the year grew and intolerably grew, a portent without horror but full of tragic desire, a doom without reason but full of the truth of sorrow! O, if only I too could have sunk into a grave and left all my fondness and foolishness in the sieve of time! How lovely was our home that year ere folly overtook me: the limes breathed, the furze burgeoned, the cuckoo cried. And there was no doubt Aunt Agatha saw, or thought she saw, some embodiment of a desire or a fantasy from a realm unknown, and day by day a conviction grew in me that she was open to communications of which I, too gross, too crudely human, was not aware, and shall never be. What were they? Whatever they were, if Aunt was bewitched she was beautifully bewitched, she throve like one who had access to some secret fountain of immortal youth. Withal, she was so cunning whenever I got to the point of questioning her that I could not but conclude there was more, far more, in the mysterious business than Fanny knew, or than I was ever likely to know.

One night I sat in the garden long after Aunt had gone to bed. I sat on until the moon, fully risen, cast such a trance of light that it paled white faces and deepened the black shades. There was not a puff of air, not one breathing sigh; a fleck of down from a feather would have fallen straight without wandering; and yet the two windows of Aunt's bedroom were closed. There was no light from either, but in that moonlight, one could not even imagine that darkness would ever come again. Then I went and stood under the quicken tree, for I do not like to remain still in the fullness of moonlight, not for very long. I have a feeling that it may do one harm. What harm? I don't know, I am not timid or superstitious, but it is the same mood in which I cover up mirrors during a thunderstorm, and don't walk under ladders. Silly, perhaps, but I must do these things. And I do believe that the moon's light mysteriously caresses the passionate nature of women, for desire of love came to me there, love that I had never known and often despaired of. I was not attractive, as Aunt Agatha must have been, as she was even though she was twice my age; I was neither delicate nor dainty. She had never married, yet it was certain that she must once have been wooed by heaps of men. I was already thirty, no man had ever wooed me, but I was romantically stirred by the projected visit of Aunt Agatha's godson, Johnny Oliphant. He was captain of a vessel trading in eastern seas but now being refitted at Bristol, and in a day or two he was coming to us at Copson for a week. As I stood under the quicken tree in the moonlight my thoughts were of him whom I had not even seen. Already he was pleading for my love. Divine foolishness!

Suddenly I had to look round. I saw nothing, but my heart

was beating with a wild ardour. For a moment I had the fearful thought that I was stifling in the marvellous light, that I was about to fall dead. In terror I looked up to Aunt Agatha's room. At that moment the right-hand window gently rattled. I had fleeting time to wonder why a casement should rattle in that windless air, when I saw my aunt come to the window in her lacy gown and open its fellow. Amazingly she leaned out and murmured softly 'Ah, you have come!' There was, I could swear, not a scoop of wind in the entire world; not one draught in all the flaring heavens; but I saw and heard the hanging creeper above the window sharply shaken. A look of apprehension floated across the pallor of her face.

'Roland, take care!' she breathed. 'O, take care!'

She put her hands on the window-sill as if watching some peril that was hidden from me, then with a sigh of passionate welcome she lifted her arms like a woman embracing. But, unless she embraced a vision that my eyes could not see, there was nothing there. A moment after she pulled back the casement, closing it. I saw no more, and the returning silence boomed with the pounding of my heart. I covered my face with my burning hands. When I looked up again all was as before, white moonlight, still trees, stolid house. I crept back to the candle-lit room. Fanny Fittle had gone to bed, I was alone with my awed thoughts.

Was my dear aunt haunted or cursed? I could not think so. I had seen only a gesture, a gesture of love that embraced nothing, nothing but an illusion. Yet the name! The name, familiarly spoken, was that of the farmer in whose grave she had dropped her offering of forbidden flowers! The man to whom malicious rumour had given her as a mistress, though I knew there was not even a possibility of truth in the malignant tale!

In a while I had to go up to my bed, and when I came to my aunt's door, passed swiftly in terror. I swear I heard the noise of dishes and knives and whisperings. Not until dawn did I fall asleep.

When I woke and recalled the events and emotions in the moonlit garden they seemed preposterous; the sun shone, and my aunt hummed so happily about the house. I could not forbear asking if she had slept well.

'I had a delightful night,' she replied, 'and you?'

'Yes,' I said. 'Did you dream?'

'No. And you?'

'I don't think I was dreaming,' I said. 'Do you ever dream, Aunt?'

'Sometimes, Polly. I had a funny little dream two or three nights ago. I dreamed I was looking towards the church from our garden. It was sunset, and there was a blackbird singing on the very top of the gilt vane on the steeple. I said to it, "You must stop singing now," but it would not stop and so I looked about until I found a bow and arrow. The bow was black but the arrow was golden. I took up the bow and arrow and I called out to the blackbird, "Now you must be quiet." But it took no notice of me, so I fitted the arrow to the bow and shot it off at the blackbird.'

I had to giggle at the notion of Aunt Agatha shooting a bird!

'Did you kill it?'

'No. The arrow sailed slowly high up into the air, a most lovely curve, glistening, and then it began to swoop down towards the blackbird, and just as it was going to pierce it the bird opened its mouth, caught the arrow with its beak, and settled down again as if nothing untoward had happened. It was extraordinarily clever, I never saw anything so clever in my life! And then the bird came flying to me here from the steeple and laid the arrow in my hand. O, I felt so ashamed. What a pity that we cannot interpret our dreams!'

My dear aunt looked so simple, so innocent, that I could have wept. But then my emotions had been fearfully torn by the sight of that moonlight rendezvous.

'It does not seem very difficult to interpret,' I ventured.

'What do you think it means?' asked my aunt eagerly.

'The bird and the church are obvious,' I said. 'The bird is Farmer Bird. A black bird – he is dead. It is all symbolic of what happened last year when you laid the flowers in his grave. And so on.'

I saw from her manner that Aunt Agatha had already thought it out for herself.

'That is very clever of you,' she said. 'I think it does mean that. But the arrow, the arrow!' And she repeated eagerly 'What about the arrow?'

'It must mean the flowers . . .'

'Yes? The chrysanthemums I took. They were yellow. I ought not to have taken them, so he brings them back!'

'And yet,' I went on steadily, 'it might mean Cupid's arrow.'

Aunt Agatha was bright-eyed as a child listening to a new tale.

'Cupid's arrow, Polly! You mean . . . love?'

'Yes, Aunt, of course I mean love,' I said sharply.

'Love!' echoed Aunt Agatha. 'That's very strange.'

'Tell me about it, Aunt,' I blurted out. 'Tell me, I am worried. I was in the garden last night and I saw . . . everything. It frightened me.'

'Frightened you? What did you see – a ghost?'

'No, not a ghost.' I told her what I had seen her do, of the words I heard her speak, of the rustling creeper, of the window shaken.

'My child!' said my aunt tenderly. 'You must have been dreaming!'

'Am I dreaming now?' I asked. 'Were you dreaming then? Of course you were not, nor was I. But something is happening to you about this Roland Bird – tell me, Aunt; the farmer that died – as if his curse were following you. It sounds fatuous to ask if he is haunting you or if you are bewitched by him, but for pity's sake tell me, Aunt, what it all means, and I'll help you.'

She was so silent for some moments, I could hear the watch on my wrist ticking sharply, and a bee buzzing in the window filled the room with uproar.

'You can't help, darling,' said my aunt.

'But, Aunt, let me try,' I pleaded.

'I don't want any help. I am very happy, the way I am. My happiness is mine, no one can touch it. No one can share it. I am not cursed or bewitched: how could you think it, dear Polly?'

That is how my astonishing aunt talked to me. I tried once more, as casually as I could manage, though, by God! the utterance almost choked me:

'Then you do see this Roland Bird. What do you do?'

'Ah, Polly,' my aunt replied. 'You must not ask me that.'

Either my aunt was mad or I was mad. Yet you can never doubt your own sanity or nullify your own experience. I had seen what I had seen, my aunt had not utterly denied it, and it was incredible. But people live and have experiences which do not tally with your own. There are those who affirm, those who deny, and those who ignore. I was to learn that though I might ignore my aunt's ghost I could not ignore her obsession. I could deny her thought, but I could not deny her experience. I could call it foolish, I could not affirm it false. And in the face of her new bloom, her calm happiness, my fears for her sanity were but a mockery of my own. And yet . . . was I really living in a house with a woman who was visited by a ghost, a ghost that she welcomed and loved, that she even – God help her – tried to feed! What is the human heart made of? I mean in its quality of love? For a while I could think of nothing better than to offer my aunt some purgative medicine. With a serene smile she waved me off – and I took it myself.

Then, plump into the midst of this unnerving puzzle dropped Johnny, Captain Oliphant. Only for a week, one tiny little week out of the ten thousand days and nights we had lived unknown, so that I scarcely knew him long enough to be able to describe him, but he was not like a sailor man, no 'Avast there!' or heaving-ho! – he was much more like a nice lawyer.

On the first day we went roving in the hills. He kissed me and I kissed him. Of course I told him all about Aunt's queer behaviour, and he was sympathetic and he was kind.

But on the second day he had thought it all over, and he was more matter-of-fact. He said she was 'batchy,' that it would be better to cut the creeper away from the casement and fit some pegs in the loose window. And we said we would do this together, unknown to her. Then we went roving on the enchanting hills again and forgot about it. I was alone with him and already I was in love with him, desperately.

On the third day he asked me to marry him, and I said I would. He said, 'Thank you, Polly; thank you, Polly; you shall never regret it. I love you dearly.' And I said, 'I love you too.' So banal, and yet so moving – God keep me simple. I promised to marry him when he returned from China in the spring. And I promised to be at Marseilles to meet him then. I promised this, I promised that, I promised anything – and I gave, too. He was my handsome Johnny. I went to his room and slept with him, and all the days and nights he was with me we were but one. Happy, happy time. And then we did something I wish we had not done; unknown to Aunt we clipped back the creeper from her bedroom window, and secretly fitted two tiny wedges in the casement. I wish we had not done it.

I was unable to go with him to Bristol; although he was ardent and I was longing, he went away alone, and I could hardly describe him now. One little week out of all our ten thousand nights and days! Just before he sailed he sent me a ring of diamonds, and a power of attorney to help me prepare a home against his return, a home like Aunt Agatha's; for that he loved and the pretty country too.

After he was gone I let my aunt's secret alone, I did not probe any further. My own secret filled all my life, and I kept that from her as long as I was at Copson. In three weeks or four I went back to London and settled down for the autumn and the long winter that was to pass before spring could come.

One of the letters he wrote me had a long analysis of Aunt Agatha's affair; he had worked out a theory about it.

'I trace it this way: she was in a state about butting in at that man's funeral and bowling things over like she did, and thought she would be haunted or cursed in some way. Well, when you *think* you are going to be haunted you very likely *will* be. But this rumour that happened along about her being his fancy – you can see that this gave a romantic turn to her idea. No doubt about that. It's all auto-suggestion, of course. She was not annoyed by that rumour; as a matter of fact, she was secretly pleased. Doesn't matter a bit whether it is true or not. If you are to be haunted you might just as well be haunted nicely and agreeably, and that's the whole bottom of her queer fancy. He would not curse her, but he might haunt her, and if he haunted her as a lover he would be welcome. And so he did, and so he was. That's the way I trace it, for if you *think* you are haunted you *are* haunted. Religious history is full of such cases. She thinks he is in love with her now, and pretends that he comes to visit her. Well, you saw what that amounted to? Of course we can't talk of ghosts, ghosts don't exist, it is a clear case of romantic hallucination. Good for her! She's an old maid and it does her no harm.'

I left it at that; it seemed but half the truth, but the other half might be odious, so I probed no further. My own secret I kept, though Aunt and I corresponded regularly. In a very short time I could not fail to notice the sad tones faintly echoing in her letters. No, she was not as well as she had been. Tired easily. Old age, she supposed, or the sharp winds.

I comforted her and promised to visit her at Christmas, but long before then I was hurriedly summoned to Copson, where I found her far gone and hopelessly ill.

She had just incredibly faded away, a thread of bones,

all her lustre gone. What had happened? What was the matter with her? No one knew, not even the doctor, or Fanny Fittle, or anybody. I bowed my head in grief upon her pillow.

For some days she lingered, not so much Aunt Agatha as a pale wraith of her, and before she died she spoke to me of the thing that was destroying her. She lay staring towards the window. It was a gaunt, gloomy day, not ominous but passive, with neither wind to hearten nor sun to encourage. The brightest thing, the only bright thing, was the pale smoke twirling from the village chimneys.

'He makes no sign,' she whispered, 'he has gone.'

'What, Aunt?'

'Gone for ever.'

'Who has gone?'

There was reproach in the eyes that looked up at me: 'You saw us – didn't you? – one night – didn't you? You saw, didn't you? You said you saw.'

So eager was her desire for confirmation that I had not the heart to deny her moonlit Eden.

Sadly she murmured on, 'He found me. I had gone to the grave against his command, he said, and for that his spirit would always follow me, he said. He came; he forgave me, he said. It was strange, beautiful, but it has come to an end.' The thin lips sighed. 'It is hard to feel so forsaken. There is no sign from him now, is there? I was sad about it for a while, rather sad, Polly, but I am all right again now.' And she fondly pressed my hand.

God knows what Roland Bird was like in the life. No Endymion certainly. He may have been an oaf, a fat ox – he probably was – but it did not matter. He had been but the crooked key which unlocked for her a glade in the Hesperides, and she had walked there until our rude hands – Johnny's and mine – had carelessly wrecked the dream.

All her possessions came to me. Except for a small legacy to her godson Johnny her little fortune was mine, and her house was mine, but for a while after her death I could not bring myself to live there, not alone, and so I left Fittle in charge and went back to London. I wrote to Johnny in Sumatra all about it. Now, of course, there was no more need for me to seek a house for me and Johnny. I arranged for some alterations to be made in the new year; some things I discarded, adding others, but it was always the same old house from the very doormat to Fanny Fittle herself, my home and Johnny's. I wrote to him in Rangoon all about it. Every week I had letters from him somewhere in the eastern world, the kind of letters that simple men write to their sweethearts, full of affection and longing. Probably he would be a little later than he had thought. Probably he would not be at Marseilles until the first week in May, but I should have definite news immediately the situation was clear. And he sent me a letter from Tokyo on Easter Monday – and that was the last I heard from Johnny.

I was in fear from the very first – I am sure, now, that it is the vengeance of that baffled ghost. We had betrayed Aunt Agatha between us. It was only I who saw the bush fluttering on a windless night, and heard the casement shaken, but together we had cut back the tendrils and stayed the window's clatterings. And who knows by what slender means the soul moves to its difficult desire, or what its desire may be? I was in fear from the first, and now I am sure: something rocks on in anguish and takes its toll from our lives.

I came back to Copson at midsummer and here I shall abide. I did not even wear black. I knew he was dead, so what was I to Johnny, or he to me? I had known him for a week of days, a holy Eden, but now I cannot recall his appearance. There is so invincible a blank now that at times I have said to myself, 'No, I never knew any Captain Oliphant. I am like Aunt Agatha, who thought she was loved by a man who was dead.' And then, when my mind tries to pierce through the void to that divinity we knew, there interposes itself the figure of a man with a cocked hat and a sword by his side. That is how a sailor should be, I suppose, but my Johnny was drowned in only his shirt, one dark night, his ship mysteriously colliding with another. Only seven men were lost, but my Johnny was one of them, drowned in the white foam that flowers in the Chinese seas. That was not fate, he was never unlucky! It was vengeance.

I should have been his bride, but I am nothing now. I look out of the lattice here in my bedroom and see moonlight and the quicken tree. The creeper hangs again where once it hung and brushed the mullions airily. Long ago I took out the wedges from the window. I can faintly hear the hymn that Fanny Fittle is playing on her mouth-organ; I hate the sound, but my aunt tolerated it, and so do I. I always have my supper here, in this room, alone. The table is set for two, even now. Poor credulous fool! Whom do I long for? The casement is softly shaken and the creeper writhes, but no one comes, nor will ever come, for me.

The Presser

Two or three years after the first jubilee of Queen Victoria a small ten-year-old boy might have been seen slouching early every morning along the Mile End Road towards the streets of Whitechapel. Johnny Flynn was a pale boy of pinched appearance – for although his black coat was a size too large for him, his black trousers were a size too small – he was not very well, and he was tired. Plodding along from his aunt's house miles away in Hackney, he sometimes drowsily ran into things: things like sauntering policemen (who were ductile and kind) or letter-boxes (that were not). A policeman genially shook him.

'Ay! Where ye going?'

'Going to work, sir.'

'Work! What work do ye work at?'

'Mr Alabaster's, a tailor, sir.'

'O, a tailor! Mind he don't put ye under a thimble and suffocate ye. Get along with it, and don't go knocking people down's if ye was popping off to Buckingham Palace!'

Johnny wanly smiled as he said, 'No,' and 'Good morning, sir.'

It was generally a letter-box, though, and after such a mishap one day he had gone into a public lavatory. There he had seen a bad word chalked up on the wall – a very bad word. Johnny Flynn knew all about bad words although he had never uttered them; his mind shrank from them as a snail shrinks when you spit on it. But this time he went on his way with the bad word chanting in his mind – he could *not* but listen to it, he was absorbed by it; and the very next letter-box he came to he said it out boldly and loud, seven times, to the letter-box. And one day he dropped his packet of dinner into the mouth of one of these letter-boxes.

Well, when he came to Whitechapel there was Leman Street, and off Leman Street there were other streets full of shops with funny names over the windows, like Greenbaum, Goldansky, Finesilver and Artzibashev, and shops full of foreign food that looked nasty and smelled, or full of objects that seemed vaguely improper. There were hundreds of clattering carts bedazing him, and women who were drunk at eight o'clock in the morning sat on door-steps with their heads in their hands. And they smelled, too. Very soon now he reached a high dull building that hoarded a barracks of prolific Jewish families, and ascending one flight of its sticky stone stairs he came to a standstill outside a door in a dark passage. There he had to wait until Mr Sulky, who was the presser and had the key, arrived. Mr Sulky was a big dark young man with a pale pitted face, who lodged in an eating house, went for long walks on Sundays, and passed for a misogynist. The rest of his time he spent in pressing trousers with a large hot-iron goose.

Johnny said, 'Good morning, sir.'

Mr Sulky said, 'Huh!' but he always said it with a faint smile.

The first business in the tailor's workshop was to light the fire, a great fire maintained with coke. Then, to sweep the room clean of its countless fragments of cloth and cotton. Heaping these in a wooden box, the boy staggered with it across the dark passage into a smaller apartment with a window, the very symbol of gloom, looking down into a dank yard where he could see people all day long going to the privy. The room contained only a colossal pile of cloth clippings covering the whole floor, and it was his unending task to sort these into their various kinds. The pile never lessened, it seemed to grow with absorbent inexorable growth. Sometimes he could scarcely enter the door to get into the room; and that implacable mountain of rags was watered with the tears of his childish hungers and despairs. He emptied the box and returned to the workshop.

Eight or nine women came in and began their work of making trousers. A massive table stood in the middle; the women sat round three sides of the room on old empty boxes – these were less comfortable than chairs, but more convenient. The room was large and well lighted from two windows. In summer the windows were a blessing to the women, the hot fire an affliction; in winter it was otherwise. Sometimes they sweated, and sometimes they sneezed or they coughed, but they never shivered. Each woman had a pad of needles tacked to her bodice, a pair of scissors and skeins of thread in her lap, and her hands were busied with the garments of men she knew nothing about. Each had a wedding ring on her nuptial finger, the beginnings of a hump on her shoulders, and the deuce knows what emotions in her heart. They were mostly young women, but they looked old, whereas Mr Sulky and Mr Alabaster were young and looked young. It reminded Johnny of the question propounded by a famous advertisement:

> Why does a woman look old
> sooner than
> a man?

And the answer was something to do with soap.

His favourite was certainly Helen, she was handsomest. Johnny liked her, she had a pretty freckled face and a big bosom, and was tall and fair. Johnny admired her, though she was not kind to him and effusive like old Mrs Grainger. Indeed she was in some ways, he thought, rather unkind and slightly haughty, but her smile was lovely. She was married to a bottle-washer named Smithers, and they had a little girl Hetty, six or seven years old, with weak eyes and heavy boots, who often came and sat on the stairs waiting for her mother. Mrs Grainger was a wrinkled crone who got drunk on Saturday nights in order to import cheer into her fading hours. Beer, she declared, was better than soup in her belly.

When Johnny first came to work with them she catechized him.

'You're a weeny little chap. What's your age?'

Her hands were shiny and lumpy, she was thin, but she had a plump behind.

'I'm ten years,' replied the flustered boy.

'God's my mercy! You ought to be at school, your age. Why don't you go to school?'

'I'm not well,' said Johnny.

'Nobody's well in this world. We're all alike.' The old woman hawked and spat into her snuffy handkerchief. 'What's the matter with you?'

'I don't know,' Johnny Flynn confessed.

'How d'ye know you're not well then?'

'I can feel,' said Johnny.

'What can you feel?'

'In my liver,' the boy whispered. 'Inch and half lower than it ought to be, and we can't alter it. My mother's a widow.'

'So your father's dead?'

'Yes; she lives in the country.'

'And where do you live?'

'With my aunt and my uncle. Down at Hackney. He's an engine-driver.'

'That's grand! D'ye like it?'

The boy reflected. 'I don't know,' he said slowly.

'Well, God's my mercy!' tittered the old woman. 'You must go out in the fresh air all you can.'

In the corner a girl sat machining seams. Mr Sulky took a hot goose from the fire to the table and pressed trousers under a damp rag that soon rotted the air with the odour of steaming cloth. This was a necessary evil, for although all the others were engaged in cutting out, preparing, stitching, binding, button-holing, and generally compounding trousers, the art of finishing the garment lay with the presser, the prince of a tailor's workshop – and that was Mr Sulky. No civilian, from a bookbinder to a bishop, would dream of donning a pair of trousers that had not been pressed. A

Hottentot might, or a skipjack – yes, conceivably even a bookbinder might – but certainly not a bishop. Let it have buttons of gold, fabulous fabric, silky seams, and trimmings of rapture, fused in a noble equilibrium of cut, but until it has been baptized with a wet rag and punched with a hot iron it is nothing.

Mr Sulky (who passed for a misogynist) whistled airily as he bumped and hissed with his iron, and then began to chaff the women.

'Well, ladies!'

Heavy scarlet lips gave him the pout of a sardonic man, but his face was a kind face, very pale and very bare. Not a hair or the sign of it was to be seen on his chin. Or on his arms. At work he cast off his coat, waistcoat and collar, and wore only a striped shirt and a belt round his trousers. He kept on his neat buttoned boots, turned up his stiff cuffs, and his cuff-links tinkled as he jerked his arms.

'What devilry have you all been at since yesterday?'

The ladies glanced at each other, and tittered.

'Nothing, Ernie, so help me God,' cackled Mrs Grainger. 'Ask Helen.'

'Bah!' The presser clouted his goose down upon some innocent trousers.

'O dear, ladies,' cried the provoking old woman, 'he's got a wink over his eye this morning.'

Mr Sulky, somewhat baffled, stuttered, 'Born devils! And you're the worst of the lot.'

'No, Ernie, no.' The old woman's glasses twinkled re-assuringly at him. 'I had my dues, thank God, years ago.'

'Your dues!'

'Many a time, and I can't deny it,' said the old woman.

'Ah, devils born, I tell you,' groaned the presser.

'And the men! Dear lord!' Mrs Grainger shot at him. 'You can't even make your own trousers.'

Mr Sulky made a rude reply, and the women laughed quietly though they pretended not to. It made Johnny laugh, but at the same time he was ashamed to laugh – and he pretended not to. Once, a boy at school had told him a rude joke, and it was such a cunning comical joke that he had had to tell it in a whisper to his father. Father had giggled. 'Don't tell mother,' implored the boy. And father had said, 'Pooh, no. No fear!' But Johnny was sure that he had gone and told mother at once, and he could not bear to think of it.

There was no more joking after Mr Alabaster came in, for he was the master. Mr Alabaster had short bow legs, a pink face, and florid hair that curled dandily. So did his voice, for he lisped. Very cheerful he looked, and was seldom harsh to anyone. At the table opposite Mr Sulky he stood with a measuring tape around his shoulders, a pair of shears or a piece of pipeclay in his right hand; and having made chalk marks on whatever piece of cloth was before him, he cut trousers out of serge, flannel, duck, vicuna, tweed, any mortal cloth you could think of, all day long. A very clever fellow. A thoughtful man, too. He would never allow Johnny Flynn to stay in the workshop during the dinner hour. Summer or winter, rain or shine, out he had to go.

'You muth get the fresh air into you,' Mr Alabaster said. 'Itth good for the lining of the stomach, or I shall have the poleeth on me. You can go under the railway arch if it rainth.'

No one but Mr Sulky had the privilege of staying in the workshop during dinner time: that was the edict, the injunction, the fixed rule. Then how was it that Mrs Smithers stayed there sometimes? Johnny would like to know. Mr Alabaster did not know of it, but Johnny knew and the women knew; what was more, although they never enjoyed that favour themselves, they were glad when Helen did. Johnny was glad, too, in a way, because of course her husband was a nasty cruel man who slogged her about, and it was best for her not to go home more often than she had to. Mrs Grainger used to advise her about Smithers:

'Give him in charge, my gal; turn him out, or sling your hook. He's a dirty foul thing, and the Lord gave him to you for a walking wickedness.'

16

'How can I do that?' asked Helen. 'I'm married to him, and there's little Hetty.'

'O, God's my mercy!' Mrs Grainger was baffled, but still emphatic. 'Give him in charge and sling your hook. What with the men and their women and the holy marriage bells, you can't tell your head from your elbow. It ought to be made impossible, and then there'd be some sense in Christianity.'

Well, the boy would go and walk in the streets. Unless it rained he avoided the railway arch because someone had done murder there, and someone else had painted a white skeleton on the wall; so he walked about. There was the dreadful den where the Jews brought their fowls to be strangled; knots of gabbling women dangling dead birds or birds that were going to be dead, the pavement dribbling blood, and feathers falling, sticking in the blood. And in the bakehouse next door you could watch a man flinging limp matzos, like pieces of white velvet, into a big oven, and another man drawing them out as stiff as china plates. Soon he opened his packages of food – wedges of bread and slips of meat folded in a sheet of newspaper. Scrupulously he sniffed the meat, and not caring for that smell he dropped the meat into a gutter and chewed the bread with resentment. Yesterday it was pickled pork, and the day before; it would be pickled pork tomorrow, and the day after, and the day after that. Whatever it was he had it for a week; six days it savoured, and did all that it was not expected to do. His aunt was a wise and busy woman who could not prepare a fresh meal for him every day; it was not to be thought of and it was not necessary. Every Saturday night she bought for his separate and sole consumption a little joint of meat, cooking it specially for him on Sundays; and every week his stomach turned sour on it after a day or two. The image of that evil ort of flesh reposing undiminishably in the larder tormented him even in dreams. It never entered his mind to complain to his aunt, and if it had done so he had little of the spirit of complaint. If he was not exactly a Spartan, he was, you might say, spartanatical. Things happened to you; they were good, or they were bad – and that was the truth about everything.

Now this neighbourhood was full of little Jew boys, and it was the custom of little Christians to submit such heathens to mockery, often to ill-treatment. In the early days there Johnny Flynn had called after some of them, 'Sheeny! Sheeny!' Sweet knowledge, how we live and learn! It was no joke to be the one pure Christian boy in a street full of belligerent bloody-minded Hebrew serpents who pretended to run away when you made a face at them, but who, as soon as you pursued them, turned diabolically upon you and dashed your Christianity into discomfiture and blood. Perhaps it was these very misfortunes that made Johnny Flynn so fond of evangelical hymns. Whenever he experienced any joy – and that was not seldom – he would lift up his heart and sing to himself that he was

> 'Sweeping through the gates of the New Jersualem,
> Washed in the blood of the Lamb.'

Or if it were sorrow that he felt – and that, too, was not seldom – he would murmur the

> 'Sweetest carol ever sung:
> Jesus, blessed Jesus.'

But maybe it was really an emotional gift from his mother. Always on Sunday eve she had taken him to an undenominational chapel run by some hooded sisters and a preacher with gaunt eyes who sometimes preached himself into a fit. At some stage of the service the sisters would come round and interrogate the worshipper.

'Are you saved?'

'Yes, ma'am, thank you,' Mrs Flynn would reply.

'Praise God. Is your little boy saved?'

'Yes, ma'am,' said mother, with bright hope in her eyes, 'I *think* he is.'

'Praise God, sister.'

But when the lady had passed on Johnny would bend and growl at his mother:

'What d'you tell her that for?'

'Well, you *must* be saved, Johnny, you know you must.'

'I ain't going to be,' he would say wretchedly; 'never, I won't be.'

'Now don't you be a bad boy, Johnny, or you'll go to the fire. Of course you must be saved; whatever next!'

Then, seeing him so cross, she would press his hand fondly and he would love her again, so that when they stood up to sing 'Sweeping through the gates' he would join in quite happily and admire her sweet voice.

Ah, in such matters he was on the side of his father. Father was an atheist; he had even joined the Skeleton Army – a club of men who went about in masks or black faces, with ribald placards and a brass band, to make war upon the Salvation Army. Yet when his father had died – twelve months ago – and a friend had made a small wooden cross, painted black, to put on his grave, Johnny had painted his name and dates on the cross in white paint with a thin brush that vexed him to madness, for the hair of the brush kept sticking out at the angle of the pressure applied and looked like an L. Moreover, Johnny had decided that his father should have an epitaph; so he cut up a piece of a cardboard box, gave it a border of black ink, composed a verse, and tacked the card to the cross with some little nails.

> I am not gone I am only a sleep.
> Where Jesus heavenly mansions keep
> Grieve not for long nor trouble be
> And love each other because of me.
>   J. F.

He wept while he composed this piece of deathly poetry, and whenever he recalled it afterwards he wept again. His mother, too, liked it so very much that tears came into her eyes. In a few weeks rain had soaked the card on the cross; the sun had bleached it and discoloured the ink so that it could hardly be read. When some of the tacks came out the card curled over and exposed an advertisement on its back of somebody's baking powder.

Long ere day was over the boy regretted his rash disposal of the meat; devastating hunger assailed him and he yearned for any scrap, even a dog's. At such times it was the joy of heaven to him if Mrs Grainger beckoned at tea-time.

'Johnny, I want you to go and get me a haporth of tea, a haporth of sugar and a farthingsworth of milk. There's threehapence – you can have the farthing for yourself.'

Nice, nice old woman! With his farthing he would buy a few broken biscuits; and he would borrow a pinch of her sugar and dip his biscuits in her milk. That did not happen every day. At other times it was a desperate joy to stand in front of a grocer's window, to divide the display in half, and to ponder long and exquisitely which half he would take if a choice were given him. Would you have marmalade, potted tongue, cocoa, and condensed milk – things like that – or would you have pineapple, cornbeef and split-peas – candles being no good? Desperate schemes for obtaining any of these, or anything else eatable, simply assaulted his longing, but he had no courage to test them again after he had once stolen a salted gherkin that made him vomit. He would turn away and glare along the pavements and gutters, hoping to find an apple-core or a rotten orange. Once he had the odd chance to pick up a playing-card, which he tore into pieces. Mother had warned him against the sin of card-playing; she had warned him against everything immoderate and immodest – strong drink, little girls, stealing, smoking, swearing, and such like. Yet whenever Mr Alabaster or Mr Sulky sent him out in the evening for a can of beer he could not resist taking a stealthy gulp or two of the liquor. Hunger was awful. In a daze he soaped seams for Mr Sulky or sewed on buttons for Helen and Mrs Grainger. If there was nothing else to be done he had to go to the ragroom and sort clippings from that maddening pile. Kneeling down beside his box among the soft rags he would dream over the fine doings he had had on Queen Victoria's Jubilee day. That *was* a day! All the scholars went to school in the morning to pray, to implore God to confound and frustrate certain nameless nations, to receive a china mug with the Queen's face twice on it, a medal with her face again – in case the mug got broken – and a paper bag containing half a sausage-piece and a great piece of cake. Lord, how grand! He ate them all over again and again. Then you marched out to the park with flags, and the park was full – millions of kids. There were clowns and jokers and sports, and you had your mug filled with tea from a steam-roller. Hundreds of steam-rollers. And then he forgot everything and fell asleep sprawling amongst the rags until he was awakened by angry Mr Alabaster.

'Hi! hi! Thith won't do, you know. I don't pay you for thleeping, it will bankrupt me. It won't do at all. You and I must part. God bleth, aren't you well?'

'Yes, sir.'

'Well, then! God bleth, do you think I am a millionaire with hundredth of pounds. I can't understhand you, and it won't do. You and I will part, my man.'

But at the end of the day the kind Mr Alabaster would sometimes give him a penny to ride part of the way home in a tram. With his penny Johnny hurried off to buy a cake or a pie, and thereafter walked cheerfully home. Often that penny became such a mighty necessity to him that as he knelt alone among the rags in the gloomy room, the pose, the quiet, and the need induced a mood in which he mumbled dozens of prayers.

'O God, make him give me a penny tonight, only a penny; make him give me a penny, please God. Amen.'

As if to impregnate his plea with suitable flavour, he crooned over the hymns he knew. Then again, 'Please God, make him give me a penny. Please this once, like you did before, and I won't ask you again. Amen.'

Not often were these prayers answered, and directly their failure became apparent he would descend weakly to the street, his whole body burning with ferocity against so frightful, so callous, so unseeing a god; and he would gasp out horrible blasphemies, until he came to a shop window where he could pause for a long rest, divide up its delicacies, and mystically devour them. In such delight he always forgot his anger against Jehovah.

One morning Helen came to the workroom at a very late hour. Mr Alabaster regarded her sternly as she came in, until he saw she had a black eye horribly bruised, and knew she had been crying. She whispered a few words to Mr Alabaster before going to her seat, and he lisped, 'O yeth, yeth. Dear me! Itth dreadful, yeth. Dear, dear me. All right.'

Mr Sulky did not utter a sound, not one terrible word, and the whole room became silent. After his first and only glance at the disfigured woman, Mr Sulky pounced upon his task with a fermenting malignity, the wrath of one whose soul had been split by a shock that drained him of charity and compunction, and his hot iron crashed upon the apparel before him as though it contained the body of a loathed enemy. Windows trembled at each mighty jar, implements on the table spitefully clattered, and paper patterns fluttered off the walls as if casting themselves to perdition. Mr Alabaster looked across protestingly.

'My word, Ernie! I thay!'

The presser ignored him. Snatching the iron from its stand, he flashed across the room, flung the cooling goose into the heart of the fire, took another in its place, tested it with a spirt of saliva that ticked and slid into limbo, and resumed his murderous attack on the trousers.

'Stheady, Ernie! God bleth, you'll have the theiling down on uth!'

Mr Alabaster's pipeclay was jolted from the table by the next concussion. Mr Alabaster was master there, but he was a timid man; Sulky could eat three of him, and Sulky was a pearl amongst pressers; so Mr Alabaster put on his coat. If Sulky was going mad he could go mad in peace and comfort.

'Muth go up the town this morning. Be back after dinner. Look after everything, Ernie. You know. Don't . . . ah . . . don't break anything, Ernie.'

The ignoring Mr Sulky signalized his master's departure by a volley of ferocious clouts upon the garments he was handling. Then he stopped. Although the sewing-machine whirred in its corner, the quietness of the women was perceptibly tense. Helen bent low over her work. Johnny knew that she was still crying, and he could not bear to see this, so he tiptoed from the workshop into the room across the passage and flung himself into the melancholy business of sorting the clippings. Canvas, buckram, silesia, cotton, silk, tweed, serge, flannel and vicuna, all fetched different prices in the rag market and had to be separated into heaps. The main heap was impregnable; it was a job that never could be finished, for the pieces always accumulated faster than the boy could sort them. It was a tide that ebbed lightly and flowed greatly, and the spirit of the boy was drowned in it. Once he had read a fairy tale about a prince in captivity who was given a barn full of canary seed to sort out in a single night or else he was to be turned into a donkey. But the prince had a fairy godmother who set some earwigs on the job, and they finished it while the prince went off to a ball and married a poor girl who was lovely and good and had cured the fairy godmother of toothache. But there were no fairy godmothers in Whitechapel, and earwigs were no use – not with cloth. And Johnny's head behaved strangely nowadays. Sometimes his head would go numb and he would feel as if he were falling out of his body and sinking into the void. Or if he only heard the ping of an omnibus bell in the city, even that gave him a horrible blow in his heart, and his heart would rattle madly. The sound of the bells was so shocking to him that when he went up to the city he always stuffed pieces of wadding in his ears. And the sight of the room full of rags affected him in much the same way:

his head swam, his knees trembled, and his heart rocked.

Suddenly the door was dashed open and Mr Sulky appeared.

'O,' he said, seeing Johnny there. Then, 'Get out of this!'

The boy slunk out into the dark passage. Helen stood at the door; she held a handkerchief to her eyes.

'Come,' said Mr Sulky, and Helen followed him into the rag room. They did not fasten the door. Johnny lingered outside; he did not know what else to do, he was a stupid boy. Hearing nothing within the room and being somewhat bewildered, he pushed open the door. Helen and Mr Sulky were folded tightly in each other's arms, silent.

'Where shall I go?' the boy timidly whispered.

The presser turned his white face towards him and with his great teeth bared he snarled:

'Go away, you idiot!'

Out shot his foot and the door slammed in Johnny's face. The boy felt that his indiscretion had been vulgar. There was something in the surprising embrace of the two people – the figure of the piteous Helen and her tender cherishing by Mr Sulky – that seemed almost holy. He crept back to the workroom where the women were talking aloud.

'Here, Johnny,' cried Mrs Grainger. 'Just run out and get me a pennyworth of pills at the post office. My consumption's so bad this morning, it's murdering me. Ask for them rhubarb pills. I don't suppose they'll do me any good – the only cure for me is a dose of poison; but God Almighty made the medicine, and I might be lucky. A pennyworth of rhubarb pills, Johnny. And tell that man with the crooked nose they're for a lady that's got a delicate stomach. Don't forget that, there's a good boy.'

When he returned from this errand of mercy Helen and Mr Sulky were back in the workshop again, looking as if nothing particular had occurred. Helen seemed cheerful. Mr Sulky whistled softly and did not bang his irons about very much.

This was one of the days on which silly Johnny had thrown

his dinner away, and as time wore on the old hunger brought him to his old despair. At seven o'clock Mr Alabaster and Mr Sulky tossed up to see who should pay for supper, and Mr Sulky won – he always did. Johnny fetched them a small loaf, some cheese, a tin of lobster, and a can of beer. He tore off as much of the loaf's crust as he dared; if he could only have got at the lobster he would have gone to prison for it. He placed the food on the table.

'Good night, sir. Good night, Mr Sulky,' then he said, moving slowly towards the door. The two men were laughing and cracking jokes.

'Hi! Here, Johnny, hereth a penny for the tram!'

O my, it was very blissful then!. Fatigue and despair left him; down the stairs he went leaping, and fled to a cookshop in Mile End Road. It was some distance away, but it was there you could buy such marvellous penny cakes, of a size, of a succulence, reeking with sweet fat and crusted with raisins. Never a thought of the Lord, never a thanksgiving prayer. Johnny unwrapped the cake and stood gazing at it, seeking the loveliest corner of entry, when a large boy came to him from an alley near by and accosted him.

'Give us a bite, young 'un.'

'Gives nothing.' Master Flynn was positive to the point of heartlessness.

'I've had nothing to eat all day,' the large boy said mournfully.

Johnny intimated that he was in the same unfortunate case himself.

'Give us half of it, d'ye hear,' the other demanded in truculent tones, 'or I'll have the lot.'

Johnny shook his head and hiked a shoulder. 'No, you won't.'

'Who'd stop me?' growled the bandit.

'Inky,' replied young Flynn. And then, as he lifted the cake to his mouth and prepared to bite a great gap in it, the absolute and everlasting end of the world smote him

clump on the ridge of his chin. He heard the rough fellow
grunt, 'There's the upper cut for yer'; the cake was snatched
from his paralysed grasp. 'And there's another for civility.'
Again the end of the world crashed upon his face from the
other side. Johnny felt no pain, not the faintest scruple of a
physical twinge, but there was such a frantic roaring in his
ears that he had to bend down with his head in his hands
and stare abstractedly at the pavement. Scores of people
were passing, but none seemed to have noticed this calamity;
and when he looked up the fellow was gone, and the cake
was gone. Dazed Johnny, after an interval for recovery, and
after imprinting upon his mind the exact spot of the occurrence and the situation of that darksome alley, walked
on grinding his teeth and registering a vow. He would train
for a whole week on puddings made of blood – and then!
Arabs gave their horses cakes made with mutton fat and they
would fly over the desert, mad, all day long; but for people
it had to be blood – and then you could blind anyone. He'd get
some blood, a lot.

The next day was cold, with a frozen mist niggling in
the streets, and when Johnny returned from an afternoon
journey to the city it was almost dark. As he ascended the
stairs he could just discern the little girl Smithers sitting
there.

'Hullo, Hetty,' he said; and she said, 'Mind where you're
coming!' She was nursing a black kitten.

'Your mother ain't done yet, Hetty, not for hours.'

The child hugged her kitten more closely, making no reply.

'Why don't you go home?' Johnny asked.

The child looked up at him, as if wondering at his foolishness.

'Somebody 'ull kick you,' he went on, 'sitting down.
What you sitting there for?'

A voice from the head of the stairs called 'Hoi!'

Johnny looked up. 'It's me,' he said.

Down came Mr Sulky. 'Is that Hetty?'

The child stood up and the man put an arm around her

shoulders. 'Hallo, Hetty. Cold, aren't you? Want some tea?'

Hetty tucked the kitten under her arm and said, 'Yes,' very softly. So Mr Sulky put his hand in his pocket and jingled some money. Then he turned to Johnny. 'You want some tea?'

'No, not much,' lied the boy.

'Well, here's sixpence. Take Hetty out to some coffee-shop and give her a good tea, anything she likes, and have some yourself if you want any. Will you do that?'

'Yes,' said the boy.

'There you are, Hetty,' Mr Sulky said; 'you go along of Johnny. He'll take you. And then come back here with him.' Bending down, Mr Sulky astonishingly kissed the child.

She and Johnny clattered down the stone stairs together and out into the street.

'You can't bring that kitten,' Johnny pointed out, 'not in a shop.'

'Why?' asked the little girl.

'They won't serve you, not in a shop.'

Dully the child answered: 'Yes, they will.'

'They'll laugh at you,' protested Johnny. 'They'll . . . they'll cut its head off.'

'No, they won't,' Hetty said.

And in point of fact they did not, although the first thing they saw on entering the coffee-house was a man in a white apron sharpening a long thin knife – a very large man. They sat down in a compartment rather like a church pew, and the large man soon came up to them and tapped on their table with his ferocious knife.

'Well?' said he, very affably.

'Two cups of coffee, please, and two dorks, please,' young Flynn timidly ordered.

Soon the large man returned with these things.

'Two coffee, two slices,' he said, and pushed a basin of brown sugar towards them. Johnny thereupon gave him the sixpence, and the man gave him threepence change.

'It's nice in here, ain't it?' said Johnny. And indeed it was; warm and savoury, with the mingled odours of fish and bacon and the sawdust on the floor. Most of the other compartments had men in them, but they took no notice at all of the children or the kitten. Hetty dropped some spoonfuls of coffee into her saucer and stood the kitten on the table. It lapped a few drops and then sat upon its haunches to gaze at the ceiling.

'Going to have some more coffee?' inquired the boy.

Hetty nodded her head and said 'You?'

'Na!' Johnny was contemptuous. 'I don't want any more coffee. What else d'you want?'

'Jam turnover,' replied the child.

The boy made a wry face. 'You don't want that. Nothing in 'em,' he declared. 'If I was you I'd have a lump of Tottenham cake. Have some Tottenham cake?'

Hetty picked the kitten off the table. 'Ernie said I could have what I like.'

Johnny took her empty cup and walked off to the counter, returning with the cup refilled, a jam turnover, and a triangle of cake that had a pink bile-provoking veneer upon it. 'Tottenham,' said Johnny. They lingered on for some time until everything had disappeared, and Johnny had to explain to incredulous Hetty that all the money was gone.

'Where d'you live?' he asked her, and she replied that she lived in Bermondsey, that her father was a bottle-washer.

'I ain't got no father,' said Johnny Flynn dismally.

'He gets drunk every day,' continued Hetty.

'I ain't got no father at all,' repeated the boy, leaning his elbows on the table and looking mournful.

'And slashes mum,' said she.

'What for?' The boy was awed, but curious.

'He keeps on trying to kill us.'

'Yes, but what for?'

'I dunno,' said the little girl. 'Mum says he's gone into bad habits.'

'When my father got drunk,' Johnny Flynn expanded, 'he was grand.'

'And 'e's a noremonger,' Hetty added.

'What's that?'

'I dunno,' Hetty went on, stroking her kitten. 'I wish we'd got another one; I don't like him. More does mum.'

'But you can't have another father! Course you can't, silly,' commented Johnny Flynn.

'Yes, you can; and mum says we will, soon. We'll have to.'

Just then a quarrel arose in a compartment near them, between a man with a peg leg and a man with a patch over one eye. They were sitting opposite each other.

'You're a liar!' bawled the wooden-leg man.

'O! Am I!'

'Yes. There you are. Now you know. I don't care what company I'm in, or what company I ain't in, that's straight from my bloody heart.'

'I'm a liar, am I?' patch-eye shouted.

'Yes, there you are!'

'And there *you* are!' cried the other, and he walloped his accuser over the head with a jar of salt.

The large man in the white apron dropped his knife and rubbed his hands together, yelling: 'Hi! Drop it. Devil and hell, where d'ye think you are – in the bull ring?'

And he hurled himself competently upon the brawlers.

'Drop it, d'ye hear! Or I'll have the guts out of you for my garters. Drop it!'

Both combatants subsided into their benches.

'D'ye see where he hit me?' said the peg-leg man, pointing with his finger to a spot on his head. 'Feel that!'

The fat host plunged his fingers amongst the greying hair. 'Jesus wept!' he murmured. 'There's a lump like St Paul's Cathedral. I'm surprised at you, Patchy.'

'Called me a liar,' the aggressor explained callously.

'Pooh, that's only his ignorance!'

'Ignorance!' moaned the afflicted one. 'He's broken my brainpan. That's done me a lot of good, ain't it?'

'O, it's just his playful heart, that's all! Now behave yourselves,' the host went on, with emollient raillery, '. . . or! You know what I'll do to you – ha, ha! you know that, don't you? I'm the king of the castle here, and an Englishman's castle's his birthright all the world over. A king can do no wrong.'

'Why not?'

'It's just a law, like everything else,' mine host explained, 'but of course it's kept private.'

'O,' said the one-eyed man resignedly, 'give him another cup of cawfee!'

During this tumult Hetty trembled fearfully, and at last Johnny had to usher her out of the place.

'I don't like these dark streets,' said she, clutching Johnny's hand and tucking the kitten under her arm.

'That's nothing,' Master Flynn assured her. 'I like fighting. Don't you like fighting? I had a scrap with a bloke last night in the Mile End Road, and I split his head open in six places. Do you know what Peter Jackson does when he trains himself? He's the champion of the world, he is.'

Miss Smithers did not know.

'He drinks blood,' Johnny informed her.

When they approached the workshop they met Hetty's mother standing in the doorway at the foot of the stairs, so Johnny told her of the grand tea they had had. And while he was also telling her about the quarrel Mr Sulky came tripping down the stairs.

'Hallo!' he cried, greeting them, as if he had just met them for the first time. 'Here we are then. This way, Nell. Good night, Johnny. Come on, Hetty.' And before Johnny could explain how he had spent the whole sixpence Mr Sulky took Helen's arm and Hetty's hand, and the three of them walked off together. And Johnny heard Hetty exclaiming:

'Mum! Look at the dear little kitten!'

Johnny never saw Helen again. Apparently she had gone away, and she would be happier now. At the end of the week the women had a 'whip round' and collected a small sum of money to buy Mr Sulky a teapot. He was setting up house-keeping – Mrs Grainger said. And when she gave him the teapot she said God bless him, and wished him the best of luck.

In a little while Johnny's tribulation came to a happy end. His mother wrote that she could not bear to be parted from him any longer; he had been away a year; he must come home to her now. His aunt was deeply annoyed at such ingratitude and wanted him to refuse to go home; but Johnny gave his notice in to Mr Alabaster, who said he was very sorry to part with him, and declared that he 'wath the beth boy he ever had'. When the joyous last day came Mr Alabaster wished him good-bye and gave him some good advice. Mr Sulky did the same and presented him with sixpence as well.

'Good-bye, little Johnny,' whispered old Mrs Grainger – and she gave him two new pennies. Johnny kept them sacredly in a box for many a long day.